One Large Coffin to Go

A Polly Deacon Murder Mystery

H. Mel Malton

RENDEZVOUS
PRESS

Cover art: Christopher Chuckry

LE CONSEIL DES ARTS
DU CANADA
DEPUIS 1957

THE CANADA COUNCIL
FOR THE ARTS
SINCE 1957

We gratefully acknowledge the support of the Canada Council for the Arts for our publishing program. We also gratefully acknowledge the support of the Government of Ontario through the Ontario Media Development Corporation's Ontario Book Initiative.

Napoleon Publishing/RendezVous Press
Toronto, Ontario, Canada

Printed in Canada

07 06 05 04 03   5 4 3 2 1

National Library of Canada Cataloguing in Publication

Malton, H. Mel, date—
    One large coffin to go / H. Mel Malton.

(A Polly Deacon murder mystery)
ISBN 1-894917-01-4

I. Title. II. Series: Malton, H. Mel, date-. Polly Deacon murder mystery

PS8576.A5362O64 2003   C813'.54   C2003-902840-2
PR9199.3.M34O64 2003

One Large
Coffin
to Go

To Norma —
in anticipation
of more Book Talk!

[signature]

Acknowledgements

Many people helped in the writing of this book. Thanks to Gillian and Steve Collins, who put up with me far longer than I had a right to expect during my stay in England, and who explained lots of English-y things to me. Thanks to Janet and Peter Gillham for train and coastal town information, and to Monica and David Hayes for their hospitality in Canterbury. Special thanks to David, who kindly allowed me to put words in his mouth. Any inaccuracies about the English stuff are my own mistakes, not theirs.

Huge thanks to Vianney Carriere, for moral and editorial support during the writing process, and to Saskia for throwing work my way that kept the wolf from the door. Thanks as ever to my publisher, Sylvia McConnell, and to my editor, Allister Thompson, for their infinite patience and support.

This is a work of fiction. While some of the locations are real, the events, characters and circumstances are entirely the figments of my imagination. (Father David is a real person, but he said it was okay—really.)

This book's for Sam.

One

Mood swings, insecurities, fears, ambivalence, impatience, and anger are all likely to surface during your pregnancy — often at unpredictable times. Why do you sometimes feel so out of control while you're expecting?
-From *Big Bertha's Total Baby Guide*

When a woman is noticeably pregnant, the normal rules of social interaction get thrown completely out the window. I learned this the hard way at about the seven-month point. Some women manage the earth-mother thing with extraordinary grace—they're radiant, their swelling bellies draw the gaze as if they've been festooned with twinkly lights, they wear that joyful, wide-eyed expression that says: "Rejoice with me in this miracle, O my fellow humans! O frabjous day, callou, callay!" I, on the other hand, turned into a fat, ferocious, touch-me-you-die kind of creature, lank of hair and greasy of skin. I was the kind of pregnant lady you'd cross the street to avoid, like a barely-controlled pit bull out for walkies with a sneering, tattooed and pierced teenager.

This state of affairs didn't happen overnight. I like to think that I started out as my usual pleasant and friendly self. It was all the attention I got that changed me. As soon as it was generally known that I was eating for two, (enceinte, expecting, a mother-to-be, a stinkin' oven with a bun), and long before my delicate condition was visually inescapable, I began attracting comment from all and sundry.

"Congratulations!" said Donna-Lou Dermott, the egg-queen of Cedar Falls, whom I met as she was dropping off a couple of dozen at the General Store in the village. "I heard from your aunt Susan that you're in the family way. Who's the father?" My jaw dropped at the sheer nerve of the question, but I quickly learned that etiquette doesn't apply if you're knocked up. Donna didn't wait to hear my answer, which was just as well, because I was choosing some words that don't look very nice in print. "Oh, I sure hope you're going to have it at the hospital," she went on. "My first was a breech birth—hurt like hell and tore me open from front to back—but they have pain killers for that kind of thing now." Then she smiled seraphically and sailed off, reminding me over her shoulder that I should eat lots of eggs over the next while.

That began it. Anyone on the planet who had ever had children accosted me on the street, in the FoodMart, the bank and the post office, sharing their horror stories, telling me what to eat and what not to eat, asking impertinent questions about my living arrangements and the identity of the father and about his reception of the news. By the time I was showing, as they say, absolute strangers had developed the curious habit of reaching out and patting me on the tummy. I learned to converse at a distance, out of arm's reach. And eventually, I developed a Rottweiler approach—the permanent snarl, the "give me any advice and it'll be the last thing you ever say" attitude.

My boyfriend and putative fiancé, Detective Constable Mark Becker, was the gentleman responsible for all this—at least in the biological sense. The moment of conception was far from blessed, though, having taken place at the tail end of a booze-sodden July evening. We were too plastered to bother with a condom—that's the truth of it, and the later realization that I was hosting a little blastula somewhere in my gut was not exactly wonderful news. But as far as responsibility was concerned, Becker and I were equally culpable. I was the one directly and immediately affected, though, and because of this I didn't actually let him in on the secret until I'd made my own decision about what to do.

Anybody who knows me will have gathered that I'm not big on babies. I have made no secret of my opinion that children should be caged until they're fifteen, and after that, let out only occasionally for exercise and lessons in etiquette. I'm in my late thirties and have never in my life gone all soft and squashy at the sight of an infant. I do not make oodgy-woodgy noises and tickle the chins of Babes in Prams. I avoid McDonald's restaurants and fun fairs and the Laingford Mall on weekends, precisely because there are always children present. One of the things I love about my remote cabin in the woods is that I am unlikely to come across any stray infants or toddlers while out walking in the bush.

You would be quite justified in wondering why the heck I didn't opt for the medical solution to my urgent dilemma. I considered it very seriously, certainly. In fact, even now, I still wonder why I didn't just call up Dr. Wright and ask her to book me for a D&C. But while I have always been willing to fight fiercely for every woman's right to choose her reproductive moment, I found that my own choice in the matter had already been made for me by past experience. Been there. Done that. This time, I wanted to keep the T-shirt. You don't want the details—stories of successful and trauma-free abortions are boring, and if you're a Right-to-Lifer, you'd hurl this book across the room the moment you realized where the narrative was going. Simply put, I decided after much deliberation to go through with the pregnancy.

"Becker," I said, "I'm going to have a baby." (I have never been one to beat about the bush.)

It was the second week of October, and we were playing a Thursday night game of pool together at the billiard parlour in Sikwan. Becker's presence had, as usual, cleared the hall of teenagers, who can smell a cop a mile away. We were alone in the small room at the back—Becker was working on a Kuskawa Cream Ale, and I was swigging Perrier. I'd explained my choice of beverage by saying that I was "cleaning out my system", but the truth of it was that my body had rejected all forms of alcohol from the moment Becker's wretched little drunken sperm buried its head in the pillowy wall of my private pickled egg. It's as if every cell in me had immediately been put on High Alert by Head Office. "Attention all Polly-bits! We have a guest, whom you are all bound to treat with utmost courtesy. You shall desist at once from any unhealthy cravings. Lungs—we know you're used to a shot of nicotine every fifteen minutes. Well, forget it. Gut—we know you're trained to require a regular infusion of fermented material. Prepare for a new order. From now on, you'll get milk and fizzy water, and you'll bloody well like it." The directive had nothing to do with me. And my sudden metabolic Puritanism played merry havoc with my mood, let me tell you.

I blurted out my news while Becker was lining up a shot. It was an easy one—fourteen in the corner pocket—and it was already an inch away, set up perfectly so he could come back for the eleven. After I'd spoken, Becker's cue sort of slipped sideways, the cue ball popped skywards and landed on top of the eight, smacking it squarely into the side pocket and ending the game in my favour.

"Shit, Polly," Becker said. "No fair—those are the kind of dirty tactics that can get you arrested." He was laughing as he said it, reaching into his pocket for another loonie so we could play again.

"That wasn't a tactic," I said.

He went very, very still. "You're kidding."

"Nope."

"You're pregnant? You're sure?" He was speaking carefully, now, moving towards me on tiptoe, as if I might be packing explosives.

"Yes, Mark. Positive."

"And you're positive you're having it? You want it?" I appreciated that he didn't knee-jerk all over me right away. I nodded, studying his face for signs of pleasure, pain, anger, elation—whatever. Signs of anything. He'd gone pale, and his expression was unreadable.

He let out a breath, a sigh, and sat down beside me, not touching, but close enough that I could feel his body heat. "How long have you known?" he said.

"Not long. It was that night we whooped it up at the Mooseview and took a taxi to your place afterwards."

I could see him doing the math. "That's ten weeks, roughly," he said. "Is there still time to do something about it, if you wanted to?" I wonder how many times, and in how many places, that same conversation has played out between two people. It conforms to the Trite-but-True rule. Life's big moments don't come wrapped in poetry and profound phrases. We humans are predictable. I had known damn well that Becker would be hurt beyond measure by the fact that I hadn't told him right away. He was nobody's fool, my policeman, and it had taken him less than a half a second to understand that I had made a decision already, without him. Maybe it would have been different if we'd been married. But we weren't.

"I think it's legal up to about twenty weeks," I said. "But it's not an option I'm interested in."

"I didn't think so."

"Is that what you want?"

"Polly, did you make your decision to have this baby on the spur of the moment?"

"Of course not! I thought long and hard about it—oh. I see what you mean. Sorry."

"Yeah. Well. Give me some time, okay? Do you want another game? You won when I scratched on the eight." We played another couple of games that night. During the first one, Becker played hard. He missed dozens of shots by over-hitting them. On a small bar-table, you have to caress the cue ball, encourage the kiss of the spots and stripes and woo the gentle tock and click and thump that comes from the perfect angle. You can't shoot good pool mad. He calmed down and concentrated after that, and it wasn't until the drive home that he brought the subject up again.

"This puts a new spin on the marriage question, doesn't it?" he said. He had asked me to marry him back in August, just before we got distracted by our mutual involvement in a municipal corruption scandal. We arrived at some pretty clear answers in the scandal case, but the matrimonial issue was still open. I wore his ring on a chain around my neck, not on my finger, and I hadn't given him an answer yet.

"I guess it does," I said.

"You wouldn't want to deal with a newborn in that cabin, Polly. You don't even have running water." That was the crux of the matter—the thing that was weighing on my mind far more than the unknown and alien things that were happening to my body. I live in a small, one-roomed building on the edge of a goat farm in rural Kuskawa. I'd moved there from the city to get away from noise and crowds and the corporate imperative, so I could pursue my craft, which happens to be puppet-making. I loved it there, and I didn't want to move. Not for Becker's sake, not for anybody's, and certainly not for the sake of what in bleak moments I considered my personal parasite. It's true there was no running water, but the well had performed its function perfectly for the five years of my residence. Granted, there was an outhouse, and it was a tad chilly in the dead of winter, but the pioneers had survived in spite of having to poop in an ice-house, and so had I. I didn't need hydro—I had oil lamps and candles and never had to worry about whether or not I could pay the power bill. My lifestyle was perhaps unconventional, but it hadn't done me any harm. In fact, I was far healthier living the way I did than I'd ever been in the city. I got lots of exercise, chopping wood and hauling water, I never caught colds, I ate vegetables grown right there on the farm, and in the dead of winter I kept my place at an even 16°C by running the woodstove at full bore. I wore lots of sweaters in the winter months, and in the summer I could wander around half-naked if I wanted to, provided the bugs weren't too bad. We discussed these points in the Jeep, driving north through the October night.

The downside to all my arguments, as Becker rather roughly pointed out when we got to the farm, was that pioneer babies, reared in circumstances similar to mine, often had a nasty habit of dying.

The night was clear and cold, and there was no moon. We stood for a few minutes, looking up. There are times when that monstrous black expanse, splattered with stars like spilled Christmas glitter, is far too big and beautiful to be real. This was one of those times. Orion was beginning to creep into the sky—my favourite winter constellation—the big guy with his splayed legs and mighty sword. I'd always considered him the harbinger of comfort, of cosy evenings curled up in front of the fire with a hot toddy while a storm howls outside. Now he seemed threatening, his sword pointing to my cabin on the hill, reached by a path that would be thigh-deep in snow by mid-February. In February, I would be seven months pregnant. I would, I imagined, be heavy and perhaps bloaty, with thick ankles and shortness of breath. Would I able to strap on my snowshoes and haul groceries from the driveway of my landlord George's farmhouse up to my place? Would I have the energy to chop wood for the fire and carry it inside?

Now we come to a thing about me, which some people probably know already. If someone tells me I can't do a thing, if they suggest that I would be an idiot even to think about it— well, I generally decide there and then to try. The alternative chilled me to the marrow. What? Knuckle under to the North American happy-baby dream of plastic cribs and Pampers and formula and washing machines and automatic everything, inside a hermetically sealed and overheated box with carpets and padded corners, baby-proofed and squeaky clean? Expose my child (there, I'd said it) to the poisonous influence of TV, the stinking breath of air conditioners and the banal subliminal coax of FM radio? No fear. I'd rather raise it in a tent.

"Do you want to come in and say hello to Susan and George?" I said. My aunt Susan lived with George Hoito—the goat farmer whose cabin I rented—in the old brick farmhouse that had been there since the original homesteaders had got tired of roughing it in the cabin and perhaps losing babies down the well. Becker agreed to visit for a while, and we found Susan by the door with a "Did you tell him?" expression written across her face in bold.

"I know about it," Becker said right away, thereby banishing any chance of a pleasant, uncomplicated chat. Within moments, Becker and Susan had launched into a gang-up-on-Polly session that lasted well over an hour. Becker wanted me to move into his condo in town and gestate in comfort and convenience. Susan, who knew me well enough to know that threats and pleading would fall on ever-more-stubborn ears, simply suggested that if the toils of winter at the cabin got to be a bit too much, I might consider moving in with them for the final month or two. George, who sat and smoked his pipe (in defiance of Susan, who told him it was not good for the baby), listened and watched me very closely.

"Polly will do what she pleases," he said towards the end. "You know this is true, both of you, and while your alliance is encouraging, you will not be able to change her mind." Susan and Becker had never really liked each other—Susan had an instinctive distrust of policemen, born of her activist history. To Susan, civil disobedience was a duty, not merely an option, and she had been arrested more than once in her youth. Becker said she made him uncomfortable. Aunt Susan was as close to a mother as I had—my parents having been killed in a car crash when I was ten. She could be fierce in my defense, could Susan, and although Becker had risen in her estimation after she was told that he wanted to marry me (rather than merely toying with my affections, as she called it), she was still perplexed as to why we were attracted to one another in the first place. Most of my friends seemed to wonder about that, actually.

Becker had by then, I suppose, cemented his position regarding the baby. Susan had worked him up into a froth of righteous indignation, which is not his best party-piece. If I wanted to have the baby, he said, he wasn't about to be un-supportive. After all, he was the father. (Not "after all, I love you", but then he would never say such a thing out loud in the presence of George and Susan. Heck, he still hadn't managed to say that out loud in the presence of me.)

"I love being a father," he said, referring to Bryan, his eight-year-old son from his first marriage, who lived with his ex-wife in Calgary. "And I'm willing to give our child everything I have, Polly. We'll talk about this some more—soon, I hope, but I hope in the meantime you'll think about someone other than yourself for once." He kissed me before he left and told me he'd take me out to lunch in a day or two. But that didn't happen, because the next day he received a phone call from his ex-wife, telling him to get his butt on a plane because his father (who lived in Calgary, too) had had a heart attack. I didn't see him again for three weeks, by which time I was picking names and thinking about how much winter firewood I would need to keep my growing belly warm.

Two

Pregnant women who continue to smoke cannabis are probably at increased risk of giving birth to low birth weight babies, and perhaps of shortening their period of gestation.
    -From *Big Bertha's Total Baby Guide*

One of the big chores in the spring, if you're a wood-burning person who doesn't want to pay $85 a cord, is to go out in the bush and cut it yourself. If you've really got it together, you'll already have a year-old supply drying in your woodshed while you're cutting the next. If you're me, you meet up every spring with a local guy called Ethan, promise him a half-share of what you take together and then hope for a good drying summer, because you'll be burning it in six months' time.

My winter's wood was still lurking in the middle of George's west acreage, where Ethan and I had stacked it in April. (George had said "take what you want—there is more than enough for us all." He cut his own in the valley, closer to the farmhouse.) Aunt Susan suggested that I might want to order my winter fuel from the Tucker brothers ("Wood R Us") and have them deliver it, to save me having to haul my own out of the bush.

"I'll help pay for it, Polly," she said, "if the cost is what concerns you." But it wasn't the price, it was the principle of the thing. Anyway, I told her, there's no way the Tuckers' truck, an enormous diesel monstrosity that belched black smoke and weighed several tons, could make it up the steep, narrow footpath that led to my cabin. While the prospect of driving George's tractor into the bush and loading up the ancient, wheeled wood-cart a dozen times didn't exactly thrill me (it never did), I figured the exercise would be good for me.

Eddie showed up to help, which was kind of him, although I suspect he might have been given some unavoidable incentive for doing so by Susan, his guardian. Eddie was eighteen by then—a big lad, whose early years had been peculiar and difficult. His mother lived in a psychiatric facility in North Bay, and his father was out of touch, living in sin somewhere in the States with a Biblical literalist. After his home was broken, Susan invited him to stay with her, and she mothered him the way she did me—without the silent "s" at the beginning of the word.

Eddie arrived as I was preparing to load the cart for the second time. My dogs were snerfling around in the undergrowth, which had taken a hard frost the night before and probably smelled wonderful. It was the frost that got me off my duff and into winter-wood-mode. I'd had a fire going for a couple of days already, using some leftovers from last year, but I knew that the demon bailiffs of procrastination were hovering nearby, polishing up their collecting jars and laying bets about the weather. It hadn't snowed yet, but it would soon.

"It's me, Polly," Eddie called, as Lug-nut announced his approach with a gentle, "familiar-two-legs-at-nine-o'clock" kind of bark. Luggy is the senior dog in our pack, a sturdy male mongrel with yellow eyes and a shaggy coat like a bad wig. Rosencrantz, a yellow Lab puppy with more pedigree than wit, looked up in surprise. When she saw Eddie, she made up for not hearing him earlier by firing off a long series of high-pitched, yappy sounds.

"Rosie! That's enough!" I sounded a tad hysterical, even to myself. Eddie pretended he hadn't noticed. It occurred to me suddenly that, by winter's end, I would be coping with a whole new spectrum of unnerving, high-pitched noises, human ones, and shouting back wouldn't be allowed.

"Susan said to follow the sound of the tractor," he said. "But I heard the engine stop as I was coming up the hill. Is it stalling out again?"

"It's running fine," I said. "I just don't see the point in running it when I'm not using it. It stinks, and it's noisy."

"Yup," Eddie said, grinning. "Like a baby, right?"

"Smartass." That was far too astute for an eighteen-year-old, in my opinion.

"No, really, I know about the noise part because we're doing the Ready or Not Tot unit in Family Studies right now," Eddie said.

"The what unit?"

"The Ready or Not Tot. It's like an automatic baby with a computer inside that we each have to take home and look after for the weekend. You know, to scare us off making real ones. Robyn had it last week. It was pretty loud."

"It cries?"

"It's programmed to act like a real baby," he said. "It starts, like, crying at four in the morning and doesn't stop unless you press a button on its back, and sometimes that doesn't work, and you have to walk with it till it stops."

"Sounds delightful," I said.

"Yeah, and the worst part is that it keeps track of what you do. Like if you ignore it, or throw it against the wall or something, the chip inside records it, and you flunk the unit."

"Has anybody actually done that?"

"I doubt it," Eddie said. "It's too real, man. Even its neck, if you don't support it right, sort of clicks, and you know you just lost a bunch more points."

"Sounds like a video game."

"Maybe. Not as much fun, though."

"Have you had your turn yet?"

"Not for a couple of weeks," he said, then grinned again. "You wanna babysit for me, to get some practice in?"

"I might just do that," I said, seriously considering it. It would be interesting to see how the dogs reacted to the creature, for one thing. "Is that allowed?"

"Yes, as long as we pay the going rate to whoever we get to look after it. We're supposed to take it everywhere we go. The girls get off on it, I think, but the guys usually hibernate when it's their turn and stay home that weekend. Especially the guys on the hockey team."

"I can imagine. And I guess it would be worse with a real one, eh?"

"Yeah. Like if you had it right now, where would you put it?" Good question, I thought. He sounded more like Susan every day.

"In one of those carrier things on my back, I guess," I said, after a moment's thought.

"What if it was a real one, a newborn?"

"If it was a newborn, I wouldn't be in any shape to haul wood, and you'd be doing this by yourself," I said. "At the going rate, of course. Thanks for coming."

"Oh, no problem. I helped last year, didn't I?"

"You did. Ten bucks an hour still okay?"

"Nah. Let's do a straight trade—I'll do this and you babysit for me sometime that weekend."

With Eddie's muscle and my pressing need to prove myself capable, if pregnant, we had all my wood hauled, stacked and tarped in five hours. The way I figured it, I'd have to agree to adopt his wretched automatic baby for a whole month to pay him what he was owed, but he seemed quite content for me to be in his debt.

After we put the tractor and cart back into George's drive shed, I helped him do the evening milking, which was his official farm chore. George kept a herd of Nubian dairy goats in the century-old barn behind the farmhouse. When I'd first moved back to Kuskawa from the city, I'd been the goat-hand myself for a couple of years, in exchange for the privilege of living in the cabin. Now I paid George a nominal rent, and Eddie was the goat-guy. I'd felt usurped to begin with, but got over it eventually. I missed the daily interaction with the animals, though. Goats are placid creatures, generally, and a dairy barn is a nice place to be. The sound track in your typical goat barn is a mixture of rustling hay, contented moans and bleats from the female residents and the occasional comical burp from Pierre Trudeau, the sire buck. In the summer, you get the burble and twitter of the barn swallows, and in the fall and winter, a rabble of chickadees lurks by the back door, looking for a handout. The barn smells of grain, warm milk and hairy goat musk (which is not at all unpleasant, in spite of what those mean-spirited anti-goat propagandists claim).

I was in the middle of filling the mangers with fresh hay when I caught a whiff of something sweet and familiar, but definitely not barn-based. I looked up to see Eddie leaning casually against the back door, surveying the hay field and smoking a joint. I'd known it would happen eventually. I am a recreational user of cannabis myself, and while I try to be discreet in the presence of those who aren't, I don't consider it a state secret. Eddie had probably figured me out long since, although I had never smoked in front of him. Now here he was doing it in front of me, and it disturbed me more than I cared to admit.

He turned around before I got to him and smiled in that wary, defiant way that young people do when they're making a statement about something.

"I would offer you a hit, but you probably shouldn't," he said.

"You're right, I shouldn't," I said. "Have you smoked around Susan yet?"

"You've got to be kidding."

"Just wondering. She won't like it."

"I figured. You don't either, obviously."

"Well, I can't say I'm delighted, my friend. But I could hardly give you the business when I smoke the stuff myself, could I? I may be older than you, but I'm not a hypocrite."

"You're not smoking it these days, though, right?"

"Right. I'm not drinking either, and I'm trying to cut out coffee, because I'm told that stuff is not good for kids, one of which I happen to be incubating. But I suppose you're not a kid any more, are you?"

"Not technically."

"You've done all the growing you plan to do?"

"Jeez, Polly, you're not going to say it'll stunt my growth are you?"

"Far be it from me. But if you smoke a lot of it, you'll get lethargic and forgetful and asthmatic."

"And if I smoke a little of it?"

"You'll laugh at movies you'd hate if you were straight, and you'll think up great ideas that will disappear like smoke if you don't write them down. But you'd better respect the hell out of it, because if you don't, you'll wind up doing something stupid. It's illegal, don't forget."

"I know that."

"Good. You don't smoke tobacco, do you?"

"Hate the stuff."

"And booze?"

"The occasional beer—you know that, Polly. I'm not an idiot."

I sighed—a long, heavy one that I felt all the way down to my boots. "Okay, Eddie. Interrogation over." He had pinched the joint out soon after our conversation had begun and stashed it in an inside pocket. "Just please, please be careful with the stuff, okay? Treat it like birthday cake or chocolate truffles—nice on special occasions, but if you use it all the time, it loses its magic."

We finished the barn chores together in companionable silence. I watched Eddie out of the corner of my eye, kicking myself for acting like a scientific observer, but I couldn't help it. I wanted to know how stoned he was. He wasn't chuckling to himself or muttering, which was a good sign. I watched his large, capable hands as he milked Donna Summer and Julian of Norwich, George's two best producers, whose yield of high-butterfat milk sometimes bordered on the amazing. Long ago, George and I had established that the goats tended to give more milk if you sang to them while milking—a phenomenon that wouldn't stand up in a lab study, perhaps, but certainly proved itself when we experimented, logging the daily production carefully and noting which songs affected which goats in a positive way. Eddie sang a Hawksley Workman tune to the goat named Donna Summer, and Julian got "Swing Low, Sweet Chariot". I joined in on the gospel tune in harmony, and old Julian, cavernous of belly and hairy of chin, gave us almost two pounds of milk. Eddie had a pleasant tenor voice and wasn't shy about using it, unlike most teenaged boys.

"Are you planning on breastfeeding?" Eddie said as we carried the full milk pails up to the dairy house. I almost swallowed my tongue. Not, I would venture, a remark that Eddie Schreier would come up with unless his inhibitions were altered. However, it wasn't as if he was asking out of prurience—he seemed genuinely interested.

"I haven't really thought about it much," I said, "but I probably will. Breastfeeding makes sense—I mean if the body produces the stuff, it seems a shame to waste it, hey?"

"It's just that the Family Studies teacher was talking about it the other day," he said. "She said that kids who are bottle-fed end up getting earaches and stuff because there's, like, natural antibiotics in mother's milk and not in formula. Just thought you should know." I was amused by his concern, and rather touched. This was something I did know, actually— during the first few days after a goat bears her kids, her udder is full of rich, yellowish colostrum—chock full of antibodies and nutrients that milk-replacer doesn't have. That's why George always let new kids nurse for a couple of weeks before starting them on the instant milk-mix. It hadn't occurred to me until that moment, though, that I, being a mammal, would be manufacturing colostrum myself. I had a sudden and profound flash-forward, imagining a heavy, warm bundle in my arms, its lips suctioned onto my nipple. It was weirdly sexual, and I could feel myself blushing.

"Hey, Polly, you want me to come sing to you when it's feeding time?" Eddie said, leering and waggling his eyebrows. "It might boost your yield, eh?" Yep. Definitely stoned.

I cuffed him across the head with my free hand, almost spilling the bucket of milk.

"That's exactly why some people call it dope, Eddie," I said.

Three

Plan any holidays or trips well in advance and try to avoid long-haul flights in the second half of pregnancy. Planes can be very cramped, and the pressurized cabin can cause swollen feet and discomfort even in non-pregnant passengers.
-From *Big Bertha's Total Baby Guide*

I joined Susan, George and Eddie for dinner. Becker was still away in Calgary, and I had not heard from him directly, except for a brief message sent to Susan's email account from an Internet café.

```
To: goataBene@kuskawa.com
From: mbecker@hotmail.com
Subject: Pls. Fwd to Polly
Date: October 25

Dear Ms.Kennedy,

I would have called, but there was no point, as
Polly doesn't have a phone up in her cabin, and I
didn't want to put you to the trouble of trying to
find her. My father passed away yesterday, and
the funeral is on Saturday. Please tell her I will be
back in Laingford on October 31.

Sincerely,
Mark Becker
```

How's that for a nice intimate note? Second-hand, no less. "Have some compassion, Polly. He's just lost his father,"

Susan had said, seeing my reaction.

"It's not that I don't sympathize with him in his grief," I had said. "I just wish he'd sent something a little more personal, that's all." Anyway, I asked Susan to send a message back with my condolences, which I assume she did.

I would have liked to have met Becker's father. What's that Oscar Wilde line? "All women become like their mothers, that's their tragedy. No man does. That's his." That may very well be true, but I'd never had the chance to check it out, as Becker's mother had died three years previously. Now that Becker was an official orphan, like me, his resemblance to either of his parents, in terms of temperament, could only be a matter of hearsay. However, I suspect that many men resemble their fathers to some degree. Becker hadn't talked about either of his parents much, and I hadn't felt comfortable pressing him on the subject, as I'd made it quite clear that I wasn't interested in discussing my own. I'd made a careful study of his parenting techniques, though, the previous summer, when his son Bryan had stayed with him for a week while his ex was away on a trip. I wasn't pregnant at the time, but I was considering marrying the guy and had put him under the powerful lens of the Polly-scope.

Bryan was a cute kid, as kids go, and obviously devoted to his father—almost pathetically eager to please him. Becker had appeared to be a loving father, too, but there was a hard edge to him in his dealings with his son—a kind of no-compromise sternness that made me wonder if his own father had been a trifle strict. What I did know about Becker Senior (Edward) was that he had been born somewhere in England, the only son of an air force captain. He had been evacuated to Canada during the Second World War and sent to live with a family on a farm near Calgary, which was where he met Becker's mother.

I figured that if Edward had undergone the trauma of being sent away, alone, at a tender age, to a foreign country, it might well have left him with some parental/abandonment issues and rendered him undemonstrative.

There you go—a canned psychological assessment of a man I'd never met, patched together from scant information extracted from his son. Edward might have been the most doting, adoring father in the world, of course, but now I'd never know. Becker hadn't appeared terribly eager to take me out to Calgary to meet him. He'd said it was because his father had never forgiven him for divorcing Catherine, Bryan's mother, and still treated her as his daughter-in-law. "We'll have to ease him into it," Becker had said. "It would help if I could introduce you as my fiancée, and not just my girlfriend." Which, as you can imagine, had turned into a bit of a tiff, as that felt an awful lot like pressure from my perspective.

*   *   *

It was Eddie's night to cook. He was pretty good at it, having been in the culinary arts program at Laingford High since Grade Nine. Susan, George and I sat in the living room, enjoying the scent of frying garlic emanating from the kitchen. He was bashing around in there, singing a Shepherd's Pie tune and obviously having a great time. I know what that's like—cooking when you're slightly stoned is wonderful fun.

George was sitting in his favourite chair next to the woodstove, puffing on his pipe and scratching the tail feathers of Poe, his pet raven. Poe had been around forever—a massive creature, far more intelligent than Lug-nut could ever hope to be. The bird perched on the armrest of George's chair, emitting little croaks of pleasure as George fiddled with his nether regions. Poe would never let me do that. The bird was picky when it came to human contact. He obviously considered George a kind of honorary raven, but the rest of us were roadkill as far as he was concerned. He had perched on my shoulder a couple of times in the past, a distinction that always made me feel grateful, but if you were smart, you'd never reach out and kind of offhandedly pat his head. At least, if you did, the term "off-hand" would become painfully literal. Luggy and Rosie had the sense to give him a wide berth, and anyway, the two-legged person throwing food around in the kitchen was far more interesting to them than the malevolent creature by the fire.

"There's some snail-mail for you as well, today," Susan said, getting up suddenly and going out to the bureau in the hall, where the day's post was stacked in a wicker basket by the door. She had been completely bewitched by the computer age and seemed to take great delight in dissing Canada Post, which I found rather unfair. After all, getting an email message from somebody isn't half as much fun as receiving a mysterious envelope, bedecked with stamps (especially if they're foreign) that you have to open physically before you can find out what's inside. For me, real mail is like getting a Christmas present, all wrapped up in sparkly paper and lots of tape, whereas email is like someone saying "here" and handing you an unwrapped widget with the price tag still on it. No comparison.

Susan returned with a large manila envelope, a fat one. "Looks like it's from the U.K.," she said, obviously intrigued. It would have been mean to wait until I got home to open it, so I didn't. I knew what it was about, anyway, though I hadn't told anybody yet.

As I've mentioned, I'm a puppet maker. That's my job, or at least that's the way I make my living, which perhaps doesn't mean the same thing, these days. I don't do the nine-to-five dance, I spend a great deal of time staring off into nothingness (we artists call that "conceptual development"), and my skills, though specialized, allow me to squeak by with the minimum of mainstream interference. I build commissioned puppets for theatre companies, mascot costumes for sports and corporate organizations, and marionettes for fun and profit. All this is one of my main reasons for living as I do, in a log cabin in rural Kuskawa with little in the way of modern conveniences—I don't need 'em, and I can't afford 'em. It's a fine life, although it had occurred to me since acquiring a passenger that my income needs might be due for re-examination. Maybe I'd have to start churning out cutesy, mass-produced hand-puppets and selling them at Kuskawa craft fairs to help pay for diapers and strained carrots. O joy, o bliss.

Back in June, I'd seen an article in *The Puppetry Journal*, a trade magazine I subscribe to, about a big, international puppetry conference planned for February, taking place in Canterbury, England. It sounded truly amazing—with speakers, workshops, displays and performances, a whole week of it, and I had fantasized about going. The article had mentioned that there were a few subsidized spots available for those professionals in the field who might have something unique to bring to the event but didn't have the cash to make the journey. Normally, I don't go in for stuff like that, my theory being that my work, while adequate and solid in its way, wasn't of the calibre to win any awards, so why set myself up for disappointment? However, in this case, I'd felt a weird surge of High Self Esteem, and acted quickly before it went away. I called up my friend Dimmy Cox, a photographer, who had agreed to prepare slides of some of my best pieces, in exchange for the construction of a slightly risqué puppet-portrait of her ex-boyfriend. I'd packaged up the slides, along with my resumé, written a fulsome letter explaining why I simply had to attend the conference and sent it off to the organizers in Canterbury. It had been a busy and difficult summer, and by the end of August, when I hadn't heard back from the conference people, I'd assumed that I hadn't made the grade.

I explained all this to Susan and George, while holding the heavy envelope in my lap, weighing it experimentally and tapping it with my fingers as if I might somehow divine what it contained by osmosis.

"So—why don't you go ahead and open it?" Susan said.

"It's probably just a bunch of promotional material," I said. "You know—sort of 'sorry we can't sponsor you, but here's some incentive stuff to make you feel even worse about not being able to afford to come.'"

"Blessed are they who expect nothing, for they shall not be disappointed," George intoned.

"Well, considering that you'll be seven months gone by February, and as big as a house, you shouldn't be travelling, anyway," Susan said. Uh-oh. She'd just used the dreaded "s" word. Shouldn't. Ought not. Mustn't. Can't. May not. Prohibited—not allowed. She recognized her mistake at once as my eyebrow shot up into my hairline and George made a little wincing sound, as if he'd been pinched.

I refrained from comment and opened the envelope.

Congratulations, Ms. Deacon, the covering letter said.

On behalf of the organizing committee for the Canterbury International Puppetry Festival (CIPF), I am delighted to inform you that you have been selected as the recipient of the Mary Chambers Memorial Bursary, an award which will cover your flight, registration and accommodation at this year's event.

We were enormously impressed with your work and hope that you will be able to bring a few samples with you and perhaps facilitate a workshop on construction techniques. Please let us know as soon as possible whether you will be attending, and we can work out the workshop details, arrangements for your flight and so on.

I do look forward to hearing from you.

Sincerely,
Phyllis Creemore,
Special Guests Committee Chair

"Hot damn," I said. "I'm going to Canterbury."

Four

Stress and worry do not in and of themselves harm a developing baby, but if you are not taking proper care of yourself, it could potentially be harmful. If you are so stressed you are not eating properly, then you may not be able to supply all the nutrients baby needs to grow properly.

-From *Big Bertha's Total Baby Guide*

All the retailers in Kuskawa manage their holiday decorating themes according to the principle of persistent overload, and it had been Hallowe'en at the Cedar Falls FoodMart since they took the Thanksgiving turkeys down on October 9. On the 31st, my friend Ruth Glass and I were there, buying last-minute ice and Clamato juice for Rico's Hallowe'en party. My friend Rico Amato runs an antique and collectibles place out on the Cedar Falls highway strip mall. The party was a new thing—Rico had in years past gone in drag to a local gay-friendly resort to howl at the Hallowe'en moon, but the place had gone belly up during a booming tourist summer (go figure), so this year he was having friends over.

"That cute Brent seems to be working out," Ruth said, referring to Rico's new roommate. We were wandering in the bakery aisle, whose shelves were bursting with jack-o-lantern cupcakes and bat-shaped cookies. Ruth brushed away a fake spider's web, which was dangling from the "Scary Bargains" sign and tickling her nose. She was enjoying the quiet of being back home, I think. Ruth's band, Shepherd's Pie, had been on tour to the Maritimes to promote their fifth CD, *Clear Cut*

Laundromat, and she looked tired.

"Well, they've only been sharing the place a month, and the Royal Doulton's still in one piece, so that's a good sign," I said. "You think we need more candy?" I was hefting a big bag of miniature chocolate bars that I'd scooped from a bin marked "Last Chance, Mom and Dad!" I'd already seen one harried parent-type rush towards the bin, make a grab and rush away again, like a seed-frenzied sparrow at a backyard feeder. But I wasn't thinking of trick-or-treaters, to tell you the truth. It was just that I wasn't drinking or smoking, so dammit, my baby was gonna have to put up with a night o' chocolate.

Ruth shot me a sympathetic grin. "We could always eat what's left over," she said and tossed the bag into our cart. Then she rolled her eyes at something she'd seen over my right shoulder and muttered "Incoming." I turned around just in time to prepare myself. It was Donna-Lou Dermott, dressed like a chicken.

"Well, hey, girls, don't you just looove Hallowe'en?" she said. She carried a wicker basket full of eggs—her own—(well, the ones from her hens, I should say) and was apparently on her delivery route. Her chicken suit was remarkably inventive. She'd wrapped herself in some kind of quilt batting and then she must have gone at it with a pair of scissors and a hairbrush, producing a tufted, feathery kind of toga. She wore an orange, cardboard beak on a piece of elastic, like an oxygen mask, pulling it down to speak so it hung like a wattle under her chin. Her face was painted bright yellow, and she wore a pair of yellow rubber gloves.

"I just ran this up on my Singer last night," she said, "and I can't tell you how many compliments I've had today."

"Fowl and fair," Ruth said, which only made Donna-Lou blink a bit.

"It's nice to see you, Ruthie. Are you still writing your songs?" Donna-Lou said.

Ruth, who hasn't been called Ruthie since high school, smiled gently, which is more than I would have managed. Shepherd's Pie does about as well as any other popular Canadian folk band these days, which is to say that they've been profiled in *Saturday Night* and *Maclean's* magazines, have won some Juno Awards and occasionally get some airplay on the CBC. "Ruthie" was a fairly big name in certain circles, but not, I guess, in Donna-Lou's.

"Yep, still doing my thing," Ruth answered. "Nice to see you, too, Donna-Lou. You still in the egg business?"

"Well, I should hope so," she said, affronted. Her feathers sort of ruffled, and I took note, thinking I would give quilt batting a try as puppet-hair. It seemed to have a kinetic life of its own. "Somebody's gotta keep food on the table," Donna-Lou went on. "Otis decided to seed the back field with hemp this summer past, and got a good crop, too, but the government confisticated it for some reason, just before harvest, so we didn't make no profit at all."

I resisted the urge to correct her grammar. "Hemp? You sure it was the legal kind?" I said.

"Well, Otis said it was, but I kinda wonder about that, now. He didn't get arrested or nothing, if that's what you're thinking."

"Of course not, Donna-Lou." I hadn't seen anything in the *Laingford Gazette* about it, and if it had truly been marijuana in Otis Dermott's field, you could be sure that the local press would have given it front page priority. On the other hand, maybe it had been the real stuff, and the government had snagged it and was storing it in the same place they stored the stuff they had grown themselves, in that government-sanctioned grow operation in a mine somewhere in Manitoba.

Canadian lawmakers are kind of two-faced about the issue, having legalized the drug's use for those who require it for medicinal purposes. They set up a highly efficient grow operation underground, a kind of hi-tech hydroponics farm, and rumour had it that the stuff they produced was so powerful, they were afraid to make it available to those who needed it. My theory was that they were stockpiling the stuff against the day when they finally legalized it and would start selling it at the provincial liquor and beer stores. "A six pack of Molson's Ex and a pack of Doobies, please." I can hardly wait.

"So, how's the mother-to-be?" Donna-Lou said. "I see you're porking up a bit already. That's good, dear, but you mustn't let your weight get away from you, or you'll never be able to lose it after." She reached out a rubber gloved hand and pinched my upper arm, like she was testing bread dough. I felt a growl start deep in my throat, unbidden and menacing. Donna-Lou sensed it and backed off. Chickens are naturally wary of dogs, they say, especially Rottweilers.

"Well, anyway—here you go—and Happy Hallowe'en," she said, handing each of us a couple of foil-wrapped chocolate eggs before scuttling away.

"Left over from Easter, I'd wager," Ruth said, poking at hers. "Celebration overlap."

"Hey—chocolate is chocolate," I said, unwrapping mine with undignified speed and popping it into my mouth. "A little stale, but perfectly palatable."

Ruth's eyes followed the retreating form of the chicken-lady as it disappeared into the canned vegetable section. "You know, forget the witches and ghosties and ghoulies—that has got to be the scariest thing I've ever seen."

"Mmm-phmn," I said, still chewing.

*   *   *

Rico and Brent lived in an apartment directly over Rico's store, the Tiquery, and it was stuffed with pieces he couldn't bear to part with, or perhaps simply couldn't sell. There were two ponderous Victorian sideboards in polished veneer, a fat horse hair chesterfield with carved wooden lion's feet, and dozens of those little occasional tables designed to feature one crocheted doily, a china shepherdess and not much else. For the party, Rico had put away the china figurines, and the little tables were cluttered with bowls full of munchies instead. I found myself grazing mindlessly, like my bovine cousins, stuffing candy corn, potato chips and chocolate-covered pretzels indiscriminately into my mouth.

If you have any more sugar, my girl, you'll be bouncing off the walls in a minute, I heard my mother's voice whisper in my inner ear. Oddly, my maternal ghost was not talking to me but was rather having a severe word with my Sprog, my private dolphin, who probably was experiencing a bit of a sugar high. Still, as far as I could determine from what Dr. Cass Wright had told me, the fetus, at thirteen weeks, was quite incapable of doing any wall-bouncing just yet. At this stage, the child would be about three inches long and weigh almost an ounce. She would have eyelids, fingernails and toenails, and a bit of spontaneous movement, but not enough to be breaking ornaments or pulling down pots of hot water on herself. Or himself, I guess, but if the ghost of my dead mother had chosen this moment, after more than twenty years of silence, to tune in from the ether, and had chosen to address my progeny as if it were female, then that was that. I had no doubt she knew her stuff. My mother had never, in my ten years of having known her, been wrong.

"It's a girl, I think," I muttered to Ruth, as we mixed up a couple of caesars in the kitchen—a virgin version for me and a hefty, vodka laced one for her.

"Do you want it to be?" she asked.

"Heck no, I just want it to be healthy," I said in a sickly sweet parody voice, the kind that you hear on television commercials for disposable diapers. Theresa Morgan was with us, decked out in full witch regalia (she belongs to a coven that meets regularly at a spot by the rapids in Cedar Falls). Theresa used to be my Aunt Susan's shop assistant at her co-op feed store and had recently taken the place over when Susan sold it. She was in the process of turning it into a vegetarian café, which we all hoped would be successful. The feed store had run into trouble after an American chain called Agri-Am opened up an enormous franchise a couple of doors down and undercut the co-op's prices, luring all her business away. Theresa figured that nobody was likely to open a big-box veggie café in Laingford any time soon, so this was a relatively safe venture.

She had dropped in just for a while, as she was presiding over the Samhain ritual that year. Theresa wasn't wearing a pointy hat, I might add, and didn't carry a broom. She was dressed in a dark, flowing robe, with interesting symbols embroidered in silver around the waistline and hem, and her neck was festooned with things on strings—crystals and wooden ankhs and a sturdy silver half-moon. I had been invited to come along, but I'm not big on rituals of any description, having had my fill of that kind of stuff as a child-Catholic.

"You sound a little sarcastic, Polly," Theresa said, pouring half a bottle of red wine into a beaker the size of a gravy boat. Rico and Brent came in at that point to top up their martini glasses. They were both in discreet drag, the kind where you can't really tell, unless you look very closely. It was a Hallowe'en thing, although if Kuskawa society were a little less repressed, I imagine Rico would have enjoyed indulging in his hobby on a more regular basis. Brent made a great girl (if you overlooked the prominent Adam's apple), and his makeup was perfect.

"What are you three up to in here?" Rico said. "Doing the cauldron thing? All hail Macbeth?"

"Hey, no fillet of a fenny snake jokes, please," Theresa said. She tended to be a little sensitive around that time of year. It's a religious season for her, after all, and Hallmark had co-opted it pretty thoroughly, which must have been as painful for her as Rudolph and Santa can be for devout Christians. "Polly was just being cynical about motherhood, is all."

"I'm just grumpy because my choice of recreational substances has been severely limited," I said, and it was quite true. One of the hardest things for a dedicated drinker and smoker is suddenly to be unable to indulge for reasons of altruism. I didn't particularly want to give these things up—that was the problem. I resented that I had to and resented that my body appeared to agree.

"Hey—I've got a joke for you," I said. "Three expectant mothers are sitting in a doctor's waiting room, right? They're all knitting little sweaters."

Ruth snickered. "Ruth, that's not the punchline," I said.

"Sorry—carry on."

"So the first mom reaches into her purse and takes out a pill bottle and pops a pill into her mouth and then continues knitting. The other two ask what she's just taken. 'Oh, it's calcium,' the mother says. 'I want my baby to have good, strong bones.'" I was doing the sweet parody voice again. Ruth and Theresa were listening, but both looked wary for some reason, and I realized I was speaking a bit loudly, so I toned it down.

"So, the second mother does the same thing—puts down

her knitting, reaches into her purse, pulls out a pill bottle, takes one, and then picks up the knitting again. Again, the other two ask her what she's taking. 'Oh, it's iron,' the woman says. 'I want my baby to have strong, healthy blood.'

"Then the third mother puts down her knitting, right? She reaches into her purse and pulls out a bottle and takes a pill and puts it back and picks up her knitting again. 'What are you taking?' the other two ask. 'Oh, it's thalidomide,' the mom says. 'You see, I can't knit arms.'"

There was a nasty little silence. Ruth and Theresa looked at each other and then back at me. Brent made a small snorting noise and left the room. Rico muttered "uh-oh" and followed him out, as if there were some sort of imminent girl-scene about to happen, and he didn't want to witness it.

"That is such bad karma, I can't even tell you," Theresa said, finally.

"It's only a joke, Terry. I think it's funny," I said.

"Never mind that it's incredibly sick," Theresa said, "but to hear it come out of your mouth, Polly—that's really disturbing."

"It is kind of in bad taste," Ruth said.

"Oh, jeez, you guys," I said. "If I wasn't pregnant, you'd have howled. Of course, it's in bad taste. The best jokes usually are. And I tell politically incorrect jokes all the time, remember? This is me, here. Me. You're supposed to be able to bend the rules among friends, and that's what we've always done. Why is everybody treating me like a badly behaved teenager all of a sudden?" And then, of course, I burst into tears. It must have been the chocolate.

* * *

"Sometimes I wonder if you lie awake at night, thinking up

33

ways to piss me off," Becker said, three days later. He had returned from Calgary and was up at the cabin for what I was hoping would be an intimate little dinner, just the two of us. I was preparing the kind of food one feeds to a person whom one wants to pamper. I felt guilty about having trampled all over his feelings by having waited so long to tell him about the baby. I felt bad about my stubborn intention of staying in the cabin. I hadn't had a chance to show my sympathy about his father's death—and I wanted to make him feel loved and appreciated. We may have been in disagreement about a few things, but I did care about him and about our relationship. I had made a splendid beef stroganoff, with sautéed baby vegetables and crusty homemade bread. To top it off, there was an apple pie to die for. I can be quite the Suzie Homemaker when I put my mind to it.

I had been nesting, in my own modest way, and as well as wanting to soothe Becker's feelings, I wanted to persuade him that my home was a perfectly reasonable place to care for a newborn. It was a place in which I could whip up a wonderful meal. A cozy, homey cabin that may have lacked electricity and running water, but was still a haven of peace and domestic delight.

I had insulated the roof, for one thing, in a burst of energy following the news about the Canterbury Conference. There was a small crawl space between the ceiling of the cabin and the roof, which had previously been filled with a mixture of sawdust and mouse droppings. I'd cleaned it out and replaced it with RU2000 pink insulation—not a huge job, really, and Eddie had helped. I was hyper-aware of the fact that I appeared to be doing more physical activity than usual, the kind that normal people would consider inappropriate for a pregnant lady, but I didn't regard it as a deliberate effort to piss anybody off. It was just that

I was not interested in being treated like a china doll and wanted to remain as independent as possible, for as long as possible. Aunt Susan had uttered dire warnings about climbing up the ladder to get into the crawl space under the eaves, the kind of warnings that, if you heeded them, would render you completely useless, lying in bed and shivering with fright, not risking so much as a paper cut, in case it harmed the baby. So, against all advice, I'd insulated the roof, and the difference it made in terms of cabin-coziness was significant. I wanted Becker to take note of it and approve. I wanted him to change his mind. I needn't have bothered.

"There's still a small matter of hauling wood inside and keeping the stove going," he said. "What happens if the fire goes out during the night, and it's thirty below outside?"

"The baby will be sleeping with me," I said. "It's not as if it's going to be stashed in a crib on the porch, Becker."

"What if you roll over in the night and squish it?" Oh, please. I knew then that we were diametrically opposed in terms of the most basic child-rearing theories, and we probably always would be. I hauled out my binder full of the notes I'd taken over the past while—the results of my "baby research" at the library, some downloaded off the net, some taken from Dr. Spock, others from more modern sources. I flipped to the stuff relating to studies about the benefits of infants sleeping with their parents and read out a paragraph or two. It didn't help much. The major problem was that he had experience already, and I didn't. Therefore, every opinion he held carried more weight with him than any theory I'd found elsewhere.

"Anyway, Mark, the baby's not due till the end of April. It's hardly likely that we'll have thirty below temperatures that late in the year." And on and on it went.

What complicated the evening's discourse was the fact that

I was, as I had promised, babysitting Eddie's automatic baby. I hadn't planned it that way; in fact, I had forgotten all about it and invited Becker over with the assumption that it would be just me and him, and the dogs, of course. Eddie had sprung it on me that afternoon, lugging the carrier-seat it came with, plus a list of instructions and a diaper bag all the way up the hill, where I had been in the planning stages of a new puppet.

"Polly—hi," he had called in a singsong voice which I knew meant a favour was about to be asked. He had a wrestling tournament that night, he said, and I had no reason to disbelieve him. Eddie was doing well with his wrestling, getting advice and coaching from Constable Earlie Morrison, Becker's partner. Earlie had been a pro wrestler once upon a time and was now a kind of big brother to him. A wrestling tournament, with all its out-of-town testosterone blown in on a visit, would not be a wise milieu for a baby doll, however significant the Family Studies unit might be on Eddie's educational vector. I'd said I would look after the creature for the evening, provided he came and picked it up again after he got home.

The instructions were simple. If the doll cried, I was to pick it up and walk with it. If it was wet (it had some sort of computerized pee-release inside its belly, apparently), I was to change it, and at certain times I was to give it a bottle of formula. The computer would be able to analyze what was put inside it—there was a powdered mixture of stuff I was supposed to prepare and administer four times throughout the evening. Eddie told me that some of the guys had fed the baby beer. The computer took note of the fact, and the Family Studies teacher had not been amused.

"No weird stuff, okay, Polly?" Eddie said, quite seriously. "I need this credit to graduate."

"I promise I won't feed your baby beer," I'd said.

"And be careful when you pick it up—support its head, I mean. My buddy Grant got nailed for child abuse that way."

"I promise I won't shake it senseless," I'd said. However, the creature proved itself to have rotten timing, and later in the evening I could have shaken its little microchips loose, if my temper had won.

Needless to say, Becker was not thrilled when I told him about my plans to travel to the U.K. in February to go to the conference. In fact, he went kind of postal.

Most of his distress, it appeared, came from the fact that I was preparing to board an airplane. Becker had received a new assignment upon his return from Calgary, a kind of secondment from his regular duties with the OPP, and though he was vague and mysterious about the details, I gathered it had something to do with airport security. The September 11th terrorist attacks were still fresh in everyone's minds, and Becker wasn't the only person who was voicing a mistrust of air travel. I knew that the airlines were reeling with the shock of the thing and that the numbers of people flying anywhere at all were alarmingly low. Everybody knew that governments worldwide were stepping up airport security measures in the wake of the tragedy, and Becker apparently had some background in the field, previous to his career as a provincial police officer, which led to his new assignment. "Research and Development", he called it, funded by the Canadian government. He wouldn't say much more than that.

"I know about these things, Polly," he said. "You have no idea how easy it is for people to board an airplane with weapons, explosives, you name it. You couldn't pay me to board a plane at the moment, and I'm sure as hell not going to let you do it either. Especially when you're carrying my baby." My Baby. Not Our Baby. Sigh.

"But if you're working to improve security, you'd think that you, of all people, would have more confidence in the whole thing than the average person, not less."

"That shows how much you know," he said. "You're not going, Polly."

"Wanna bet?"

It was at that point, of course, that the wretched automatic baby started howling. I'd stashed it in the bedroom at the back, hoping against hope that I wouldn't have to explain it to Becker, who, I knew, would not regard it with delight.

"What the fuck is that?" he said. I explained as succinctly as I could as I went to get it. It would not shut up. Becker's face darkened. "You need this?" he said. "Like you want to practice dealing with a screaming baby? Polly, I have been there—I know what this is like. I don't need reminding."

"I don't have this thing here to remind you of anything," I said. "This is a favour for Eddie."

"And how does it feel?" he said. He was looking at me with profound curiosity.

"You just have to walk it," I said. "It will stop soon." It didn't. So I went through the drill, referring to the printed instructions the thing had come with. I changed it. It still screamed. I heated up some water on the propane stove and mixed up its formula and tested it for temperature against my wrist the way the pamphlet said and stuck the bottle into the pursed, plastic mouth, and it was only then that the horrible recorded shrieks were silenced.

"You know, you could have taken the battery out," Becker said sardonically. He had been watching me with an odd smile on his face, and he hadn't offered to help. Not that there was much he could have done, I suppose, but he could have offered to hold it while I was making its formula stuff. It shrieked louder if you put it down. But no—he just sat there with his arms crossed, watching me.

"If I'd done that, Eddie would flunk his course," I said. "I told him I'd look after it."

"Your grip on reality appears to be getting loose," Becker said. "Here you are, playing baby dolls in a shack in the bush, and meanwhile, there's a real baby growing inside you, and you're planning to go on a trip to God knows where, and once again, all you're thinking of is yourself and nobody else."

From that point on, the conversation degenerated into a childish shouting match that did neither of us much credit. If the baby had been out and about at that point, instead of being safely wrapped up in its placental duvet, I think we might have torn the poor thing to pieces, each tugging at a limb like toddlers fighting over a toy. While we were yelling at each other, I recalled that old King Solomon story, the one about the mothers fighting over a baby before King Solly suggests that it be chopped in half to let each person have a bit. If I had been there, I'm not sure that even then I'd have been willing to let go of my share.

Luckily, we had reached the dessert stage by that point, so I can't say that dinner was ruined, although my stomach was distinctly unsettled by the time he stomped out, leaving half his apple pie uneaten on the plate. It didn't go to waste, though. Moments later, I found myself finishing it off—after all, I was eating for two.

After Becker had gone, I found Lug-nut and Rosie curled up together on the bed in the lean-to bedroom, their ears laid back and their eyes wide, tails thumping in that "it wasn't my fault" kind of way. I telescoped forward to a day when the kid would be present in body as well as spirit, a hearing, thinking person whose parents had just been shouting at each other.

Becker and I argued a lot, there was no doubt about it, and while we always made up at some point afterwards, the process of disagreement was rarely conducted in a mature fashion. I knew how damaging that kind of atmosphere could be to a child—how small people naturally assume that the tempests raging in the household are of their own making, how they slip into the self-assigned role of scapegoat, of perpetrator. Heck, I read the newspapers, I know how it happens. Becker and I didn't need to come to blows in order for the climate between us to reach the level designated "emotionally traumatic" by the authorities. Abusive, even. I curled up on the bed beside the dogs and stroked their fuzzy heads and spoke soothing words to them.

"It's okay," I said. "It's okay, it didn't have anything to do with you." Then it occurred to me that I couldn't say the same thing to the little fetus currently doing multiple-cell gymnastics in my belly. I placed my hand over the general area—which at thirteen weeks was already beginning to swell, a pleasant tightening, as if the muscles were binding together like some kind of protective armour. The argument I'd just had with Becker had everything to do with the baby—or at least we wouldn't have had such a nasty one if the baby wasn't a fact. If I married him, was that likely to change, or would we still grapple with control issues at every turn, bickering like children over every diaper change, every new tooth, every aspect of the process? If I were to capitulate and do what Becker wanted, tie the knot and move in with him, ditch the conference and concentrate on motherhood to the exclusion of all else, including my work and my independence, would that guarantee a healthy, well-adjusted child? Would the child's mother then become a faceless wife, an acquiescent brood mare? Okay—I know that those are extreme notions, and quite unfair to Becker, but I'm only telling you what I was thinking. Chalk it up to hormones. The fact is that while I had decided to have the baby, I was determined to have it on my own terms, and my fight with Becker had finally clued me in to the hard fact that I couldn't do the motherhood thing entirely by myself. There was one all-important factor that had only just registered. The baby itself. Himself? Herself? Whatever—no woman is an island. At least, no pregnant woman is. She's an archipelago.

Whatever decisions I made in the next seven months had to be made with the understanding that for the next twenty years or so, my choices would be affecting two of us. Three, perhaps, if I loosened my hold on the reins enough to let the child's father have a vote, but those choices could no longer affect just one person only. This hit me with such profound force that it took my breath away.

I patted my belly. "Sorry about all that," I said to it. "I'll try to make sure that doesn't happen again. In the meantime, how 'bout another piece of pie?"

Before it could answer one way or another, the automatic baby, forgotten in the corner, started howling again. Sibling rivalry is a terrible thing.

Five

Nearly every new parent feels exactly the same way you do. A baby changes everything, from your lifestyle to your schedule to your desire level. But you can get the old magic back with a little attention and some tricks from other parents who've been there.
-From *Big Bertha's Total Baby Guide*

We were having the weirdest winter on record— ridiculously mild, with hardly any snow to speak of. Oh, we were blessed with a couple of inches of the white stuff at Christmas time, a kind of cosmetic icing that fell thick and wet and broke tree branches with its weight, but it disappeared under a warmish rain by New Year's Day. In the second week of January we had a thaw (which was redundant, as there was nothing to melt) that made it feel like March, with blue skies, a lemon-yellow sun and enough warmth to fool the trees into setting leaf buds. George said he'd never seen anything like it, and the weather-gods must have arranged it in order to make things easy for me, pregnant and barefoot up in my cabin.

And truly, the lack of snow and mild temperatures did make it easy. It was quite cold enough to need the woodstove, of course, but there wasn't that feeling of being in danger of freezing to death overnight. When the temperature drops to more than twenty below zero Celsius, some of us get that tight, back-of-the-throat fear that makes you stuff the wood box before bed, then worry all night that the wretched thing is going to overheat and fry you in your sleep. There was none of that—the red juice in my thermometer rarely fell below minus five Celsius. Because there was no snow, the travel along the hill path from cabin to farmhouse and driveway was no trouble at all, except that I found that my centre of balance had shifted. Walking on a slope, even a gentle one, with some recently gained frontal poundage put everything a tad off-kilter, which meant that when going downhill, I had to lean back very slightly, as if I were carrying a heavy basket of peaches.

A couple of days before Christmas, Becker took me out to dinner before hopping on a plane to Calgary to spend the weekend with his son, Bryan and his ex-wife, Catherine. He said he had stuff to do concerning his father's estate, and initially, I felt no jealously about this. I hadn't seen much of him since he'd returned from the funeral, anyway, as he was spending most of his time in Toronto on his airport security assignment.

We'd gotten together for meals and the occasional movie when he was in town, of course, but the distance between us was growing as quickly as my belly was, and we hadn't made love since I'd told him about my pregnancy.

"I feel like you don't want me near you any more," he had said to me in early December. "It's like you've got a part of me inside you now, and that's all you want." I could have replied with a similar remark—that I felt he didn't want to touch me any more, now that my body was preoccupied with knitting together the cells of his progeny, but I didn't say it. Anyway, I was frankly not interested in sex—so maybe it was my fault after all. The more remote we became, the less we talked about it.

George, Susan, Eddie and I would be celebrating the holiday together, as we had done since Eddie had come to live with Susan. We were all able to steer more or less clear of the Christmas imperative that makes some households vibrate with tinsel and tension from November 1 to December 25. I'd had trouble choosing a Christmas gift for Becker, though. I thought about a book to begin with—books are the best presents, in my view, but Becker wasn't much of a reader, except for computer manuals and the occasional Stephen King horror novel. He kept a bunch of magazines and comic books in the rack in the bathroom, and Bryan's room in his apartment (kept kid-like for when the boy came to visit) boasted a small bookshelf full of Becker's old childhood classics, but he really hadn't acquired much in the way of reading material since he was a teenager. I wandered around the mall for a couple of days before Christmas, grinding my teeth at the ruthless, piped-in music blaring over the speakers, which I was convinced had a subliminal track running through it—"buy, buy, buy, you pathetic creatures, buy lotsa stuff to prove you love somebody."

I found myself in the Big Chain Bookstore but couldn't face actually spending the forty-odd bucks on the new Stephen King hardcover, which Becker might have read already, for all I knew. I checked out the health and family section and considered (for one very brief moment) giving him a copy of *Father to Be*, but I didn't think he'd get the joke. I was feeling a bit dazed by then, the mall having worked its evil magic upon me, making me consider quite seriously the purchase of a package of shiny, seasonal decorations—the kind of thing you gaze at in surprise when you get home and say "I don't remember buying that." I was surrounded by junked-up, frantic, jingle-bell-frenzied moms and kids, and more than a little aware of the fact that soon I too would have to learn the balance of can-have and can't-have. I'd have to learn the language of momhood: "Don't touch that, you little brat, or Santa's not gonna leave you nothing."

As for Santa, I figure he must have a hell of a time trying

to decide what, precisely, to give all the bazillions of little children who expect him to cough up the goods every year. It's hard to buy for somebody about whom one knows little except their naughty-or-nice scores. I knew Becker's, sort of, but I bet Santa had a better handle on him than I did, even though I was the one carrying his baby. I was still wearing Becker's engagement ring on a chain around my neck, and I was so used to having it there that I barely noticed it any more. It had been a long time since I'd taken it off the chain and tried it out on my finger. Anyway, my fingers were too swollen (a pregnant lady thing) for it to fit by then.

The elegant kitchenware store had a lot of nice glass and pottery and culinary doo-hickeys, but I felt that if I gave him something like that, he would take it as an indication that I wanted to move in with him, or that I was thinking in domestic terms. Too much like a wedding gift, too much like an answer to the ring question.

I ended up getting him a CD, the latest Barenaked Ladies album (which was a safe bet, as he had one or two by the same band already in his truck) and a pair of locally-made leather moccasins. Yes, I know. One step up from a tie, but I was desperate.

When we finally got around to making that curiously formal exchange, he admitted to having had a hard time as well, when it came to choosing something to give me. He'd settled on a book—a *For Better or Worse* comics anthology, and a large box of expensive chocolates, which we both knew I would eat compulsively, all by myself, in about three hours.

We were doing this ritual, pre-Christmas dinner at the Mooseview Resort—a pricey place, and not insignificantly, the cradle of the evening wherein we had engaged in unprotected sex. After you have fallen, go back to the garden, I guess.

"I have something for you, but you don't need to open it now," Becker said, as we were finishing a shared piece of chocolate cheesecake, which had been billed "death by decadence" on the menu. "It's just a token thing. There's lots I wanted to get, but I kept second-guessing myself, thinking you'd take it the wrong way."

"I know what you mean," I said. "And thanks for saying so." I was a bit surprised by this remark, actually, as Becker wasn't usually so frank about his feelings. "We should have mentioned it earlier, I guess, and agreed not to exchange anything." He seemed shocked by this and slightly annoyed.

"That's not what I meant," he said. "I want to give you everything, not nothing."

It sounded like soap opera dialogue; I couldn't bear it, and I'm afraid I sighed out loud. I might even have rolled my eyes, showing my best sensitive and tactful side. I apologized at once.

"Did you know that every time you say or do something bitchy these days, you immediately chalk it up to hormones and being pregnant?" he said, in a dangerously light, conversational voice. "It's really interesting. I can hardly wait to hear what kind of excuse you come up with after the baby's born, and you're back to normal."

"I'm not sure what normal is," I said, trying to match his tone. It came out sounding as brittle as the wine glass that he was holding, which looked ready to shatter in his white-knuckled grip. "I used to be a childless woman, and I'm not likely to return to that state any time soon."

"You chose it, Polly."

"I did. And I'm guessing that you'd probably have preferred me to make a different choice."

He sat back, exasperated. "Of course not, that's not fair. I just wish you'd include me a bit more, that's all."

"By moving in with you and marrying you, you mean."

"Or by taking into account that I'm involved, at least."

"You're the one who's going to Calgary for Christmas." Ouch. That one just popped out by itself. I'd known about it since the summer, when Bryan had gone out west with his mother, and Becker had promised to visit and spend the holiday with them. I'd always accepted it and insisted that to me Christmas was no big deal, and Becker should by all means spend it with his son. Maybe it was the residue of the mall experience that made me suddenly want Becker to stay. Or made me pretend to want that. I don't know—maybe I was just being bitchy, and the hormones had nothing to do with it.

Well, he got mad, and I don't blame him. The rest of our spat-dance included all the requisite steps, from hissing at each other like snakes over the paying of the bill, through the sullen silence in the truck, treading the light fantastic over our mutually guilt ridden apologies just before we got to the farm, to the balm of the make-up kiss and hug, the shamefaced and hurried exchange of our meaningless parcels, and the fragile goodbye.

"I'll call you as soon as I get back," Becker said. It was snowing, the only snow we got, it turned out, until the night I left to catch a plane for England.

*   *   *

By the middle of January, I had, as Susan had predicted, expanded. I wasn't as big as a house—more like a small cabin, as I still had three months to go before lift-off. I was having dreams by then of splitting apart like a burnt sausage, and my skin was so sensitive that I could feel the slightest shift in the air, as if the atmosphere around my body had grown hands. If you've been involved in this kind of show already, you know the drill. My ankles were thicker by the day, I had to pee every four minutes, and I felt physically co-opted for some purpose that had very little to do with me at all. One of the many books I'd acquired said "You don't really have the baby, the baby has you." Yep. Preparing for my trip to England helped to take my mind off my body, for which I was grateful.

The organizers of the conference had requested that I take along a couple of samples of my work, and it was a difficult decision, as I knew I couldn't afford to take a great big pile of puppets with me. They'd asked me to do a marionette construction seminar, with an emphasis on methods for making and manipulating moving parts. I wanted to have some good pieces to use as examples, but most of my favourites had been sold. Still, one of my most inspired creations had been a puppet I'd made of a policeman (which bore a marked resemblance to Becker), and Constable Earlie Morrison, Becker's partner, had it hanging in his bathroom. I knew I could borrow it back from him for a little while, and it wouldn't take much to alter it for its debut on the Canterbury stage. It had originally been designed to conceal a little pop-up version of the male member, a functioning moving part, you might say—perfect for the seminar. The original extra piece had been omitted from the finished puppet, for reasons of delicacy on the part of the artist and the eventual owner, but it would be no trouble to mold a new one and attach it.

I had decided to use the month of January to construct a companion for the policeman puppet, and I would use these two in my seminar. They would both be reasonably lightweight—the heads being constructed out of a thin layer of air-dry clay over a *papier mâché* base, the arms and legs of carved wood, and the hands and feet of clay as well. I usually make puppet bodies out of a core of dowel (in order to have something to screw the joint-mechanisms into), pad them with quilting, then sew a canvas skin over top. Packed properly into a box, with lots of soft stuff wedged in the gaps, they wouldn't come to any harm in transit, I figured. The policeman puppet had a beautifully made (if I do say so myself) little uniform, complete with hat, boots, belt and a teeny tiny gun—which I'd found in the dollar store in downtown Laingford.

The companion puppet turned out to be (pause as everybody says out loud that they saw this coming a mile away) a pregnant lady. I don't go for subtlety in my work, you'll have gathered. The thing is that I work with whatever is uppermost in my mind (it makes for in-the-moment creativity), and so the modelling of hands and head and feet was done in a fairly abstract way—I was merely making a female figure, and it wasn't until I'd finished the lower leg and foot of my little person and noticed that the poor thing's ankles were all puffy that I realized what I was doing. Too late to quit, by that time, as January was streaking by. While constructing the torso, I left a small, hollow space in the belly, about the size of a squashed navel orange. I lined it with red felt and put a soft, padded door on the front of it, held shut with a tiny brass catch from the hobby shop. This made perfect sense at the time. It meant, of course, that I would have to make a small pair of bloomers for the creature, in order to preserve what little dignity I'd left her, and I designed the costume she wore, a maternity tent, to lift easily. And needless to say, I then had to sculpt a baby. This one, at any rate, I would have complete control over. I planned to attach a string to its head.

Six

Babies resemble grandparents and great-grandparents because, just as there are many seeds hidden in the earth, so there are seeds hidden in mankind, which give us the features of our ancestors. That's what they used to say.
-From *Big Bertha's Total Baby Guide*

"Why is it that passport photos always make you look criminally insane?" I was sitting in the Slug and Lettuce Pub (drinking soda pop, I might add) with my photographer friend Dimmy Cox. I contemplated my picture, the one I'd had taken at Shutterbug, the local photo shop, which now adorned my brand new passport. I looked sullen—no, worse than sullen—I looked like a terrorist.

"My theory is it's because passport photos are usually taken by people who would rather be doing something else, and they make you feel uncomfortable," Dimmy said, sipping a Kuskawa Cream Ale. It looked ice-cold, condensation beading on the outside of the glass, golden yellow and delicious.

"Hey, can I have a sip of that?" I said.

"You think you should?"

"A sip won't hurt," I said. "I just want to see if it tastes okay." I did truly want to know that, because ever since I had become pregnant, my body had taken it upon itself to reject beer in no uncertain terms. Beer, my favourite beverage, and Kuskawa Cream, my beer of choice, had made me gag back in August. I had brand loyalty issues at stake here. Just because I was abstaining for the requisite nine months, didn't mean I was on the wagon for life. I just wanted to experiment. After all, I was going to the United Kingdom, homeland of perfect beer. I couldn't help remembering something my mother had said, many years ago, that had somehow stuck in my mind. "When your grandmother was carrying us," she'd said (which was back in Ireland, before they'd emigrated), "her doctor prescribed a pint of Guinness every day. He said it was good for pregnant ladies—full of vitamins." Of all the things I remembered my mother saying, this was one of the biggies. "Guinness is good for you," spoken in all seriousness.

I lifted Dimmy's glass, looking around me before I did it to make sure nobody was watching. Taking even a mouthful of alcoholic something or other while pregnant is considered a serious crime. I didn't want to offend anybody. I took a sip, and it was gorgeous. Yummy. Nectar, in fact.

"You be careful," Dimmy said, watching me. "You don't want this kid coming out with one of those thin upper lips and eyes too far apart—the fetal alcohol syndrome thing."

I bristled. "One sip of beer won't be doing that, Dimmy," I said and told her what my mother used to say.

"Yeah, I think we're maybe a bit overprotective about that stuff over here," she said. "Still, you want to give yourself every opportunity to have a healthy baby, right?" I nodded glumly. My having been forced by circumstance to abandon my cherished vices still rankled, and this was the first time I'd been in the pub since July. Maybe it hadn't been a terribly good idea meeting Dimmy there. I was clearly not over-endowed in the impulse-control department. This would mean that in England, I'd have to avoid pubs—and what kind of insanity was that? England—the place where the word pub was born, those warm rooms in every village, cozy and ancient, with dozens of wonderful, dark and powerful brews just begging to be sampled. It was going to be torture.

"Back to this passport," I said, handing back Dimmy's glass with more than just a twinge of regret. "It just arrived, and I'm glad to get it in time, but you know, I'd kind of expected it to be more imposing, somehow. More official. It looks like a cheap notebook from the dollar store." The small, blue booklet was softcovered, stamped in gold, certainly, but with none of the heft I'd imagined. "It looks like something you could lose really easily."

"You better get one of those body purses," Dimmy said. "You know, the kind you strap below your clothing, to put your travellers' cheques and passport in."

"I'm going to England, not India," I said. "I don't want to do the paranoid traveller thing. I can just see me having to undress every time I want to buy a newspaper."

"I think you'd be safe carrying your cash in the usual place," she said. "Anyway, it's just a thought. Canadian passports are very much in demand, I hear."

"You think I need one of those little Canadian flags to put on my backpack?"

"You're taking a backpack? No suitcase?"

"Well, I was hoping to do a little hiking while I'm there."

"Polly, you'll be seven months pregnant by then—you won't want to be hiking. Anyway, February in England will hardly be hiking season."

"I'm not planning to do any mountain climbing. I just want to be able to travel around without worrying about luggage," I said. Okay, maybe I was being unreasonable, but it was my first time going anywhere, and I had a romantic image of walking along one of those footpaths England was famous for, brandishing an old hickory walking stick and enjoying the view.

Dimmy knew me well enough to let the subject drop. The

more she tried to convince me that hiking in England in February was a bad idea, the more inclined I'd be to do it.

Later that afternoon, I did go to the luggage place and pick up one of those body purses. It was white cotton and looked like a rather spinsterly piece of underclothing, with curious straps and a little zippered pocket. However, it held my passport quite nicely, as well as the modest number of travellers' cheques I'd bought at the bank.

*   *   *

About a week before I was due to leave, Becker showed up at my door, carrying a mysterious package. He had the same expression on his face that Eddie had worn when he'd arrived at my doorstep with the automatic baby. He wanted something.

I was in the middle of packing up my puppets. I'd found a sturdy case at a junk shop—a hard-shelled thing with a nice leather handle, which had once upon a time been used for a brass instrument, a horn of some sort. I'd torn out the insides and lined it with styrofoam, carved to conform to the shape of the little bodies it would contain. In a fit of morbid creativity, I'd then finished the interior with satin, so it looked an awful lot like a small, two-person coffin.

"What the hell is that?" he said.

"It's a packing case. I'm taking a couple of puppets with me for a seminar I'm doing." I was hoping he wouldn't look too closely at the policeman puppet, which he had seen before, acknowledging that it looked a teensy bit like himself. He had not seen it since I'd remodelled the missing appendage and wired it up. The little trousers had a peek-a-boo slit in the fly, and a discreet line ran from the tip of the tiny member to the complicated cross-piece at the top, from which the puppet was manipulated. With a flick of a finger, the puppet penis could spring to attention. I'd showed it to Susan the night before, and she'd almost wet herself. Becker, though, might not find it quite as amusing as we did.

"You're gonna have trouble with that going through customs," he said.

"I hope not. The conference people told me to get a carnet—you know, a set of import papers that describe what you're bringing in, and I did that. Here it is—it should be okay." The carnet had cost me a pretty penny, but international regulations required it. I had photographed the puppets and made a list of the materials from which they were made, as well as estimating the value of the things. The puppets were deemed "professional equipment", and it wouldn't cost me any extra duty or tax, as long as I had the carnet. The official I had dealt with suggested that I keep the estimate of value low, because I'd been told I had to give them a deposit equivalent to the duty and tax payable if the goods had been exported for sale. It was sort of like a bond—I didn't really understand it, but then there are times when it's best just to do what you're told. I scratched out what I'd originally written ("priceless"), and wrote $200 instead, which was low-balling, big time. However, a $200 ransom, which is how I thought of it, was all I could afford.

"You're really going through with this trip, aren't you?" Becker said, which struck me as a monumentally dumb thing to say. I had my passport, my ticket, my knapsack (with a little Canadian flag sewn on) and my puppet case and the official carnet. It wasn't as if I was having cold feet, for pity's sake. I'd be gone in seven days' time.

"Yes, Becker. I'm really going through with it."

"Nothing I can say to make you change your mind?"

"Nope."

"You wouldn't be interested in hearing about the rumours of terrorist activity at Pearson International Airport?"

"That's not fair, Becker. You're just making that up."

"Am I? How do you know? I'd know better than you in this case, at least, because I've been working with the people in security down there."

"I know you have. And I know as well as you do that if the rumours were true, they'd shut the airport down and send us all home. So quit fretting. I'll be fine."

"Didn't the airline make a fuss about letting you fly when you're, um, like that?"

"Like what? Fat, you mean?" We were getting spatty. Well, I was. I suspect that Becker was trying to be patient in the face of it.

"I mean," he said, after a tiny pause, "when you're so far advanced in your pregnancy."

"As of next Monday, I'll be twenty-eight weeks gone. You're allowed to fly up until week thirty-two. I made sure about that. I even have a note from Cass Wright about my expected delivery date, in case they ask."

"Which is the first or second week of May, right?"

"Right. No worries, Mark."

"What about cabin pressure, low humidity, stuff like that?" I was impressed. It was almost as if he really cared—like he'd done his homework and was truly worried about me and the child I was carrying, and not just freaking out because he wasn't in control of the situation.

"They suggested an aisle seat at the bulkhead," I said, "so I made a special request. Not that I know what a bulkhead is, you understand, but I'm trying to do this by the book, you know. I'm not really the perverse little puppy you think I am."

"Could have fooled me."

"And they say I'm supposed to drink lots of fluids during the flight—and walk around a lot so my ankles don't swell up—although if I'm drinking fluids, I'll be walking to the bathroom every two minutes during the whole flight, anyway."

"Bathroom—that's what the bulkhead is, Polly. You won't have far to walk."

"Oh, great. Put the pregnant lady next to the can—isn't that like being stuck at the table by the kitchen door when you're dining alone? Charming."

"You'll probably be thankful for it."

"So you've accepted that I'm going, then."

"Oh, yeah. Of course I have, sweetheart. Just making a last ditch effort." He hadn't called me sweetheart in ages—not since that night about a week after I'd told him about the baby, when he'd got roaring drunk and held me in his arms, stroking my bare tummy with a freckled hand and rocking me back and forth while he held back tears. We hadn't made love that night—he couldn't, truth be told, but it was the closest we'd been in all the ensuing months. Hearing it gave me a twinge below, down in the places where I used to play, as Mr. Cohen would say. I touched the back of his hand gently with one finger.

"I'll be fine, Mark," I said again.

"I hope so. And if you're really going, I have a favour to ask you."

"Uh-huh?" I was actually hoping the favour he wanted was a sexual one, because I was all of a sudden quite willing to provide it, but that was not what he had in mind.

"You know that we cremated my dad, back in October, right?"

"Yep. You told me that." I was still a tad unhappy that he had not asked me to fly out to join him for the funeral. It would have been something at least, seeing as he'd never let me have the chance to meet the old guy while he was still alive.

"Well, my sister and I were going to scatter the ashes at his fishing cabin up at the lake, near Jasper, but we decided not to."

"How come?"

"Ever since I can remember, Dad talked about going back to England—to Sussex, where he was born—just to visit, not to live. He always talked about it like it would be as good as winning the Stanley Cup, like he would win something there that would make him happy. When Mom was alive, he always said he'd take her back to visit his mom. He never did, though. He didn't even go back for her funeral, in 1980."

"Where in Sussex?" I asked. Not that I knew Sussex from Wales as far as geography was concerned, but I could see where this was leading, and I wanted to find out how far Sussex was from Canterbury. "Eastbourne," he said. "A small, seaside town, I think. Picturesque, probably. Worth a visit. There are these white cliffs there—you know the song 'The White Cliffs of Dover', the one the Andrews Sisters used to sing? Like those, I guess. He used to go up there and look at the sea and play when he was a kid, a place called Beachy Head, I think."

"You want me to go and scatter his ashes there, don't you?"

"My sister and I talked about it on the phone last night. She's cool with it."

"This is something you two should be doing, not me, Mark. I didn't even know your dad."

"I know you never got the chance to meet him, and I'm sorry about that. You would have liked each other." I refrained from mentioning that I'd wanted to meet him, and Becker had made it almost impossible to do so.

"So, why don't you hang on to the ashes a bit longer, and go over there with your sister in the summer and visit your family, or whatever? It's not that I wouldn't be happy to do it,

Mark. It just seems a kind of ceremonial thing, and it would be meaningless if I did it."

"It won't get done, otherwise, Polly," Becker said with some bitterness. "I'm a lot like my dad in more ways than you can imagine. I'd just talk about it and talk about it, and Dad's ashes would just sit there in my bedroom closet for years and never get back to Sussex, ever."

"Isn't it illegal to sprinkle human remains in public places?"

"Officially, it might be. But nobody needs to know." ·

"And how do I get dear old Dad through customs, Mark? You got a carnet for him?" I didn't mean to sound so callous, but then he was the one who was so all-fired serious about customs issues.

"Hey, it's just a little bag of ash, and I've got a photocopy of his death certificate and his cremation form from the funeral parlour. It should be fine. You can just say you're returning the ashes to his birthplace for interment. It's done all the time."

"It is? Golly. And do you have relatives over there in Eastbourne who might be interested in being involved, or do I just hike up there to Beachy Head by myself and cast him to the winds?" Hike. I'd said the word hike, and suddenly had a lovely picture of a solemn walk along a blustery clifftop, the wind whipping the waves into stiff peaks, the salt air on my lips and my hair blowing out behind me like a scene from *The French Lieutenant's Woman*. This might take care of my hiking yen quite nicely, with the minimum of fuss.

"Dad was an only child, but Grandma had a sister who still lives in the area, my great aunt Edith."

"Are you in touch with her?"

"No, I only met her once, when she came over for Mom's funeral in '97. She was pretty frail and had never even met

Mom, although they wrote lots of letters back and forth. I think they started that after my grandmother died. Mom used to say that Edith was lonely all by herself over there. Dad was surprised she made the trip for Mom's sake, though."

"Did you let her know when your dad died?"

"We sent a letter, but she didn't respond, but then she's really old, and her connection was really with my mom. She still might be alive, anyhow. I'll find out and get you her address. So you'll do it, Polly?"

"I suppose so," I said. "There's a little free time in the conference schedule, so as long as this place isn't too far from Canterbury, I could probably swing it."

"Yesss," he said and did that clenched-fist, pumping-arm thing people do when they've won something. He really seemed hugely pleased, like I'd just given him the best present in the world. There was a curious gleam in his eyes, as if he'd been expecting me to say no and couldn't believe that I'd agreed. It felt great to make him happy so easily. God knows I hadn't been excelling in that department recently. With a conscious air of ceremony, he handed over the cremated remains of Edward Millbank Becker, tightly wrapped in plastic and nestled in a little blue velvet bag, complete with travelling papers. It weighed more than I expected, a couple of pounds, actually, but I suppose the bony bits of an adult male human, even after a spell in a fiery furnace and a session in a big crusher-thing, would still add up, bulkwise. I handled the package gingerly, the way I'd handle a baby if someone suddenly handed me one without warning. Ashes to ashes. It occurred to me that I had just added enormously to my status as a courier of metaphor—I would be crossing the Pond as a representative of three stages of humanhood, a beginning, a middle and an end.

At the time, it struck me as enormously significant.

Seven

The rule of thumb for expecting moms is wear whatever makes you feel good—and comfortable. Beyond that, it's best to wear separates such as a skirt or pants with a top to accommodate frequent trips to the bathroom. Layer your clothing to cope with sudden temperature changes, from the arctic blast of an air-conditioned airport to the stifling heat of a crowded bus.
   -From *Big Bertha's Total Baby Guide*

The night before I left for the U.K., Susan and George threw a little going-away party for me. I'd never had one before, although when I toured theatre I'd travelled around North America pretty extensively. My only parting from Aunt Susan of any previous celebratory significance was the day I left Laingford for a Toronto art school, back in the eighties. Then, my hair was dyed electric green, and we both knew I needed to be elsewhere, however remarkably well we got on. We had both expressed frank relief at the thought of a separation. This time it was different; there was a bewildering air of regret in the room, as if the people seeing me off expected never to see me again.

"I just have a bad feeling about this trip," Theresa Morton told me privately as I took her coat in the hall. She wears a cloak these days, a Harris tweed thing of enormous width and weight, like a blanket. Beneath it she was wearing black, a pleasant, floaty thing with jet beading.

"Thanks for telling me. I'll be fine, Terry," I said. "Nice dress."

"It's vintage," she said. "Rico found it for me."

"He and Brent have been here about half an hour. They came early with lots of grocery bags, and they've taken over the kitchen. It smells wonderful in there."

Rico and Brent were determined to iron out any negative wrinkles in the evening and were performing very funny TV chef impersonations and whipping up something naked in the wok. George and Susan were having a blast being the audience, I think, although the raven had retreated long ago to the barn. Eddie was chef's assistant and was playing his own riff off the Rico and Brent Show with prodigal flair. He was stone-straight, too—I asked. His exhibition was natural, not chemical. This confirmed for me a long-standing suspicion that he was destined for the stage. Lug-nut and Rosencrantz were doing a creditable job as busdogs, keeping the floor very clean.

Later, we all gathered around the long harvest table in the kitchen to eat a shrimp and noodle dish that was so good we couldn't help but gobble it. Dimmy Cox had come, and Earlie Morrison. No Becker, who had called at six to say he had to finish a seriously overdue report and couldn't make it. He was sending Morrison in his stead, he joked, and did I mind if Morrison drove me to the airport tomorrow night, as this report was taking longer than he had anticipated? We both knew perfectly well that Earlie had been invited in his own right as an honorary member of the family, being Eddie's wrestling coach and friend, so the joke, meant perhaps to be self-mocking, came off sounding mean. I was annoyed that he was ducking out, and I spent most of the evening trying not to let it show.

At the serving-out, George had proposed a toast to "Polly's first trip to the Old Country and a successful conference and safe return". After everybody took a swig (I didn't touch my ginger ale, because you're not supposed to toast yourself, Brent said), I replied in kind.

"I'll be back in a week, so I hope you're already planning my coming home party, which had better be as good as this one." It got a laugh, but there was still an uneasy feel to things, and I wasn't sure if it was real, or if I was projecting some personal apprehension onto everybody else. I couldn't shake the feeling that the general cheer was false. It reminded me of the "NDP victory party" we had for Aunt Susan one election night years ago, when she'd been utterly buried under a Tory landslide. I thought about mentioning this, but didn't.

The whole trip had developed for me like a Polaroid photo labelled "escape", and while that didn't change my mind about going, it did make me pause to wonder what exactly I was running from. A decision, you think? Nah—too easy.

"I've arranged a Hotmail address for you, Polly," Susan said from across the table, over coffee and dessert.

"A what address?"

"Hotmail—it's an email account so we can keep in touch when you're there."

"I'm travelling light, Susan. It's not like I've got room for a laptop in my knapsack. I'll send you a postcard or two, don't worry. And I'll bring you back something from Fortnum's."

"There's such a thing as an Internet café," Theresa said. "That's a great idea, Susan. Then you can put us in a newsgroup and keep us all in the loop."

"What loop would that be?" I said. "I won't have time to write a travel diary, guys. For pity's sake, it's only one week."

"Lots can happen in a week in your third trimester," Rico added in a fake English accent.

"Yeah, do you have all your medical info with you, Polly?"

That was Dimmy. "Health insurance? Bet you had to pay a bundle, eh?" I ignored that one. I had paid a lot—through the nose, as a matter of fact. Not an item covered by the Puppetry Festival's Mary Chambers Memorial Bursary, I might add.

"Look, I'll send an occasional email when I can, and Susan can pass on my love and regards to you all, but believe me, the silence will mean everything's fine. I promise I'll let you know if there's a problem, but there won't be."

"Postcards are nice to get," Earlie said, accepting a black coffee but turning down seconds on the tiramisu. "I used to collect them when I was a kid."

"Hey, so did I," said Dimmy. "I have a cousin in Maine, and we've had a contest going for years to find the most boring postcard in the world. Right now, the winners are an exterior shot of the Parry Sound Hospital and some mall parking lot in Kennebunkport." So the melancholy moment passed. Good thing I didn't blurt out my memory of the NDP "we lost the election" party. Bad karma, as Theresa would say.

*   *   *

My flight was scheduled for nine p.m., and baggage check was at eight, so Morrison was coming to pick me up at five-ish. Becker called to say goodbye an hour before that. It was a long phone call, and I felt a lot better about things after our final exchange of endearments and our gentle hanging up. Of course, Becker and I have never been ones for loving nicknames, so I suppose endearments is the wrong word. He was hardly a Boojums, and I'd stopped calling people Darling after I quit the theatre biz. He called me Polly. I called him Mark, and more often, Becker. Still, the tone of the "Polly" and "Mark" by the end of the conversation was deeply satisfying. The report he was working on was important—career-moving important—to do with the airport security thing, and I understood that better after listening for a bit. And at the end, he said he loved me. Right out loud, even. I wish I'd been there.

Of course, it snowed for the first time since Christmas on the drive down to the city.

"I love the way the weather gods time their stuff," I said, mostly to relax myself, as I'm not the world's happiest passenger. Actually, I was relieved that Earlie was at the wheel and not Becker, who drives his Cherokee a tad aggressively, as if it were a tank. The road was slick with wet snow, and visibility was crummy. Morrison's car is one of those big, boat-like sedans, with an automatic transmission and bench seats as wide as sofas. He drove the speed limit in the slow lane, like I do, and his windshield wipers were new, so it wasn't so bad, but I was still making liberal use of the phantom brake, and he could see me doing it.

"At least you're getting out before it gets ugly," he said. "Over there, in mid-February, you'll probably see flowers—snowdrops and crocuses."

"This early? Really?"

"Yeah, England's had a mild winter, too, you know."

"Mmm. Some sun would be a treat." The winter had thus far been grey and dark in Kuskawa, and if there's no snow, the meagre light has nothing to reflect it back and gets swallowed up by the trees and rocks.

"Are you really planning to do some hiking? Dimmy mentioned you were thinking of it."

"Hiking may be too strong a term," I said. "I do want to see the sea, just to say I've seen it, you know. And throw a rock in it or something. And I'd love to visit an old ruined castle."

"There's lots of those," Earlie said. "I took dad over a couple of years ago."

"I didn't know that. Got any travel advice for me?"

"Neither a borrower nor a lender be."

"You're a bit young for Polonius, Earlie. Laertes, maybe."

"The loyal brother to the girl? No way. Not the brother—way too whiny for me. Cast me as Guildenstern, and I'll sit in the wings and share beers with your dogs."

"You never struck me as a Shakespeare buff."

"Oh yeah, I try to get down to Stratford once in a while and take in a play. You see Kenneth Branagh's *Hamlet*? I've got it on video."

Deconstructing Branagh took us all the way to Barrie, where we stopped at Tim Hortons for a pee and a coffee.

"You want anything?" Earlie said as I set off at an urgent pace in the direction of the ladies' room.

"One large coffee to go, triple cream, half a sugar, please." That was my personal mantra according to the litany of the Hortonite. Earlie's was "small black to go"—the shortest version in the repertoire, while Becker's was "medium double-double" and Susan's was "medium coffee with milk, please, one sugar." We all had them, and they fell trippingly off the tongue with long accustomed use.

South of Barrie, the snow stopped suddenly, as if we'd passed through an invisible shield, designed to cut the greater Toronto area off from the real world. The pavement was bare and dry, and I could see in the twilight that there was a fair bit of green in the fields surrounding Canada's Wonderland. The amusement park's bleak, fake mountain rose from a nest of bare-branched trees—a grey and alien structure in the middle of what used to be prime agricultural acreage. Wonderland acts as a kind of city signpost for southbound drivers—a sentinel from which one could imagine George Lucas-type Star Wars army drones pouring out at the sound of the city hall alarm, fifty kilometers away on Queen Street.

Morrison took the toll highway to the airport, and the traffic was light. We arrived a whole hour before the recommended time for baggage check, which meant I'd have to hang around in the terminal for a while. This didn't bother me, as I fly so rarely that it counted as a pleasant diversion, but Morrison seemed to want to linger and see me off.

"You don't need to stay, Earlie," I said. I wanted to go and choose some inflight reading material and wander around the duty free by myself. I could feel my whole mind letting go of great wodges of anxiety and home-related unfinished business, as if it were peeling off my body in layers, like wet wallpaper. "I'll be fine, and the weather's not going to keep off Toronto forever, so you'd better drive while the driving's still good."

"You won't get distracted by something and miss your flight, right? And you'll call as soon as you land?"

"Call who?"

"Call me," he said, to my great surprise. He thrust a business card into my hand. I didn't even know he had one, though I suppose all constables of the Ontario Provincial Police are given them as standard issue. "Put that somewhere where you won't lose it," he said. "I've been designated the official correspondent to Polly Deacon, woman at large— oops, sorry. No offense intended."

"Official correspondent?"

"The Hotmail thing," he said. "Or postcards—whatever. George asked me to have one more stab at making sure you stay in touch. He thought you'd be happier sending a word my way, rather than feeling pressured to call home, or feeling that everybody's being nosy. Becker would be better, I said, but

George didn't think so. I said it was a long shot, but I'd try. I'll relay any stuff you send to the interested parties."

"Who are the interested parties?"

"Everybody's on email, Polly, except you. There's Rico and Brent, Theresa, Dimmy, me, Becker and George and Susan. That's six computers. People care about you, Polly. You should let them. I'll be posting regular updates, if you care to send any."

"If I find an Internet café in Canterbury, Earlie, I promise I will send you an occasional word or two, just to make you happy." I stowed the card away in my purse, where my ticket and passport were zipped into an inside pocket. During the journey, I had checked them dozens of times to make sure they were still there. I'll never be a seasoned traveller in the sense that I will never be blasé about my official paper-stuff.

"And here's something for you to put in your pocket," Earlie said, reaching into his own and pulling out a handful of change. He fished in his palm and then pulled out an old brown coin, a little bigger than a quarter, wafer thin.

"I don't know where the heck this came from originally, but I've carried it around for years," he said. "It's a ha'penny—an English half-penny, 1919. It won't buy you much, but maybe it'll be good luck."

"You're not afraid I'll lose it?" I said as he dropped it into my upturned palm. King George V's head on one side and a figure enthroned on the other. When it was minted at the end of the First World War, I imagine it would have bought something—a slice of bread and cheese, maybe, or a newspaper. In England now, it would be considered worthless, although an eighty-three-year-old coin here at home was considered a collectible.

"You won't lose it," Morrison said. There was a little pause. I wasn't sure if that was a declaration of faith or an order.

Didn't matter. I put it into the pocket of the incredibly attractive fat pants I was wearing for the flight. Tilley stuff. Drawstring-waisted, tough and very baggy. I could have hidden an Uzi in there, and the pockets were nice and deep.

"Thanks, Earlie. See ya in a week." I felt moved to give him a hug and did so. Our mutual girth meant that we had to stretch like giraffes to touch cheeks, which must have looked hilarious to any curious bystander, but I didn't care. Suddenly, I was missing Morrison, although he was right there, which meant that I was having a maudlin episode—brought on, no doubt, by the personal hormonal martini I was currently mainlining.

"Okay—I'm outta here. Take care of yourself, Polly, and have a good time, okay?"

"'Kay. Safe home, Earlie." Then he was gone, leaving me in the middle of Pearson International Airport, rubbing my fingers over the surface of the ha'penny in my pocket, standing beside an airport luggage cart containing one big knapsack (maple leaf proudly displayed) and an old instrument case, containing two puppets, one male, one female, labelled "fragile". I watched his back until he was swallowed by the crowd. I must have had a similar label attached to my forehead, because a moment later I had company. He was a big guy, simply oozing vegetable magnetism, one hand on my knapsack and the other on the puppet case, just about to heave them off the cart.

Eight

The ultrasound test provides obstetricians with a unique opportunity to evaluate the fetus at different stages of his or her development. No x-rays are used, only sound waves. As far as we can tell to date, ultrasound is perfectly safe. Still, this procedure should be performed only when the information obtained will help in the prenatal care of your unborn baby.
-From *Big Bertha's Total Baby Guide*

H ey, leave that alone!" I yelled, at the top of my lungs. His eyes bugged out as if I'd kicked him in a very private place, and he dropped the bags and ran. You'd think, wouldn't you, that yelling something—anything—loudly in an airport, in this day and age, would attract some attention. It didn't. At least, not in the "is something wrong—can I help you?" category. The crowds, which in the moment before had been quite thick and animated, burned off rapidly and silently, and I felt myself standing alone, ringed like a fire-juggler at a buskerfest. I stared back at a few faces, then hauled my gaze off into the middle distance, where the almost-thief was disappearing behind a pillar.

"That guy tried to grab my stuff," I announced, generally. "He ran away." An airport security guard pushed through and approached me somewhat warily. I was suddenly aware that, with my khaki fat pants, my big belly and multi-layered Polly-Goes-on-Safari outfit, I could easily be taken for more than flesh and less than sane. I didn't muck about.

"My name is Polly Deacon, and I have a nine p.m. flight

on Canada Jet to Gatwick," I said quietly to the security guy. "Canadian citizen, my papers are all here. Someone just tried to do a grab-and-dash on my bags. I'll give you a description, and maybe you can nab him before he gets someone else."

I think the guy appreciated my businesslike attitude, because he immediately let go of some of his extreme surface tension and pulled out his radio.

"What'd he look like?" he said.

"White—about five foot three, muscular and heavy-set, shaved bald," I said. "Very light blue eyes and a squashed nose. I didn't see what he was wearing."

"Black track pants and a Dodgers T-shirt," said a man in a turban nearby. "I saw him run."

"Thanks," the security guard and I said in unison. He relayed the information to somebody at the other end, got the name and number of the witness who had spoken up and directed the crowd to disperse. Then he turned back to me.

"You have a flight in an hour and a half?" he said. "We'd better get you checked through early so you can make a statement and still catch your plane."

"A statement takes an hour and a half?" I said. He gave me a tired look.

"If you're lucky," he said. "Come on. I'll try and get you through fast."

*   *   *

Usually, you hand over your ticket and have a nice brief chat with the ticket-person about seating and departure gates and so forth, and then off you go. This time there was an awkward little pause. The ticket person cleared her throat, stepped back and then turned off the conveyor belt, just as my luggage moved to her side of the counter.

"I'm sorry, ma'am. Your ticket number seems to have been selected for a random security search," she said. I heard a little hiss of annoyance from my friend the guard, whose name tag said Marcel. "I need her for a statement," he said. "She don't need that crap. She's okay."

"Yeah, and make me lose my job, why don'tcha?" she said back at him. Then she looked me in the eye. "No big deal," she said. "It could happen to anyone. Don't sweat it, if you've got nothing to hide. They're on their way already."

"Who are 'They'?" I said.

"Gate Security." And then they were there—two of them, a man and a woman. They each took possession of my bags, the man took the knapsack and the woman took the puppets and off we all went to a little room. Marcel came with me to the door, arguing with the male gate-guy about custody rights. It was truly unpleasant, and I wished with all my heart that I hadn't sent Morrison off so quickly.

The female guard stayed in the room with me while there was some argument outside.

"So you pick random people to search, I guess, eh?" I said, in what was meant to be a conversational tone. My hands were shaking, and I felt sick.

"Yeah, we do." She referred to the clipboard she was holding. "There's a flag in here says you're pregnant. We need to check that, of course."

"Excuse me? You want a urine sample?" She laughed, thank God. If you're dealing with people in uniform, it's always a good thing if they have a sense of humour. "You're not shy, are you?" she asked. Oh, jeepers. Couldn't be.

They took a quick look in my knapsack, tossing my underwear and socks aside and peering into my overloaded toiletries pouch. They confiscated my nail file, but didn't pay much attention to the blue velvet bag with Becker's Dad inside. I told them what it was and showed them the official "these are human remains" papers, and they nodded and carried on searching. I guess it's common for people to transport human ashes from place-to-place—just another day at the customs office. Anyway, they were far more interested in the puppets and their carrying case. It was as if the thing had "Suspicious Parcel" written all over it, and in spite of my expensive official carnet, they took the whole thing apart, piece by piece. They ripped the lining out of the case, looking for explosives, maybe. They even cut into the foam padding, leaving little bits of the stuff all over the table. I managed to stop them from performing a Caesarian section on my pregnant lady puppet, and I was allowed to demonstrate how the little door in her belly opened to reveal the small baby inside. It was an adorable little object, the puppet's baby, about the size of your thumb, painted pink, curled up and sucking its thumb. The female gate-person even said "awww" when she saw it.

"What's it made of?" the guy said.

"*Papier mâché*," I said. "It's hollow—nothing inside it, I swear."

"We'll have to run it thought the X-ray," he said, taking the whole mess with him, puppets, baby, case and all. While he was gone, I was required to prove that the bulge of my belly was not a bunch of dynamite, taped on. This involved a certain amount of disrobing, and it was enormously uncomfortable, for both me and the woman guard, who I think was beginning to feel some regret about the whole thing. This may have been my imagination only, but it made me feel a bit better. She did not subject me to the indignity of a cavity search, for which I was thankful. I saw the box of rubber gloves on the counter by the door. I knew what could have happened.

The male guard returned with everything intact, more or less. They hadn't seen fit to operate on the baby, and I popped it back into its proper place in the puppet's belly, then did my best to put the whole case, padding and puppets back together. I was also pathetically grateful for their not having completely destroyed my work, and it wasn't until after it was over that I realized how angry I was. Still, they were just doing their jobs, I suppose—as the woman said a couple of times on our way back to the luggage check counter.

They led me to the head of the lineup, butting in front in a most un-Canadian way to put me first. They stood by as I checked my bags properly, then handed me over to a waiting Marcel, who was looking grim. Everybody in the line-up was staring. I felt like a criminal.

"We didn't get him—your guy, I mean," he said. "But we'll keep an eye out for him."

"Look, I have to get on a plane," I said. "The thug's probably downtown by now, and anyway, he didn't do any damage. Unlike some people." I glared at the retreating backs of my gate security friends.

"Yeah, that was a tough break," he said. "Don't take it personally, though. It's a new policy, post 9/11, eh? They're just doing their jobs."

"Uh-huh. So you might as well go off and do yours. You have my name and address and the description of the guy— you don't need anything more, and I need to go. If you catch him trying to rob anybody else, send me a postcard."

"Yeah—okay," he said and backed off a bit. Maybe he could see my inner Rottweiler getting ready to attack—it was a wise move, anyway. I could feel myself growing fangs. My invaded luggage was finally on its way into the hold of the plane, but my stomach was growling like a bear, and I had fifteen minutes to find my departure gate and strap myself in.

"Have a nice trip," he said to my back as I stumped away.

*　　*　　*

I know it's not terribly cool to be a fearful flyer, especially since there are dozens of under-twelve airport veterans who treat the whole process as if it were a boring old preschool game. People who don't mind air travel often regard those who suffer from aero-anxiety with a kind of patronizing superiority. They will quote statistics at you, pointing out that your chance of dying in a plane crash is far smaller than your chance of being struck by lightning or winning a lottery. They will emphasize the words "safe" and "comfortable" and "perspective", and will make you feel like a stupid child. But the fact is, for me anyway, that I do not fear death by plane so much as I fear the experience of flying. I know that it's reasonably safe—more so than driving Highway 401 in a blizzard, which is certain suicide. It's the enclosed and powerless feeling that paralyzes me. It's the sensation of being shut up in a metal box miles above the natural habitat of the earthbound human, where the air is as thin as Kate Moss and oxygen-free. It's the fact that I'm not driving, and the driver, him or herself, is someone I have neither met nor even seen, and who might be someone I wouldn't trust if I did. It's the restriction and the surrender that I hate. Of course, media reports of hijackings and fiery crashes don't make this discomfort any easier, either.

The logic of the calm air traveller goes like this: "This machine is proven to be reliable, statistically, and I have always arrived at my destination safely, well-fed and well-watered. If I took a boat, it would take a week, and instead, I'm here in seven hours. This is a good thing. QED."

My logic stops at the statement about the machine. Strapping yourself helplessly inside a locomotive machine of any kind is an act of faith in human perfection, and my degree of faith in that is thin enough on the ground, never mind in the air. Perhaps my Catholic early years are to blame for this serious gap in my psyche. Most everybody else seems to have the ability to trust that what is made by men is worthy of its intended use, and infallibly made to boot. That's why we use leaf blowers and Sea-Doos without a thought to the ethics of their existence, and we flick the power switch on without giving a toss how the hydro is generated as long as it arrives in time for us to boot up the system and log on. We have extraordinary faith in machines and their makers, it seems to me. Still, seeing as we're always ferociously at war about the question of who the Ultimate Maker is, and genocide and attrition make us question the existence of any just god at all, perhaps the human version is easier to believe in.

It's not that I don't believe in something, but human perfection isn't it.

*   *   *

After I'd found my seat and settled in, a female attendant labeled Natalie came to visit. I was looking over the pamphlet they'd given me with my boarding pass. *Moms in the Air*, it was called, with some very amusing illustrations. Presumably, a big airport computer somewhere had flagged my name with information about my gravid state. Then it twigged. It was far more likely that my official status as Lady with a Baby actually provoked the security search, no matter how much they had insisted on its having been random. On the other hand, I hadn't had much choice about letting them know, as it affected my insurance and ticket purchase. Turning up large without warning them first would have undoubtedly provoked a similar search, which would probably have been more justified than the one I'd just endured.

Moms in the Air assured me that everything would be fine. Commercial air travel poses no special risks to a healthy pregnant woman or her fetus. The cartoon accompanying this statement showed a happy fat lady reclining comfortably in her seat and reading a baby magazine. At least they didn't draw her knitting booties.

Domestic travel is usually permitted until the pregnant traveller is in her thirty-sixth week of gestation, and international travel may be permitted until the thirty-second week. A pregnant woman should be advised always to carry documentation stating her expected date of delivery.

I had waved my doctor's note frantically at the gate guards, but they'd hardly looked at it and had still made me bare my belly. The flight attendant was more interested—in fact she specifically asked to see any papers I was carrying about my condition, leaning across the elegantly suited man sitting next to me and tapping my shoulder. She had to do that because I was staring into nothing at the time, white-knuckling the pamphlet and reliving the search, quite unaware that she was standing there.

"I like to know what I'm dealing with, if you know what I mean," she said, when I handed over Dr. Cass Wright's "To whom it may concern" letter.

"Twenty-eighth week, eh? You'll be fine. You might want to switch with your seatmate here, though, unless he wants you climbing over him every five minutes. We're supposed to ply you with liquids."

Mr. Suit looked suitably alarmed at the prospect, and I probably did, too. He was a small man, and I would have squashed him. It was nice of Natalie to suggest it.

"Oh, certainly," my seatmate said and scrambled to undo his seatbelt and collect his briefcase and newspaper. I thanked him, and we did the musical chairs bit.

A pregnant woman should be advised to walk every half hour during a smooth flight and flex and extend her ankles frequently to prevent phlebitis. The safety belt should always be fastened at the pelvic level.

The illustration that came with this bit showed the large and smiling lady striding regally down the aisles like a loaded barge in a wide canal. In truth, I'd touched the sides on my way into dock, and I was leery of any navigation that wasn't entirely necessary.

Natalie got close and personal to make sure the belt rule was complied with, then moved on. I suspected that I was in for some special treatment, and I wondered whether Natalie would notice that I was not smiling like the cartoon Flying Mom.

"Nervous?" my seatmate said. An English accent—a thick one. I nodded. The engines had just fired up, and they were awfully loud, although nobody else appeared to think they were. Doors were being shut with dreadfully final thumps, and the pilot had just done his opening spiel over the P.A. system.

"I always think the take off's the worst," I said, "until we're in the air, and then I think being in the air is the worst until we're landing, and then I come away thinking the landing is the worst until I'm about to take off again."

"Ah," the man said and smiled, kindly. "It's like that, is it? Wear these. It's Mozart." He handed me a slim and obviously expensive portable CD player and tiny little earplugs. "Keep it hidden—they don't want you wearing anything in your ears, but you'll find it helps, I think."

He seemed to know what he was talking about, and I figured it couldn't hurt, so I slipped the little black plugs into my ears and fiddled for the play button. Of course, it was a curiously intimate moment, the one in which I checked my actions for a nanosecond, aware that I was about to commit orifice-related contact with an utter stranger. You think this is extreme? Have you ever taken a close look at the ear-receiver on a payphone? Yergh. They're made of black plastic for a reason, you know. Still, the plugs looked clean, and so did he, so I was okay with sharing.

The CD was something orchestral and glorious, soaring and soothing, and I turned it way up, gave him what I hope was an appropriately radiant smile and closed my eyes.

The next thing I knew, the cabin was level and Natalie was poking me with a snack tray.

Nine

Finding out you're pregnant is one of the most exciting moments in a woman's life. But for women who find themselves pregnant far from their families—and the familiar—the joy and anticipation they feel can be tempered by an overwhelming sense of fear.
-From *Big Bertha's Total Baby Guide*

I borrowed Mr. Fogbow's earphones on the way back down to earth, too, and by then we were old friends, and as it was a night flight, we had sort of slept together. Over our ten p.m. dinner, Norman Fogbow had introduced himself as an anthropologist whose specialty was the study of human mating rituals and practices. If he'd said it with a smirk or a leer, I would have taken it as a come-on, but he was quite serious and genuine about it and eager to make sure I didn't misinterpret him.

"I know that sounds unlikely," he said, "but it's quite true. Fascinating subject, and something we all care about, in one way or another. I've just been giving a paper at a folklore conference in St. John's, Newfoundland." He pronounced the name of the province the way the locals do—Newf'n'land— proving himself an observant man.

"What was your paper about?"

"Oh, my dear, you'd kick yourself for having asked me, once I got started," he said and gave a little barking hoot, like the barred owl who hangs out in George's swamp. He had fluffy dark hair, cut very short and going grey about the ears. His face was alert and a bit wicked, delicately-boned with a small, sharp nose. If you were flying the plane, I thought, I'd be fine with that.

"Where are you off to, if you don't mind my impertinence?" he asked.

I explained who I was and where I was going and why, thereby breaking every rule in the "Single woman travelling alone" handbook that Theresa had shoved in the outer pocket of my knapsack. During the exchange of personal information, opinions about the airline food and personal philosophies, I discovered that Mr. Fogbow taught his subject at a minor college in London, was married with two children and was not fond of airline coffee. He displayed an uncanny knack for asking extremely personal questions in a way that left one quite comfortable about giving a frank answer. Perhaps it was just because mating rituals were his area of expertise. I felt like a tap he'd turned on, and I hope I didn't bore him.

In my less-than-reticent account of myself, I had made little mention of Becker, and my ring finger was bare, so it wasn't hard for Mr. Fogbow to surmise my unwedded state, and he could hardly have missed the baby-part.

"Are you going it alone, then?" he asked, with a quick referential glance at my midriff.

"That's in negotiation," I said. "Marriage was already a question on the table—the baby came up in the middle of it."

"A bit hard on the baby," he said. "It always seems to me such a waste of potential to bring a child up with only one parent."

"Well, I suppose one parent is better than two parents at war," I said.

"If it's permanent war, yes, perhaps you're right. But the occasional skirmish is character building, in my opinion. You're not at war with your young man, are you? I see you're not wearing a ring."

"I have one," I said, fishing it out of my shirt, where it had been dangling on its chain. "I just haven't worn it yet."

"You might think about doing that while you're travelling," Mr. Fogbow said. "It would make you less vulnerable."

"Vulnerable to what? Interrogation by anthropologists?"

He hooted again, softly. "Forgive me—I'm afraid I am an incurable elephant's child. You must tell me to stop."

"No way," I said. "You're doing a perfect impression of a very expensive shrink, and it's probably good for me. After all, we'll probably never meet again after we land—but you'll have another case study in hand, and I'll feel all cleansed and re-motivated."

"I'll write up a bill, then, and post it later," Mr. Fogbow said.

Not long afterwards, he settled down to sleep, burrowing into his airline pillow and emitting a few endearing peeps of contentment as he did so. I sat there motionless for a while, until I was sure he was properly asleep, then quietly reached up to undo the chain around my neck. The clasp was stuck, and I pried it apart with what I found in my pocket—Morrison's ha'penny—then slipped Becker's ring off so I could look at it. I held it up to the light and studied it for the bazillionth time. It was a relatively harmless looking ring, really. A simple gold band, no scrollwork or twiddly bits, set with a modest diamond that sparkled pleasantly, yet didn't shout. I thought of Frodo, all befuddled and conflicted, meditating on his lordly ring. They're powerful things, rings.

What had Mr. Fogbow meant by vulnerable? I suppose it was partly that single-woman-alone thing, complicated by my being a person of pregnancy. I had always felt reasonably impervious to the dangers out there—at least, I'd always felt that it was absolutely my own responsibility to defend myself against attack, and I've always assumed that I would be up to the task.

What would wearing a ring do to change that? Mark me as protected, perhaps? A badge declaring me One-Walking-As-Two (or three, in my case)? Who needed a guardian, anyway? Not me. Somewhere deep down, a shard of memory stirred, a long ago lesson in self-defense that hurt where it touched the mind and made me pull back into myself, like a snail. We wouldn't be going there, I thought. Not just yet, not while I'm testing the gods already, trapped in this wretched airplane.

I'd told Becker that he would know my answer when I either returned the ring or began to wear it. Poor mook. All at once, I felt deeply sorry for him, and for myself, too. Why did this have to be so hard? I looped the ring back on the chain, did up the clasp around my neck, and dropped it down my front again, where it hung suspended, as ever, between my breasts (my first real set of them, actually, quite alien still, and sore as hell).

*   *   *

Mr. Fogbow and I parted amicably as we emerged into the customs area at Gatwick airport seven or so hours later. His Mozart tape had made the landing bearable, and I was feeling quite the grown-up air traveller, all calm, perky and businesslike, in spite of its being four a.m., Canadian time. We exchanged business cards before he beetled off to find his luggage. Mine said simply "Polly Deacon, Puppets" and gave my mailing address. His had lots of academic initials after his name, the college address and information and his own personal numbers, faxes and email addresses as well.

"Yes—it's a veritable Rosetta Stone," he said when I examined it. "Yours is very subfusc. I envy you your discretion."

"It's not discretion, Mr. Fogbow," I said. He'd told me to

call him Norman, but I liked the formality of his surname, and he appeared to have been equally happy addressing me as Ms. Deacon, in spite of our less than formal conversation. "It's just that I have no phone, fax or email. I'm just a happy little colonial in the woods."

"Well, you're lucky to be one," he said. "I won't say goodbye. It'll blow the chance of us meeting again, and you never know—we might." We shook hands warmly, and I slipped his card into my purse next to Earlie Morrison's.

*　　*　　*

I was in England, finally. My feet were on alien soil for the first time in my life (the U.S.A. doesn't count), and it felt wonderful. I had absolutely no trouble getting through customs. The British clearly had more respect for the carnet than the Canadians had, and I was out into the terminal and ready to party in less than an hour. A big, suspended clock told me it was nine a.m. on Tuesday morning. I was starving and not in the least bit tired.

The first thing to do was to cash a travellers' cheque and get some foldin' money. This didn't take very long, although I was annoyed to learn that there was a surcharge for the service. Later, I learned to make these transactions at a proper bank or a post office. The next thing to do—at least when I got to Canterbury I planned to do it—was to get a wider wallet. These are the things they don't tell you. English pounds are wider than Canadian or American dollars, and the notes spilled out of the top of my billfold like legal papers crammed into a standard 8.5" x 11" file folder.

I had hoisted my knapsack onto my back, not doing up all the straps and things, because I would just have to undo them all again when I found my way to the Gatwick Rail Link the travel agent had told me about, which would take me to a central train station where I could change for a train to Canterbury, Kent. According to the map, the trip was a little less than the distance between Laingford and Toronto—about a hundred kilometres. Not far. In fact, the whole of England could fit quite comfortably into the province of Ontario, and I rather liked the sense of scaled-down distance. Driving to Scotland would be like zipping up to Sault Ste. Marie to see your folks for a holiday weekend.

I wasn't due to register at the conference until that evening. I'd never been to a conference before, although I'd given plenty of puppetry classes and workshops, and I was eager to schmooze with other like-minded puppet-people. I'd boarded the plane at night, after driving through a snowstorm. All that was behind me now. I imagined Rosie and Luggy curled up on George's old plaid couch in front of the woodstove, a blizzard howling outside. Cozy. And completely not my responsibility for a whole week. Ahhh. The England I'd seen through the window of the plane was beautifully patterned like a quilt in shades of green and soft brown—no white stuff to be seen. I was looking forward to this. I even, for one moment, considered giving the heavy sweater I was wearing to the first homeless person I saw, but I didn't see any recognizable vagrants in Gatwick airport, so it didn't happen.

I stopped with my back to the wall for a moment and gazed at the seething mass of humanity before me. It wasn't long before I noticed that almost everybody I could see appeared to be talking on a cellphone. I mean everybody. Interesting, I thought, and stifled a giggle. Jet lag, I guess. The cellphones reminded me that I'd promised Earlie that I would call him when I landed. I gazed around, looking for a payphone, and feeling the tiniest bit irritated about it.

"Help you with your bags, miss?"

The man making the offer could have been the twin of my shaven-headed thug at Pearson. He was grinning at me in a very unpleasant way and reaching down to take my puppet case.

"No! Thank you," I said, yanking the case away. "I don't need any help."

"Looks heavy," he persisted. "Lady in your condition shouldn't do any heavy liftin', you know." He was as bald as the guy at Pearson, but this man had a tattoo on the right side of his skull, a kind of crest-thing, with a devil figure holding a pitchfork and above it, a line and three blobs which might have been a boat with sails. It was done in red and looked like a wound.

"Get away! Now!" I said. I didn't say it as loudly as I'd said more or less the same thing at the other airport back home, because I really didn't have the energy to deal with any more airport security guys. However, I did say it with emphasis, and the fellow's eyes narrowed at once. A sneer replaced the ingratiating smile he'd worn a moment ago.

"You orter watch out for thieves, Miss, in a place like this—you being a Canadian visitor and all. And you orter be more polite." He reached out with a hand as quick as a snake and tweaked my breast before slipping away into the crowd. I was left standing there with my mouth hanging open, mostly at the shock of the unexpected assault, but also because he'd called me a Canadian. It's true my knapsack had a brave little maple-leaf flag sewn on (to prevent people thinking I was an American, and therefore a target for anti-Yankness), but the knapsack was on my back, and my back was to the wall. How had he known?

I took a quick look round. Nobody appeared to have witnessed the little encounter, for which I was grateful. They were all too busy having conversations with people on the other end of their cellphones. I was revolted by having had my person invaded by that nasty little man, but I was hardly traumatized. I didn't need immediate assistance—I just suddenly wanted a hot bath, even though I was baking in my thick, cable-knit sweater.

Muttering to myself, I did up the straps on my knapsack, hoisted my puppet case and headed for the overhead sign that said "Railway". I was determined not to let that particular greeting spoil my arrival. I was here in one piece, on English soil. That was the main thing. I'd call Earlie and tell him so when I got to Canterbury.

Ten

Recent research suggests that pregnant women who use cellphones could cause serious harm to their unborn babies, and that the risks from cellphone radiation could be far greater than previously imagined.

-From *Big Bertha's Total Baby Guide*

Back in the eighties, when I was at art college and went home to Laingford regularly to visit Aunt Susan, I always took the VIA Rail train from Toronto, a trip of about three hours. There were several daily trains and people used them to commute to work in the city. What a concept. I'd always make directly for the bar car—a smoky and convivial little room, presided over by an inevitably wizened and tortoise-like gentleman who would bring you your beer in a cold aluminum can and pour it for you into a plastic glass so flimsy it felt like you were holding a water balloon. I met a lot of interesting people in the bar cars of trains—people who would invite you to join them for a game of cribbage, or sit down opposite you and trade lies for a couple of hours. Ah, the good old days. Now you're expected to drive, which is presumably why Toronto has one of the highest smog counts in North America.

In England, though the natives appear to complain constantly about the train service not being half what it used to be, I found it utterly enchanting. There were trains every half hour that could take you absolutely anywhere. They were cheap and they were on time, give or take a minute or two. They were clean and quiet and comfortable. In motion, they went clacketty-clack, like trains in movies, and the scenery scrolling by was infinitely fascinating. The only thing that marred their perfection was the clientele—the passengers.

I'd not been seated more than three minutes before it began. The compartment I was in was crowded, and thick with the same kind of constrained silence and averted eyes you get on Toronto subway cars, so I felt quite at home, but as soon as we were moving, the air was filled with a sudden and bewildering chorus of little beeps.

The woman sitting next to me rummaged in her bag and brought out a cellphone, pressed a few buttons and launched into an animated conversation with someone called Dorrie. "I'm on the trine, dear," she said, loudly, in order to be heard above the dozens of people around her, who were all telling Reginald and Kirsty and Gillian and Victor that they were on the trine, too. After the initial flurry of informative phone calls, things settled down a bit, except for a young businessman opposite, whose conversation with Amanda quickly reached boiling point, until he was more or less shouting, insisting that Stephanie and little Malcolm were not to touch the bleeding video machine until he got home from work at the end of the day. I was feeling dreadfully out of the loop by this time. I wondered how much a cellphone cost. After Amanda was dealt with, there was a lull of about seventeen seconds before the compartment was alive again, this time with incoming calls—presumably all the Amandas calling back. Each phone was set to play a nice little tune, from "Für Elise" (very popular) to "You Can Dance if You Want To". And so it began again. I yearned for Mr. Fogbow's personal CD player, to drown it all out.

In London, I had to change trains for Canterbury and had about forty minutes to kill before my connection. I found a locker where I could stash my knapsack and puppet case and went off to get myself a sandwich.

One of the nicest things about visiting a country that is not your own is that the most mundane things become exotic, simply by virtue of their being different. In some people, this elicits a fair bit of complaint—"eeew, that's not like we have at home." I suppose this is a natural response, if a trifle narrow-minded, but I was determined not to fall into the same trap myself. I wanted to take note of things, and celebrate them. I purchased a submarine sandwich, which the counter person identified as a baguette, for my future reference, and a coffee to go. Well, I'd said "to go" and got a funny look. "To take away" is the correct term, I was told. I would have to start taking notes.

Unencumbered by my luggage, I wandered into a toy store and spent a happy while discovering a whole raft of fun stuff that I'd never seen before. Perhaps I should buy a little souvenir for the Sprog, I thought. I could tell her later that she'd actually been there when I bought it, even though I didn't let her pick it out for herself. I found myself going all squashy at the sight of pink fluffy teddy bears and little teething toys. It was very pleasant and sort of dreamlike, and I kind of lost track of the time. I did make a purchase, which meant I only had a few minutes left before my train was due, and I headed back to the baggage locker area at a lumbering trot. I slowed my pace when I got there, though, because there was an official looking person in uniform, opening the door of the locker where my stuff was. Behind him, waiting impatiently and looking about him— presumably for signs of me—was my breast-tweaker, large as life and twice as thug-like. I lost it, big time, and ran right up to them, splashing my coffee and losing my grip on the baguette sandwich, which bounced off into a corner like a rubber ball.

"What the hell is going on here?" I yelled, grabbing the arm of the official, who was a harmless looking elderly man with watery eyes. "That's my locker, and those are my bags. Doesn't anyone around here have any respect for private property?" The old man straightened up and stared at me, befuddled.

"Oo's she?" he said, turning to the breast-tweaker, who of course had high-tailed it out of there the moment he'd seen me.

"She," I said, "is the holder of the key to this locker, who paid three pounds for its exclusive use." I reached into the pocket of my khakis and produced the small brass key for his inspection. I'd fished up the old ha'penny, too, which gleamed dully in the fluorescent light. The man picked up the key and squinted at the number engraved on it. "463," he said, as if it were an amazing oracle. "Why, that's the right one, Miss." His uniform (name tag: Reg) was rather grubby and frayed at the cuffs.

"It certainly is the right key," I said. "So how does it happen that you opened the locker for somebody who didn't have a key to it, eh?"

"Well, 'e said 'e'd lost it, didn't 'e? Said it fell out of his pocket, like."

"Uh-huh. And did he produce any ID? Did you just take his word for it??"

"Well, 'e seemed orl right. 'E was in a hurry. Terribly sorry, Miss. You won't report me, will you? I'd lose me job over this." Reg's eyes misted over. Oh, damn. Querulous old men get me every time.

"Well, I suppose there's no harm done," I said. "He didn't actually touch the bags, did he? They're still in there, right?" We both stooped to look.

"Right as rain," Reg said, smiling widely in relief. "Still there."

"Well, that's a blessing. Listen—that same guy tried to get his hands on my bags back at Gatwick airport. He must be following me." This had only just occurred to me, and it wasn't a pleasant thought. Honestly. It's not as if I looked like a wealthy traveller or anything. Perhaps the fragile label on the puppet case suggested Ming vases or something to the British criminal mind. I felt the first faint stirrings of unease, a little prickle at the back of my neck. Someone had tried to grab my luggage at Pearson, too. The world was a scarier place than I'd thought, and maybe I wasn't the invulnerable single-woman-traveller I'd thought I was.

"You don't want to be followed about, Miss. You should tell a p'leeceman." He gazed around vaguely, as if one might magically appear.

"No policemen, thank you. But I'll be on my guard from now on, I can tell you. And I won't trust baggage lockers any more, that's for sure." He looked hurt and defensive, as if I'd just insulted his profession, which I suppose I had.

"'Ere," he said. "Lockers is safe as 'ouses long as you don't lose the key."

"Which I didn't do," I said.

"No, but if you did, there's proper channels you got to go through."

"And did my friend from Gatwick go through the proper channels before you almost gave him my luggage?"

"Well, 'e filled up a form, see?" Reg produced a crumpled bit of paper from his jacket and showed it to me with a slightly trembling hand. He was rather cross. I snatched it from him and stuffed it into my purse.

"Oi," he said.

"I'll tell you what," I said. "I won't try to get my three pounds back, which I would be entitled to on the basis of your little mistake, and in exchange, I get to keep the evidence."

"But they've got serial numbers on them. Reg'll see it's missing."

"I thought *you* were Reg," I said inanely, pointing to his badge. I really didn't have time for this.

"We've got three of them, Miss."

"Well, tell Boss Reg you lost it, like the guy just did about the key," I said, tossing my wrecked coffee-cup into a nearby garbage can labelled "Bin". Then I grabbed the puppet case, hoisted my knapsack and started walking.

"I have a train to catch," I said, over my shoulder. Old Reg let me go.

Eleven

By the 25th week, sleep becomes a hazy memory. Your belly is simply too big to allow you to lie down comfortably. If sleeping on your side with pillows wedged between your legs and behind your back doesn't help, head for a comfy chair instead. As your belly reaches watermelon proportions, you may sleep better sitting up.
-From *Big Bertha's Total Baby Guide*

The whole phone-thing happened again on the train, the chorus of "I'm on the trine", and the tweeps and bleeples of incoming calls. This time I was prepared. I'd learned from the toy-shop assistant [name tag: Devona] that the item I was looking for was called a "mobile" and not a cellphone, and yes, they had a toy one, over there on the rack with the rest of the novelty Pez dispensers. It looked quite real, at least from a distance. It was a convincing size and shape, with a blue plastic body, red buttons and a little red rubber antenna like a bit of licorice. It had a tiny battery in it, and when you pressed the bell button, it rang in a loud and startlingly accurate imitation of a real phone going off. If you pressed the musical note button, it played the opening bars of "Für Elise". What's more, I got two free tubes of Pez to go with it, and it only cost me a handful of change.

I was glad of the reinforced pocket lining of my Tilleys (no—this is not product placement, I swear), because one and two-pound coins are thicker and heavier than the loonie and the toonie.

It's interesting to note that many nations seem lately to be reverting back to coinage in large denominations. I imagine it has something to do with the ease of counterfeiting bills and notes in these technological times, but I think there's more to it than that. A handful of coinage means a lot to the majority of poor, working class mooks who aren't gaining anything by the rampant imperialism of the current era. If you can't get a credit card, the modern equivalent of Roman citizenship, then ten bucks in change is more than pin money. To Hank and Bobbie-Jo, to Pierre and Raheel, Sidney and Sarah and Jajeet and Chunju, the coin is the real economy, and the fat change purse is an indication of class, rather than a fashion statement. It would not be a surprise to see a revival of the commoner's purse, the sack of leather at the belt, where coins are kept for daily use because they are the only wealth to hand.

Still, the Pez-phone was worth the four pounds it cost, because I used it and managed to clear myself some space in the train. When the mobile-phone chaos began, just after the Canterbury train pulled out of the station, I whipped out my Pez-phone, pressed the bell button, pretended to answer it, then began parroting the things I heard around me. I wasn't loud, you understand, but mobile phone carriers are acutely aware of each other, for all their feigned detachment. The three people who flanked me, one to my right and the woman and man sitting opposite, all had real phones and were presumably having real conversations. My Pez-phone conversation, which I swear was low-key, made the people opposite get up and find different seats. I put my feet up and put the phone away. The woman next to me put hers away too and turned to look me over, a sweet smile on her dumpling face.

"They are awful, aren't they? I got mine for Christmas from my daughter-in-law, so she can keep me on a lead, like a dog. She thinks I'm going a bit senile, I suppose. Still, it's a lovely thing to have if you're feeling lonely. You can call up a friend for a little talk whenever you like."

"That was her calling you just now, then?" I said.

"Yes, love. She likes to ring every few hours, especially when I go up to London, and she does fuss, you know, if I don't answer it."

"That must be very annoying."

"Well it is, rather, but I don't say so. It was a present, so it's rude not to like it." I remembered my father and mother, watching me open birthday presents at the breakfast table one morning when I was quite small. A box of Marks and Spencer underwear had been one of the gifts, and it had confused me, because it wasn't something calculated to please me, as real birthday presents should be. "Oh, good, you needed some of those, and you can't get them in Kuskawa," my mother had said.

"Best undies ever made, Marks and Sparks," my father had added. It had been a present from somebody my parents knew in Toronto, whom I'd met once at a church thing. I learned then that even when you get what you don't want as a present, it's rude not to be grateful.

"I know what you mean," I said to the lady next to me in the train. She was in her late sixties or early seventies, I think, apple-cheeked and ample, with a complicated accent and an extremely thick pair of glasses, through which she peered at me, squinting as she did so.

"You're from America then, are you?"

"Canada," I said quickly.

"Oh, I know someone in Canada," she said, delighted. "Donna-Lou Dermott. She has an egg-farm in the country. Do you know her?" I almost swallowed my tongue.

I knew that everybody in the world says this at some point to a hapless traveller: "Do you know my cousin Fred who lives in [insert home country here]?" But the chance of actually knowing the person referred to? What sort of odds exist for that? I wondered if it might be a good idea to buy a British lottery ticket on the strength of it, or maybe to suggest that my seatmate should. I lied, of course, not wanting to get into a conversation about the egg-queen of Cedar Falls. I was supposed to be getting away from it all. "No, I'm afraid I don't," I said.

"Oh, well, I suppose it's an awfully big country," she said. "Silly question, really." We sat in silence for a bit, and I hauled my backpack out from under my seat to scrabble in a front pocket for some gum.

Although my bodily system had rejected the notion of nicotine seven months previously, I still battled the behavioural legacy of the stuff, and still sniffed eagerly if I caught a whiff of burning tobacco leaves nearby. Smoking on the train was forbidden, but the scent had wafted in behind those who had sucked on cigarettes somewhere else until the last possible moment. I wanted a cigarette very badly just then, but spearmint gum would have to do. I offered the pack to my companion.

"Oh, thanks, love," she said. "You know, I haven't had a piece of chewing gum for years." She took a stick and unwrapped it carefully, as if it were a chocolate bar. "Lovely," she said. "I'm Maude, by the way."

"Pleased to meet you," I said. "I'm Polly."

"You wouldn't be going to that rally in Canterbury, would you?" she said.

Rally? Is that what they call a conference over here? Like mobiles, baguettes, bins and takeaway, another term to file away. I nodded vaguely, and found myself beginning to drift off. It was by then about noon, or seven a.m. by Canadian time, and I had not slept much on the plane. I mumbled an apology to Maude, who seemed geared up to chat on and on for the entire journey. She smiled gently at me in a grandmotherly kind of way.

"Oh, that's all right, love. I've got my knitting." She produced some wool and needles from a bag at her side and placed them ready in her lap. I closed my eyes and went into a half-doze, then heard her rustle in the bag again. A pause. A beeple or two.

"Elsie?" she said, quite softly, which was kind of her. "Yes, dear, it's me. I'm on the trine."

*   *   *

Maude poked me awake at the stop before Canterbury, which was Sittingbourne. Outside, it was pelting with rain, the countryside grey and brown, like an old photograph. It was probably stunningly beautiful in the summertime, but right then, it was depressing. What was I doing in England in February? I had to be insane.

"I don't like to wake you, love, but it's our stop next. I live in Canterbury myself, you know. The conductor wouldn't have let you sleep through, but they do rather wait until the last minute, and it's nice to have time to gather your belongings. I have your box-thing down here. A man took it off the luggage rack for you already."

I was instantly wide awake. "My box thing? A man?"

"Yes, that case of yours with 'Fragile' on it. He was sitting a little further down the carriage. He walked up the aisle just before the stop and was taking it down, quite as if it were his. I was just finishing a row, and I looked up and said how kind of him, saving you the trouble of stretching up to get it yourself. I saw you put it up there, you see. He gave me ever such a funny look, I can tell you. Mind you, my knitting needle was pointing right at his tummy, so perhaps it was that. He got off the train very quickly, anyway."

"Did he open it or anything?"

"Heavens sakes, no. He just got it down, that's all, and I tucked it under my seat, out of the way."

"What did this man look like?"

"Well, that's a bit difficult, dear, because I don't see very well. Sort of big, with a cap on, and he smelled like a fishmonger, poor man. You can never get it off your hands, can you?"

"What would he have done with it if you hadn't said anything?"

"Well, I was rather wondering that myself, you see, which is why I spoke. It was marked 'fragile', wasn't it? You can't be too careful with other people's things, to my mind. He did put it down quite quickly. I hope he didn't break anything."

"Well, thanks for that," I said. "My poor luggage seems to be attracting a lot of attention. I'll be glad to get where I'm going and be rid of it." I felt a return of the prickle at the back of my neck. Attempted theft, four times. First Pearson, then Gatwick, then the train station, now on the train. Okay, I was willing to believe in coincidence up to a point—after all, Maude knew Donna-Lou Dermott, but there must be a point at which recurring incidents begin to display a pattern. I decided then that in spite of my reluctance to use Susan's email address thing, I'd have to knuckle under after all. I'd write to Earlie about it, and he would tell me not to be so paranoid, and that would be that. I'd feel better.

We were coming into the station, and the usual flurry of preparation began, people standing and putting on coats and gathering parcels and papers.

"It was lovely meeting you, Polly," Maude said. "Elsie will

be there to fetch me, I expect, so I'll toddle. Have a lovely time at the rally, and perhaps I'll see you. Canterbury's a small city, you know."

"Nice to meet you, too, and thanks again for guarding my stuff," I said. She performed a beautiful hockey deke between two guys in suits and was off, trundling along the platform like a motivated porcupine.

It was absolutely pelting with rain. I had imagined coming in to Canterbury and being bewitched by the sight of the spires of the Cathedral, towering over the ancient city. I wanted to see the little bulgy houses overhanging the streets and sense the history, but I could hardly see a thing. There was a taxi stand outside, but only one taxi in sight. I confess I played up my pregnancy and heavy baggage a bit as I came out onto the street side of the station. I heaved a big sigh, and my performance was rewarded instantly by the woman who had just flagged it. She gallantly offered the cab to me instead.

"That's awfully kind of you," I said. "We might be going in the same direction—would you like to share?" The driver was out in a flash and stowing my luggage in the trunk. (Which, Brent had informed me a tad patronizingly during a lexicography lesson at the farewell party, is called a boot in England. I knew that.)

"Where are you going?" she said.

"The Pilgrim's Rest," I said. "It's a B&B, I think."

"Oh, yes—that's right in the old city—just off St. Peter's Street near the West Gate. I live not far from there, so yes, thanks. We'll go down together."

"Are you here to see the Cathedral?" she said as the taxi pulled away from the curb.

"Not really," I said, "although I'll have to go check it out. I'm here for a conference. Or a rally, I guess you'd call it."

"There seem to be a lot of special things going on here at the moment," the woman said. She was very elegantly dressed in the kind of tweedy outfit you'd see worn by Lady-so-and-so on *Masterpiece Theatre*. Her hair was expensively cut, and her coat had probably cost more than my plane ticket. "One can hardly keep track of it," she went on. "I know there's something rather controversial going on at one of the local churches, and of course there's the Lenten Choir Festival at the Cathedral, as well as term time at Kent University. Which one are you at?"

"Actually, it's a puppetry conference," I said.

"Oh, yes, I remember seeing a notice about that in the newspaper," she said. "Well, I hope they'll give you a chance to see the sights. It's an ancient city, with a very interesting history. And be sure to visit the Roman museum and so forth."

"I'll try," I said. Whether or not the conference schedule allowed tourist time, I had every intention of sneaking out to go soak up some history. I love old stuff, and you don't get much of it in Kuskawa, Ontario.

I felt a pleasant twiggle of excitement as the cab made its way slowly along a practically deserted, narrow street. Through the rain and mist, I could see the fronts of buildings all post-and-beamed, with mullioned windows. It was mysterious and secret—and I could well imagine the streets crowded with pilgrims and medieval personages, huddled in doorways out of the wet. This was a city of ghosts, I decided, and I was looking forward to meeting some.

The cab pulled up outside a mind-blowingly picturesque building on a small side street.

"Pilgrim's Rest," the cabbie said and hopped out into the rain to release by baggage from the back. I dug into my pockets for some pound coins, but my new friend insisted that it was her treat.

"It's a tax write-off anyway," she said.

"Well, thank you very kindly," I said—an expression I'd never used before in my life, but which popped out by itself. Quaint, it was. She gave a little quirky smile and said not to mention it.

In the space of time it took me to get from the back of the cab to the door of the B&B, I was soaked as thoroughly as if I had been dumped in the Stour River. I rang the doorbell, and there was rather a long wait, at least it seemed long. I was glad of the way the building was constructed—the upper storey loomed out over the street so that I was sheltered from the worst of the rain, but there was still cold water dripping down the back of my neck, and my hair was drenched. The door was massive, dark black wood, thick planks of it, with hinges the size of dinner plates and a great latch like the handle on a vault. There was a brass door knocker, too, which reminded me of the Boz illustration of the Marley knocker in Dickens' *Christmas Carol*. It was a friar's face, I thought, cowled and imposing, large and heavy, with a beaky nose and angry eyes. I contemplated rapping with the knocker as well, but didn't, as it was obviously centuries old, and if I broke it, I'd be in deep doo. Finally, the door opened with an atmospheric creak, and I was greeted by an impossibly tall and cadaverous figure whose face, with the light behind him, was in shadow.

"Ah, a pilgrim, and a wet one," the man said. "We've been expecting you. Come in and get warm, my dear." Gratefully, I did as I was told.

Twelve

You can still enjoy your favourite caffeinated drinks as long as you don't overdo it. Abundant research suggests that moderate amounts of caffeine won't harm mother or baby during pregnancy. Researchers define moderate as 300 to 400 milligrams (mgs) of caffeine, about what you'd get in three to four cups of coffee.
-From *Big Bertha's Total Baby Guide*

```
To: oppbeck@kuskawa.com
From: Polly1258@hotmail.com
Subject: hi
Date: Wednesday, February 13

Hi, Becker. Just to let you know I'm here and OK.
Hope all's well with you.
Love,
P.
```

The note to Becker had taken me longer to compose than you'd expect. Oh, I tried to give him more details, but every time I wrote something down about the past twenty-four hours, it sounded as if I were either crowing about the fact that I'd made the trip safely in spite of his misgivings, or conversely (in the case of the attempted thefts) that he had every reason to have been worried about me going. I'd write a sentence, then read it over, then delete it, then repeat the process. I eventually gave up and just gave him the bare minimum. It would have been easier a generation ago, when all you could send was an overseas telegram, which was paid for by the word and you could be forgiven for your brevity. I hoped the "Love, P." at the end would sweeten it up a bit. On the other hand, writing to Earlie was strangely easy, probably because I knew he would be passing the info on to George, Susan and the others.

> To: oppmorr@kuskawa.com
> From: Polly1258@hotmail.com
> Subject: All's well
> Date: Wednesday, February 13
>
> Dear Earlie,
> Sorry I didn't call you as soon as I landed. Transit and all that. I took a train directly from the airport to my B&B in Canterbury, and there wasn't time to find a phone booth. You know what? There are hardly any of those red phone booths you see on BBC dramas—I don't know where they've put them all, perhaps they're stored in a warehouse somewhere in London and only brought out when they're filming "All Creatures Great and Small."
>
> The flight was uneventful, and getting here was no problem, although there were a lot of thieves around, who all seemed to find my puppet case an item of interest. Thwarted one at Pearson, then one at Gatwick, then the same Gatwick guy at the train station, then somebody else on the train. Is this country full of crooks, or what? Next time you come over with your dad, never carry anything that looks like it might contain something valuable. I have stored it and my passport and return ticket in Mr. Frayne's big old safe (he's the proprietor of this place), and if the thugs try to steal it, Mr. Frayne says he will smack them over the head with his 11th century mattock, whatever that is. Anyway, never mind that. I'm safe and secure in Canterbury, in the weirdest little inn-place you've

ever seen—straight out of a history book.

My room is on the very top floor, under the eaves of the house, which Mr. Frayne says was built in 1430. I can't tell you how wild it is to sit in a room that has had other people sitting in it for 700 years. It's tiny and low-ceilinged, with dark wooden panelling and little diamond-paned windows. The ceiling is slanted, the floor is slanted, and it creaks at night. It's like living in an old trunk, and I love it.

I went to the registration thing last night, in an office at the University of Kent, where most of the conference will be held. Seems I lucked out with accommodation, as most of the people attending the conference seem to be billeted at the university, which is modern and not nearly as interesting as The Pilgrim's Rest, where I am. Apparently, the Mary Chambers Memorial bursary-thing which I won (goodness knows how) provides accommodation here, because Mary Chambers is Mr. Frayne's dearly departed sister, and before she died, they used to run the place together. Anyway, this B&B is way better than some anonymous room at the university, so I'm happy.

I have a bunch of seminars to attend today, so I better make this quick. I'm at an Internet café near the cathedral, tucked away behind a pub where you'd never find it unless you knew about it.

Hugs to everybody, and I hope you're not buried under a ton of snow. It's been raining here, but today it's quite mild, with lots of picturesque fog. Give Luggy and Rosie a pat for me, if you get a chance.

   Cheers,
   Polly

I'd found a Starbucks in Canterbury, which was a surprise. Mr. Frayne, who appeared to be a bachelor, had made me an enormous breakfast at 7:30 a.m.—a fry-up , as he called it—with fried bacon, sausage, blood pudding, fried tomatoes and fried bread. Actually, it was wonderful, except for the fact that he didn't have coffee, except for instant, so I'd had a cup of tea instead, which isn't nearly the same thing to a person who requires a thick, dark infusion of caffeine first thing. The Sprog didn't mind my coffee addiction, I swear. In fact, I like to think she shared it, as I'd discovered some weeks ago that if I didn't have a cup of coffee by ten a.m., she'd kick at her walls like nobody's business. Seeing as she was being deprived of the pleasures of nicotine and beer, I figured she deserved one decent vice, at least, before she entered this crabby old world. The Starbucks large with double cream was for her benefit, not mine. The beverage was getting cold, though, as I let my fingers run away with me, writing to Earlie Morrison.

After I'd sent the email to Earlie, I felt better. Making light of the luggage incidents helped to dispel the bothersome feeling of impending trouble, the internal alarm that had been making my neck prickle. I rummaged in my bag to find the conference itinerary to double-check the time of my first meeting, and my fingers touched a crumpled bit of paper. I pulled it out. It was the "Proper Procedures" form that I'd snatched from Old Reg at the train station, after the Gatwick thug had tried to get him to hand over my luggage. I had been too caught up in the Pez-phone, Maude and jet lag to have a look at it on the train the day before, and then I'd forgotten all about it. I could see the thug in my mind's eye—bald head, thick neck, squashed nose and little beady eyes. Surely he couldn't have been the same guy who'd tried to steal my bags at Pearson, could he? Nah. The Pearson guy hadn't had the strange tattoo on his head, for one thing. More likely, there was an international set of membership guidelines for common thugs—heck, they were probably unionized—and they would have to conform to the stereotype before they were allowed to operate. Yet another legacy of globalization.

I took an absentminded swig of my cold coffee and peered at the writing on the form, titled Luggage Retrieval Docket 23b. It had the BritRail logo at the top of it and lots of fine print at the bottom, the kind that says that the rail people are not responsible for loss or theft of personal belongings, etc., the kind of legalese that says more or less "you pays yer money and you takes yer chances." Still, it didn't cover BritRail employees who actively gave your luggage away to any Tom, Dick or Harry who asked for it.

The name written on the ID part of the form was Derek Smith, and he had given a street address in Canterbury—surprise, surprise. Of course, it would be "Smith"—although the Derek was an original touch. The address was probably fake—at least, I was willing to entertain the possibility that it was just a fluke that he had scribbled down Canterbury. The ID number Old Reg had copied down was most likely from a bogus driver's licence. Still, I wasn't about to throw the scrap of paper away. It might come in useful if the trouble continued. It was possible that the guy was so dumb, or in such a hurry that he actually used his real ID. They never do that in books or movies, but I knew they did that in real life. You just have to read the "stupid criminals" excerpts in old Ann Landers advice columns, like the one where a guy wrote his bank hold-up note on the back of a personal cheque.

If the guy at Gatwick and then at the luggage lockers did live in Canterbury, then he could easily be the same person who'd made the attempt again on the train. Maude had said he was sitting in the same rail car, but if he had been wearing a hat, I probably wouldn't have given him a second look. I was too jet-lagged to notice anything except the ringing of the cellphones.

The important question was: what was it about my damn puppet case that was so attractive to thieves? It wasn't enough that it was labelled "fragile". It was just a battered old instrument case. Perhaps the guy at Pearson airport and my Canterbury thug both actually believed that people carried guns in instrument cases and were both desperate to get hold of one.

Back at Pearson, the gate security people had asked the usual inane questions: "Did you pack your bags yourself?" (to which I was dying to answer "no, my Mommy did") and "Have your bags been with you the entire time?" (to which I might have said "No, I left them unattended for an hour or two in a busy airport, just for fun.") They'd taken the puppet case apart, and hadn't found anything incriminating (although the tiny penis on the policeman puppet might have properly been indicted for a lack of taste), but I suppose no airport thug could be expected to know that. Maybe they had me pegged as a likely drug smuggler. I'd searched the puppet case again myself at the B&B, but there was nothing there that gave me a clue as to what all the fuss was about. Still, I didn't want anyone breaking in to the Pilgrim's Rest and making another try for my poor puppets, which is why I was grateful to Mr. Frayne when he suggested I might like to put my valuables in the safe.

I stashed the BritRail form with Derek Smith's personal info into the little zippered pouch with Earlie's and Mr. Fogbow's business cards, drained the rest of my cold coffee and wandered out into the foggy Canterbury streets.

From the "Welcome to the Canterbury International Puppetry Conference (CIPF)" brochure:

University of Kent, Canterbury (UKC), is built on 300 acres of parkland overlooking Canterbury. It was founded in 1965 and is still growing and evolving. Modern buildings are surrounded by open green spaces, courtyards, gardens, ponds and woodland, and the view across Canterbury and the Stour valley all help to make Kent an attractive and friendly campus.

The night before, I'd taken a taxi (the same guy who'd driven me from the train station, coincidentally, whose laminated photo ID thing identified him as Rajeet) to the registration location. I hadn't seen much of the university then—just a looming bunch of buildings swathed in fog. This time I took a bus, having been given careful instructions by Mr. Frayne as to which bus to get on and where to wait for it. I was delighted to find that it was a double-decker—not one of those old fashioned red ones (which must all be in the same warehouse where they've stashed the red telephone boxes) but a modern one, all gleaming chrome with pseudo-leather seats. I went straight to the top (although the climb was a bit of an effort) and to the front, where the window offered me a vista like a big TV screen. The mobile phone crowd began to operate at once ("I'm on the bus"), and I noticed that many of them were not talking, but rather punching the keys carefully and staring intently at the little screens of their phones. I learned later that this was a feature called messaging, and that all the best mobiles offered it. Sadly, that blew my Pez-phone right out of the water. I'd have upgraded, if I'd known.

The wild thing about being on the top platform of a double-decker bus, I discovered, was that it gives you a completely new perspective, which includes suddenly being able to see into the second floors of buildings. The bus didn't run in the really ancient part of the city, so I didn't get a chance to snoop through those compelling little mullioned windows where the buildings bulged out over the streets, but it was still great fun (and rather thrilling in a prurient kind of way) to get sudden glimpses into people's kitchens and sitting rooms in the second floor flats we passed.

Just before we pulled off the main road and started climbing into the countryside, I could have sworn I saw my Gatwick/train station thug, sitting at a table, smoking a cigarette and reading a newspaper. It was only a split-second thing, like one of those pictures flashed on TV during a commercial, and then he was gone, but I got a good look at his shaven skull, and there was that tattoo—the red crest with the devil with a pitchfork and the three blobs above it. I craned my neck to keep him in sight as we whizzed past. A street sign flashed by—Castle Road—and then we were into a kind of lane with trees on both sides, like a tunnel. I rubbed my eyes and wondered if I had imagined it. If it hadn't just been my overworked imagination, it would mean that the thug had stupidly written down his real address when trying to steal my stuff from the luggage locker. This would also mean that he had been with me on the same train, which would also require me to believe that a) it was a coincidence that I happened to be travelling to his hometown or b) he had known who I was, where I'd be and where I was going, and was there waiting for me at Gatwick. The "b" option was completely far-fetched, so I chose "a", the coincidence option. After all, Maude knew Donna-Lou Dermott. Coincidence does happen. Lightning can strike twice. I scrabbled in my purse and drew out the BritRail form again. There it was—Derek Smith, 26a Castle Road, Canterbury. Just like the personal-cheque bank robber. Just goes to prove that crime is the playground of the stupid. I resolved to go to the local police if there were any more attempts on my belongings. I had him—I knew where he lived.

The Sprog chose that moment to make her wakefulness known—booting at my insides like a piece of undigested gristle. I placed my hand on my midriff and spoke soothingly to her as the bus trundled off into the Canterbury fog.

Thirteen

Pregnancy represents a true fork in the road of life. One can never know what would have happened had a woman gone the other way. To gain strength and connection with other women, share your story whenever you can.
-From *Big Bertha's Total Baby Guide*

In February, the open spaces, courtyards, gardens and the rest of the UKC campus were not exactly attractive, in fact they were invisible, but the people were truly friendly, just as the Welcome brochure claimed. I got off the bus at the big sign that said "University of Kent, Canterbury", and was immediately totally lost. I don't have a great sense of direction at the best of times, and the fog was disorienting. The cab driver the night before had dropped me at an anonymous door, through which I'd gone, registered and stumbled out again in a jet-lagged haze. I would have to ask directions this time.

I pulled out the brochure again, which I knew had some sort of campus map in it, and was leafing through it when a kindly young student-type touched me gently on the shoulder.

"Do you need some help?" she said. She was fresh faced and cheerful, carrying an enormous, book-crammed backpack.

"I'm trying to find the Cornwallis building," I said. "I'm attending a puppetry conference—if you know anything about it."

"Oh, yes, I thought there was something going on there," she said. "My college is right next door. It's not far—just up that lane and take a right and the big glass door with the pillars on either side is it." She gave me a little wave and went on her way, staggering a bit under her academic burden, and was swallowed quickly by the murk.

Thick fog in England is an interesting substance. In Kuskawa we get fog sometimes, or mist, really, as we haven't got the sea to make it the pea soup kind—just a bunch of lakes that belch out thin stuff from time to time. This fog was tangible, smelling of salt and sea, delicious, if cold and clammy. I knew that Canterbury was quite near the coast—it was touted as one of the most ancient port-connected cities in England, seven miles from Whitstable, a "popular harbour town". I thought of Conan Doyle's London fog, the kind of pea-souper that Sherlock Holmes waded about in. In Holmes stories, the fog appeared as a kind of secondary character, usually turning up to make things difficult for the sleuth, to add a kind of mysterious, dense and detached stumbling block to the task at hand. Now I understood it. "Just up that lane and take a right" was all very well, but the ground itself was hard to see, and there were trees on every side of the lane, hemming me in so I felt like a child lost in a maze and couldn't shake the feeling that I was being watched. I guess this was a carry-over from the shock of seeing the thug in the window. I don't usually let stuff rattle me, but this had. Perhaps I was on edge because now there were two of me to watch out for.

It was an enormous relief when I found the pillars and the glass door. Inside the lobby, there was a comforting bustle and movement. I reached into my bag and pulled out my name tag, a little plastic pouch on a string which held a card with the Canterbury International Puppetry Festival (CIPF) logo on it, a Muppet face with the mnemonic coming out of a cartoon talk-bubble with "Polly Deacon, Canada, presenter" written below. It was my entrance pass, and I'd been warned in the welcoming letter to wear it at all times. I hung it around my neck and was instantly greeted by the woman I'd met the night before at the registration, whose label-on-a-string said "Phyllis Creemore, Canterbury, U.K., Organizing Committee". It was she who had signed the letter of acceptance and welcome I'd received back in October.

"Oh, Polly, there you are, dear," she said, sailing into my personal space like a hockey player doing a bodycheck, grabbing my arm and steering me into the boards. "Everything okay at the Pilgrim's Rest? Cedric is such a sweetie, isn't he? I hope he gave you a good room and you slept well." Cedric was Mr. Frayne. It would take me a while to get used to calling him that.

"Yes, he's very kind," I said, trying to move back a little. She appeared to be fascinated by my belly, and her hand hovered nearby, ready to administer little pats. "I'm quite comfortable, thanks."

"Oh, goooood," she said. "And you are coming to the opening address, aren't you? Mr. Blaise Killington from UNIMA will be speaking about puppetry used as a form of disassociative civil disobedience in third world countries—you know—agitprop theatre and all that. He's been arrested ever so many times, so it should be interesting."

"It sounds it," I said. UNIMA, which stands for the Union Internationale de la Marionette, is basically *the* international puppetry organization. If you do puppets, it doesn't make sense not to join.

"And I am so looking forward to your session—it's tomorrow afternoon, isn't it? Is there anything you'll be needing? Oh, and we'll need your PowerPoint disk today so that our technicians can do a trial run."

"I'm not using PowerPoint, actually. A flip chart and a table will be fine." She looked at me as if I were out of my mind.

"Not using PowerPoint? Everybody uses PowerPoint."

"Not everybody, Phyllis. I don't even have a computer."

"Oh." She stepped back and examined me, chewing a fingernail as she did so. Reassessing, perhaps. "Oh. Well, then, that makes everything much easier, doesn't it?" I got the implication. Not having bells and whistles also makes things much more boring. I began to feel a little niggle of doubt about my presentation. Should I have brought slides, at least?

"How many people will be attending, do you know?" I said.

"Well, there are several sessions running concurrently, so I expect you'll get anywhere between ten and thirty," she said. "You're in one of the lecture rooms—very modern, you know. All the latest equipment."

"As long as there's a flip chart—or a blackboard, I suppose, and a table, that'll be fine," I said.

"Right," she said. "A flip chart. I'm sure we've got one of those stored away somewhere. We don't use them very often. As for a blackboard…" she went off in a gust of giggles, as if I'd suggested using stone tablets and a chisel. "We haven't had blackboards for years, dear."

"Oh," I said. Sometimes it's hard being a Luddite.

Phyllis steered me towards the Hospitality Room, where a breakfast buffet had been laid out, with tea and coffee, juice, muffins and fruit. As I'd made a pig of myself over Mr. Frayne's fry-up, I didn't think it seemly to gorf out on another breakfast, but there were fresh strawberries, which I couldn't resist, and I discreetly wrapped up a bran muffin in a paper napkin and stowed it in my bag for later. The conference goers appeared to be a hungry lot, and the table was under siege from all sides, so I figured that the spread wouldn't last more than a few minutes.

I chose a small single-serving tin of apple juice, rather than a coffee. I didn't want the Sprog to get too excited, especially if I had to sit in a lecture hall chair for goodness knew how long. I retired to a corner to sip it and watch the crowd.

Puppetry people are a strange breed, when you get them all together in one room. I suppose any special interest group is the same—it wasn't as if this were a symposium of actors or models, who tend to be rather decorative. Puppet people are frequently those who love to perform, but have perhaps found it more fulfilling to be the genius behind the strings, or the person under the counter with their arms above their heads, rather than being out there by themselves on the stage or screen. They are frequently eccentric looking, and usually muscular about the arms and shoulders. (It takes a great deal of strength to hold a five-pound puppet above your head for an eight-hour rehearsal, or longer if it's film or TV work.)

I was just finishing up my tin o' juice when I saw someone across the room who looked awfully familiar. It took me a moment or two to realize where I'd seen her before. She turned around and looked directly at me, and I swear it was like looking into a mirror. She looked uncannily like me, or I looked uncannily like her, I suppose. She was pregnant, too. When our eyes met, I could see hers widen in the same kind of recognition. We moved towards each other like people in a dream and met in the middle of the room, hemmed in on both sides by other conference goers.

She wasn't wearing a tag-on-a-string. "Well, that's odd, isn't it?" she said, shaking my hand cordially. "We might be sisters."

There comes a time in every reader's life when they will be asked to suspend their disbelief to breaking point. If this moment were something I was reading in a book, I'd begin harbouring grave doubts about the plot-building capabilities of the author and might even consider throwing the book away and picking up a good thick reference text instead. However, seeing as this was happening in real life, I didn't have that option, so I searched quickly though my mental archives to see what I knew about the Author. Frankly, the Author and I are hardly on speaking terms, and I'd never bought the Old Man in the Sky theory, so there wasn't much point in regarding this ruthless succession of coincidence, serendipity, weirdness, what have you, as God's Will. I was aware, though, that from the moment I'd surrendered my body to the inexorable process of hosting a bundle of dividing cells, destined to become a person, I'd been confronted at every turn by moments of "how weird is that?" In fact, I was coming to expect it, which is dangerous, because as soon as you start looking for signs, you'll find a whole bunch.

My double looked into my eyes. We both had the same colour and a similar cut of hair, our faces were not identical, of course, but eerily similar. We were even the same height, and though she appeared to be further along in her pregnancy than I was, we were both wearing the same kind of khaki trousers.

We formally exchanged names. She was Alma Barrow, and she was there, she said, under false pretenses.

"I'm not exactly part of the conference," she said, "but I did so want to hear Blaise Killington, so I thought I'd just trot up here and try to blend in with the crowd." Our voices were not similar at all. She had a dense, almost impenetrable accent—a flat and adenoidal sound that placed her somewhere in the Midlands, an accent that spoke of centuries of coal dust getting up the nose.

"Do you live in Canterbury, then?" I said.

"Oh, no—I'm from Birmingham. I'm here for this week's pro-life rally, down near the Cathedral."

"Ah," I said, on my guard at once. Anti-abortionists, at least the activist kind, are not my favourite kind of people. I felt obscurely disappointed, as if she were indeed my sister and had turned out to be a bit of a loony.

"Oh, it's all right," she said. "I'm not one of them. I'm the president of our own little chapter of pro-choice activists in Birmingham, you see, and I'm planning to infiltrate the ranks of the pro-lifers to do some pamphleteering and so on. We can't let these fanatics win, you know." Her eyes held a fanatical light of their own.

"I'd heard somebody mention a rally, actually," I said, remembering that both Maude on the "trine" and the lady in the taxi had asked me if I were attending it. I suppose my pregnancy must have made them think I had a vested interest in the issue. "A big rally, is it?"

"Well, I expect so," Alma said. "It's not nearly the hot topic here that it is in America, but the anti-types have been mobilizing just lately, picketing clinics and so on, and there have been one or two nasty incidents with providers being harassed. Oh, I do hope I haven't read you wrong—you're not one of them, are you?"

"No, I'm pro-choice," I said. "Although I've never had the energy to do anything overt about it."

"Well, somebody's got to," Alma said. "The rally this week is going to be quite well-attended, we think. We have to make sure the voice of reason is heard, or else before you know it, it'll be outlawed and we'll have back lane abortions and knitting needles and things again."

"Well, I admire your dedication," I said, a little distantly. I wondered if the fact that she was pregnant herself made it harder or easier to promote her views, but it was hardly a polite question to ask someone I'd only just met. Alma answered it for me in the next moment, patting her belly contentedly.

"Of course, this one is wanted," she said. "But not every baby is, as you no doubt know. I've got three more at home, but not everybody has a mother who likes to look after her grandchildren. And you know, this works as a wonderful disguise. Pro-lifers simply assume that every pregnant woman on the face of the earth is an anti, don't they?"

It was an interesting point, but I didn't have time to answer it, as the crush of people in the Hospitality Room was thinning all of a sudden, everybody moving through a set of double doors that had opened into a large lecture hall. We moved together to join the throng.

"You don't mind if I sit with you, do you?" Alma asked. "I don't know a soul here, and they'll throw me out if they think I haven't registered."

"Of course," I said. "Why are you so eager to hear this Killington guy, anyway?"

"He's going to talk about street demonstrations," she said. "You know—the kind where they carry great big figures of political leaders and so on through the streets—that sort of over-the-top activism. I want to get a few pointers, because Samantha—that's an artist friend of mine in our group—she's made a big effigy of a baby for me to carry during the march tomorrow, with "Wanted Baby" written on its nappy. I'm hoping to ask him afterwards if he has any advice for me."

"Golly," I said. "That's brave."

"And very un-English," Alma said, with a certain amount of satisfaction. "I'm expecting a bit of bother about it, actually, and I want to be prepared."

"You're doing this all alone?"

"Well, the others are with me in spirit, but nobody in our group could get away except me," she said, her voice a little tight, as if she weren't entirely happy about being a lone voice in the wilderness.

I had a mental image of Alma in the midst of a horde of roaring anti-abortionists, her agitprop effigy being pummelled to death by the kind of signs-on-sticks that pro-lifers carry—those ones with graphic pictures of aborted fetuses on them.

"I hope you'll be careful," I said.

The auditorium had filled up, and the only empty seats we could find were quite near the front. It was a big room, laid out in a half circle, amphitheatre style, with comfortably padded, raked seats. The lectern was off to one side, and a big screen filled the central area. Obviously, Mr. Killington was going to be using PowerPoint. Perhaps I could pick up a few pointers, too. I felt thankful that my own modest little puppetry session would be on a much smaller scale, in a small lecture room with a flip chart.

The lights in the auditorium dimmed, and a slim, dapper gentleman walked up to the podium to make his introductions and welcome. In my belly, the Sprog did a double backflip, then settled down to digest her apple juice. The Canterbury International Puppetry Festival (CIPF) had begun.

Fourteen

It seems there's more and more pressure these days to buy your baby just the right toys to broaden her horizons and make her a little genius by the tender age of six months. Don't fall into the "baby won't learn as much if I don't buy this toy" trap.
-From *Big Bertha's Total Baby Guide*

"The puppet has always had a totemic power," Blaise Killington was saying. "The audience, young and old, instinctively accepts the premise that the manipulator is a servant of the animated object, someone in the background, merely. The object, the puppet, takes on a larger-than-life aspect, which allows it to express a viewpoint that might not otherwise be tolerated, coming from a human performer."

He was winding up a truly fascinating forty-minute lecture, and my mind had not wandered once, though the Sprog, exerting a little pressure on my inner self, had suggested that a visit to the ladies' room might be appropriate when a break was called.

"This is most evident from the behaviour of the police during the street demonstrations last year in Karachi, when their first action, upon engaging with the crowds, was to pull down the puppets we were using and stomp them into the ground." On the screen, a short film clip of the Karachi demonstration appeared, the police in riot gear, and the puppets, huge creatures with arms on sticks, were indeed the objects of the first assault. The puppeteers, I noticed, did not exactly escape punishment, either. A man in charge of one of the figures was shown having his head stomped at the same time his puppet's head was being ground into the dust. It made my flesh creep.

"Just recently, several NGOs in the war-torn regions of Afghanistan and Pakistan have approached UNIMA for help with setting up a program to help kids deal with post-traumatic stress issues, using puppets," Killington went on. The screen showed a picture of a woman in a head scarf working a friendly-looking hand puppet, which looked just like her. The small child beside her was focussed entirely on the puppet, speaking to it in an intimate way that tugged at the heartstrings. "We know of course that puppets have been used extensively to help children articulate and work through the trauma they've experienced—notably in cases of sexual abuse. Kids will tell things to a puppet that they would never tell an adult. It's proved invaluable, and the program in Kabul has been enormously successful." There was a smattering of applause at that.

Killington received a huge round of applause after his address, and Alma moved in immediately after the lights came up to talk to him. "I'll see you later," I said. "Gotta pee."

"Me, too," Alma said, grimacing, "but I must catch him before he disappears. I hope to see you later, Polly. It's been fun meeting you."

"Yes, and if we don't bump into each other again, best of luck with the rally," I said. "I hope the anti-abortionists don't stomp on your head." Alma chuckled and then waded off into the crowd, using her substantial belly as a battering ram. I headed for the exits, looking for a washroom sign.

In the rest room, I noticed that the toilet paper dispensers were made by Kimberly Clark, a North American manufacturer which had a factory in Laingford, back home. This evinced in me an absurd and surprising little twiggle of patriotism. I was glad to see that, in spite of what Brent Miller had said, English washrooms did not all have user-fees. He'd earnestly suggested I keep a handful of change on hand for bathroom breaks. "It's where the expression 'spend a penny' came from," he had said. "It costs money to use a toilet, eh? My aunt told me that."

There was a demonstration of *wayang kulit* puppetry, Indonesian shadow puppets, that I wanted to check out, but that wouldn't happen for twenty minutes, so I headed for the outdoors. During Killington's speech, the fog had lifted, and a little pale lemon sun was working its way to earth through a gap in the clouds.

It was a huge campus. The blurb had said there were three hundred acres of it, and there were a lot of open spaces, which were probably gorgeous in the summertime. In February, it was pretty bleak, and there was a chilly wind coming off the open fields beyond the visitors' car park out front. From where I stood, I knew I had my back to Canterbury, facing towards London, basically, though the breeze was fresh and wonderfully salty. Students scurried to and fro, all with backpacks, all looking about twelve years old. Behind me loomed the Cornwallis building, which housed the lecture theatre and Phyllis' state-of-the-art seminar rooms. Off to my left were more buildings, all in that 1960s concrete bunker style, imposing and a little bit military, with bulky exterior walls and long, thin, castle-like windows very high up, with turrets at the top. In the distance were the student residences, attractively laid out to form a sort of village. To see the vista of Canterbury, the Stour Valley and the Cathedral, I'd have to walk south-east, through the campus to the hill on the other side. I decided to save that for another time, but I was looking forward to it.

I had a sudden, profound urge to march into the registrar's office and sign up for something. University campuses always affect me that way. They stir up in me a long-contended-with urge to throw myself once more into the swamp of academe, to follow a schedule and do what I'm told and listen to lectures and take notes and concentrate on nothing more important than a paper or an exam. They make me feel safe, or at least wrap me up in the feeling that safety is possible.

In truth, I have never actually completed anything other than Grade Twelve. I was at Art College in Toronto for one-and-a-half years, then got bored and transferred to Theatre School instead. Halfway through my theatre course, I got bored again and quit to work for a puppet theatre company out east. Although I like the idea of university, and the romantic notion of classes and student life, I'd never really been any good at it. The discipline always defeated me, once boredom set in. It was like those nice fresh notebooks we all had as kids in elementary school—the ones we swore black and blue we'd keep clean and free of mind-wandering doodles. The ones that were covered with scribbles and "Kilroy was here" cartoons by December. I still had occasional dreams of monumentally important things unfinished. Standing there on the campus of the University of Kent, Canterbury, I felt again that faintly shameful yearning to earn myself a proper degree, a piece of paper that would make me worthy, that would impress Aunt Susan and would guarantee me a life of gainful employment, instead of the hardscrabble existence of an itinerant puppet maker.

I sat on a stone bench in a courtyard in front of the elegant grey building and fought the urge for a cigarette.

*   *   *

"Excuse me, are you Polly Deacon, by any chance?" I turned to see a man standing there, whose tag-on-a-string identified him as Richard Seth, Canada.

"That's me," I said.

"I thought you must be," he said. "Juliet Keating said you were here doing a workshop and told me to look out for you." Juliet was the artistic director of the Steamboat Theatre, a childrens' theatre touring company based in Sikwan, a town south of Laingford. I'd worked there the previous summer. Juliet and I weren't speaking, as it happens, and I was surprised that she'd bothered to mention my name to anybody, particularly someone so, well, delicious. His skin was a rich bronze, he was dark and mysterious, and he had the kind of bone structure you do actually write home about. "Dear Earlie," I composed in my mind, "I've met a perfectly beautiful man..."

"What did you think of Killington's talk?" he said, sitting down beside me after we'd introduced ourselves.

"It made me think I wasn't doing enough serious work to change the world," I said. "It made me feel guilty, as a matter of fact." He laughed, a nice, light, ringing laugh.

"I know what you mean. Like I suddenly wonder if I've got this gift that I'm supposed to use for world peace, and instead I'm building foam rubber props for a production of *Hunting and Fishing Is Our Heritage* for the Ontario Federation of Guys With Guns."

"Yikes. You're working on that one? I read about it in the *Laingford Gazette.* I almost swallowed my tongue."

"It's government funded, eh?" Richard said. "Big bucks for Juliet."

"And they're going to include copies of the *Ontario Firearms Handbook* with the teacher's guides, right?" We laughed together about that. Better than weeping, I guess. It was nice to meet somebody from home, actually. It wasn't that I was homesick or anything—I'd only been on foreign soil for forty-eight hours, but if you start waxing nostalgic about a toilet paper dispenser, then there must be something going on.

We agreed to meet later in the student pub for a beverage and to gossip about Juliet and her crew at Steamboat. Richard was fresh out of the theatre tech program at Ryerson and knew many of the same people I did. He smoked, too, and after asking if I minded (are you kidding? Blow it my way, won'tcha?), he pulled out a pack of DuMaurier Lights and lit up.

"I brought a carton with me, duty free," he said. "Last time I was here, I tried to adapt to British cigarettes, but they all tasted funny, like someone had boiled the tobacco in cabbage water before drying it. I tried a dozen brands, but eventually had to find a specialty shop in London that carried Canadian brands. Cost me a fortune. I was going to quit before I came over this time, but it didn't happen. I tried the patch, but it just made me crave band-aids."

"Try getting pregnant," I said. "Works like a charm."

*   *   *

The *wayang kulit* demo was amazing. I've always been fascinated by shadows. I remember my mother being awfully good at creating animal hand-shapes in front of a candle or a lamp bulb, throwing fantastic shapes against the wall. She taught me how to do a camel and a bird when I was very small, and I have always cherished a mental image of a big bird and a little bird, her hands and mine, flying together across the blank wall in the dining room, eons ago.

When I was doing touring theatre, there was one rather memorable and wild night of partying (which may perhaps have included the modest use of some recreational substances) during which a couple of us, with the help of a hotel room lamp with the shade pulled off, entertained the cast for about two hours straight. We'd put the show tapes on someone's portable tape deck and had done a hand-shadow puppet version of the play we were touring, becoming increasingly more hysterical and inventive as we went.

In formal shadow puppetry, the audience only sees the shadows of the puppets, thrown onto a screen by a light or a fire. Its history is ancient. Many think it originated in Greece, although Chinese records show forms of shadow puppetry being performed two thousand years ago. In *wayang kulit*, intricate flat puppets made of wood, paper and animal hide are manipulated in front of a light thrown onto a muslin screen, usually telling stories from Hindu mythology. In Java, audience members sit on both sides of the screen—either to watch the shadows, or to see the puppets and the manipulating puppeteers.

The demonstrators explained their techniques as they went and did allow us to move back and forth so we could see the effects. They allowed us to give it a shot, as well, and it was great fun. They had some of their puppets for sale, too, and I couldn't resist buying one, a perfectly flat, exquisitely delicate, paper and balsa wood figure that looked, in an Indonesian sort of way, awfully like my pregnant-lady puppet. At least when the time came to take it back across the border, the security people wouldn't be inclined to tear it apart, looking for bombs. There's a lot to be said for working in two dimensions.

*   *   *

The shadow puppet demonstration had also put my mind at ease regarding my own lack of high-tech props for my workshop. They didn't have PowerPoint (they had no slides), just their screen and their puppets. All I had were my two puppets, resting quietly in their case back at the Pilgrim's Rest, ready and waiting for their shining hour. My session was scheduled for the next day at one p.m., after lunch.

Before leaving the building, I went in search of Phyllis Creemore, to see if she could direct me to the room I'd be lecturing in. It turned out to be a very small, intimate classroom at the end of a long hallway next to the main auditorium. There was no raked seating or stage—although there was a slightly raised platform at one end of the room, with a simple table and—yes!—a flip chart.

"I found one, you see," Phyllis said, having led me to the location herself. "There were several, actually, in a storeroom in the basement. I've got you some nice, thick markers as well, dear. I hope that'll do you."

"It's perfect, Phyllis. Thanks," I said.

"Now you're sure you won't be needing anything else?"

"Nope, I'm the soul of simplicity, really. I just hope somebody comes."

"Oh, they'll come, all right. We don't often get marionettists at these things, you know. Too many strings to pull to get you here." She giggled again—an incongruous sound coming from such a matronly person. "Actually, there may well be a visitor or two from town as well," she said. "I had a call from someone this morning asking when and where your presentation was going to be. You're quite famous, my dear. We do allow the public to attend some of the sessions, provided they pay something at the door."

"Oh? That's flattering," I said. "Any idea who they were?"

"They didn't say. Sounded like one of the teachers from the comprehensive," she said. "I could hear children in the background, anyway."

"That might be awkward," I said. "One of the puppets I've brought is a little indelicate."

"Oh, don't worry about that," Phyllis said. "We've had a no-children policy here, ever since the time we offered a Punch and Judy show for the kiddies on the Cathedral grounds and got had up by the local authorities for propagating violence in our youth. It was rather embarrassing. So now, no children allowed." She bustled away, leaving me with the amused notion that an international puppetry conference that didn't allow children anywhere near it was, well, peculiar. Like one of those model train displays presented by a bunch of deadly serious old men who wouldn't let anyone under thirty-five anywhere near their stuff.

I set off back down the hallway, hoping to find a kind student who might direct me to their watering hole, where I was supposed to meet Richard Seth. If it was dark enough in the pub (so nobody would notice that I was pregnant), I had decided I would treat myself to a half pint of Guinness. After all, my grandmother had sworn by the stuff for pregnant ladies. I just hoped that I wouldn't be "had up" by the local authorities, for corrupting the young.

Fifteen

The sacrament of baptism for a child is an occasion involving the whole family and should include both relatives and friends. Make sure you know what it means before you commit to it.
   -From *Big Bertha's Total Baby Guide*

To: Polly1258@hotmail.com
From: oppmorr@kuskawa.com
Subject: RE: All's well
Date: Thursday, February 14

Dear Polly,
Everyone says to say Hi, and your Aunt Susan sends a special Valentine's Day greeting. She says you'll understand the joke, because you guys don't do Valentine's Day, which makes no sense to me, but what the hey. George says he's giving her a bunch of flowers anyways.

   I don't like the sound of these guys trying to steal your bags, so take it easy and watch your back. Don't forget that every city in the world has a crime rate, even though it may look old-fashioned and quaint. Don't go down any old English alleys by yourself.

   It's snowing a lot here now, and we've been busy with people driving like maniacs on Hwy 11 and spinning out. Susan said not to bother you with this, but I knew you'd be pissed off if you didn't hear about it until later. Our young friend Eddie got himself into a load of trouble on Tuesday night, and some people are saying it's partly your fault, although I know that's not true. Seems he was driving George's pickup truck (the one you drive) and was going real slow on a back road when some guy comes up behind him and Eddie didn't have room to move over and let him pass, so the guy overtakes him and loses control and spins out into the ditch. Eddie stops to help him and the guy takes a swing at him. Road rage, I guess. Anyway, happens me and Becker were called to the scene and Becker searches the kid and finds a couple of joints on him. So we take both of the guys in, and the road rage guy gets off and Eddie gets charged. There wasn't anything I could do, and you know how my partner gets when I disagree with him. Anyway, the stupid kid did have dope on him, although he swears he wasn't driving stoned. So his court date comes up next month and you'll be back by then, but I thought you should know. Don't sweat it—he'll probably just get a fine and probation. He did make damn sure that we knew he didn't get the stuff from you, though, although some people think he did. I know better.

In other news, you might be interested to know that Brent and Rico are trying to get the local United Church to marry them, of all the fool things. No way it'll happen, but they're getting interviewed by that Calvin Grigsby from the paper, and it should be interesting watching the shamozzle over that one. I'll save you the clipping.

Your aunt and George are fine. I'm going over there tomorrow night for dinner and a game of cribbage. If you write back soon, I'll take your latest along. I'm at work right now so I got to make this short. I'm using Becker's computer because mine's on the fritz. He hates it when I use his stuff. We're heading out on snowmobile patrol in half an hour. The sledders are out in full force, even though there's no snow base on the trails and the lakes are still open.

> They're dropping into the drink faster than we can pull them out.
>
> Take good care, and best regards.
>
> Earlie Morrison.
>
> PS. Your Rosie caught her first mouse yesterday and boy is she ever proud of herself.

Getting a letter from home, even if you've only just left the place, is utterly heart-warming. Even if it contains bad news. I was so mad at Eddie that if I'd had him with me, I'd have smacked him. Talk about a dope. I knew damn well that Becker was the "some people" who thought I was Eddie's source of pot, and I couldn't help noticing that he hadn't bothered to reply to my message, short though it had been. I saved Earlie's message and decided to reply to it later in the day, after my seminar was over, so I'd have some interesting material. My large cop-friend surprised me—he was a good letter-writer, and I wanted to respond in kind.

I was already establishing a routine, even though it was only my second morning in Canterbury. I guess I'm a creature of habit, although I like people to think I'm spontaneous. I was sitting in the Internet café near the Cathedral again, with my Starbucks coffee, after having stuffed myself with Cedric Frayne's morning fry-up. There was a seminar scheduled up at the university at ten, all about "Touring Tips for the Puppetry Troupe", which I'd decided to miss, as I had toured for more than a decade and didn't want to hear any more about it. Also, I'd picked up a flyer at the local convenience store, advertising the "Right to Life" march and speeches planned for that morning in the old downtown area, and I thought it might be interesting to watch. Not that I was expecting to see my new friend Alma getting her head stomped by the police, of course, but crowd dynamics interest me, and I wanted to see Alma's agitprop baby-on-a-stick. I took my coffee with me and headed out into the day.

It was a glorious morning, quite mild, with the sun burning off a light mist and reflecting off the cobblestoned streets like a scene from a Merchant Ivory film. There weren't many people up and about yet, although the Internet café was buzzing, having opened at the crack of dawn. I'd dabbled in the shallows of the net for a while and read *The Times*, and it was nine-thirty already. I was wearing my old, zip-up curling sweater, a retro-piece I'd found at a second-hand store in Sikwan, and the extra layer of wool was actually making me perspire. It felt like April in Kuskawa, or May, even. Who'd have thought that Canterbury in mid-winter could be like this? Who needed Bermuda? (Actually, it was only about fifty degrees Fahrenheit, according to Mr. Frayne's thermometer, but for one of Canadian blood, in winter, that was tropical.)

The main street, which changed its name every block or so, was almost too perfect to be real. The Welcome brochure for the conference had a blurb about the "narrow streets and period architecture", but nothing can prepare you for the extraordinary feeling of being surrounded by things built hundreds of years ago. Nothing comes close.

When used in modern building construction, the fake-o "Tudor"architectural style has always struck me as silly. I'd never realized, though, how far removed the fake versions are from the real thing. When I saw my first genuine Tudor buildings in Canterbury, I realized that the fake ones were like low budget cartoons. It was like comparing a plaster statue of Rudolph the Red Nosed Reindeer in somebody's front yard with a living, majestic, shaggy and snorting creature seen on location in Lapland.

Canterbury is called the "cradle of Christianity", and the Cathedral is considered the Mother Church of the world's Anglicans. The Welcome brochure informed me that the first cathedral was built in AD 597, when St. Augustine arrived from Rome to baptize King Ethelbert of Kent and "so pave the way for the conversion of all England to Christianity". Canterbury was obviously a kind of roadhouse theatre for invading people, Romans, Saxons, the whole gang, all using the place as a kind of stopover on the way to London, which was called Londinium, way back when. The neat part about England is that people have been bickering over the turf for almost two thousand years, and they all tended to leave their mark on the place. Not only their physical marks—buildings, battle sites, dropped change and tossed away booze bottles, but their psychic marks as well. That's what thrilled me the most. I'm not a new-age crystal rubber, you understand, but you'd have to be made of stone not to feel the ghosts of people gone before. It was in the very fabric of the place. Nothing remains of the original cathedral, except a few bits and pieces incorporated into the ruins of a nearby monastery, which I decided I would have to visit later. The construction of the present cathedral was started in 1067. The place is most famous for being the site of the murder of Thomas Becket, which led to its being the destination of Chaucer's pilgrims in *The Canterbury Tales.* I wanted to visit the shrine in the Cathedral, as well, and planned to do that after I'd watched the loony Right-to-Lifers do their stuff.

The old part of the city was still surrounded by the ruins of walls, built in the thirteenth and fourteenth centuries on Roman foundations, presumably to keep out the undesirables. At the end of the main street, there was an archway over the road, the last surviving city gatehouse, called the West Gate. I walked down the street towards the West Gate, imagining that my feet were stepping on ground that twelfth century tourists must have trod.

On the left, a bit before the gate, was an incredibly old facade that my brochure told me was the Eastbridge Hospital. It took me a while to figure out that it wasn't a medical hospital, but rather a charitable foundation built in the thirteenth century to house poor pilgrims on their way to the shrine. According to the blurb, it was still used as a rooming house for Canterbury's poor and elderly, and the chapel, refectory and crypt were open to visitors from ten a.m. until four. It was stone-fronted, crooked and utterly compelling.

A bit further down the street, there was a little bridge over a small river, a branch of the Stour, the brochure said, and leaning out over the water were a bunch of lopsided, half-timbered buildings, labelled the Weavers' Houses, a flophouse for a group of French refugee textile workers in the sixteenth century. I was just loving this. The street ahead was practically deserted, the sun was casting time-traveller shadows on the cobblestones, and I felt sort of dreamlike, as if, with a waft of wind, I might suddenly be transported back in time, to be plunked on a bridge in 1170-something, just another pregnant wench on her way to an appointment with an apothecary.

It was in that bemused mood that I knew suddenly that I was being watched. You know the sensation, as if there are a couple of eyeballs like deerflies tickling a spot somewhere between your shoulder blades. I spun round to look back down the street, remembering as I did Earlie's email advice to watch my back. There was a brief flicker of movement down the street on the other side, in the doorway of the Eastbridge Hospital. It was probably one of the residents out for a morning stroll. There were several people on the streets now, going about their business, and none of them paid me the least bit of notice. Perhaps my reverie had conjured up a ghost from the past, some medieval footpad getting ready to steal my purse and push me into the Stour. I turned back to face the gate, and heard the distant murmur of a crowd. I looked at my watch—coming up to ten a.m. This must be the march.

It was odd that they'd picked an early hour on a Thursday in February to attract attention to their cause, I thought. Still, perhaps the local authorities (who, after all, were known to shut down Punch and Judy shows on the basis that they were corrupting the local youth) had been dicey about giving these folks a permit. I knew without a doubt that you'd have to have a permit to march anywhere, especially in a place that relied on the tourist trade as much as Canterbury did.

I looked back behind me again, and there were twice as many people on the street now, as if some movie director had said "Okay, bring on the extras." They were just people out doing their daily things, dropping into shops and presumably going to work, many of them carrying Starbucks coffee cups, as I was. Some of these people were visitors, I could tell. A tourist, even in February, has a certain look—the camera around the neck, the running shoes (in England they're called trainers—so Brent had told me), the windbreakers (anoraks) and the guidebooks in hand.

The march advanced through the West Gate and onto St. Peter's Street. Someone at the head of the line was playing a trumpet—"Onward Christian Soldiers"—and everybody was marching in step. I wondered whether they would have been allowed in by the security guys in the twelfth century. Probably not. Many of them were carrying signboards, the stuff you see clinic picketers carrying, with the usual graphic photo (retouched, I think) of a bloody fetus, ostensibly post-abortion. I believe you can download this thing off the net. It's not a pretty sight. Some people were chanting "Let them live! Let them live!" and others were accosting bystanders and thrusting pamphlets into their hands. I stood and watched, fascinated by the fervour I saw in their eyes.

I accepted the pamphlet someone handed me, stuffed it into my bag and watched the passing parade. It was mostly men, I noted, middle aged men with receding hairlines, men so angry their faces were red. And older women, the kind of women you'd expect to see manning the booths at church bazaars, prim-faced and wild-eyed, with thin lips. When they chanted their slogans, their eyes slipped sideways, as if they were making sure their colleagues were being as loud and as dedicated to the cause as they were.

Alma was at the tail end of it, being ostracized by most of the people in front of her, who kept looking back at her with frowns on their faces, hurrying the people in front of them in a Keystone Cops kind of way, trying to widen the distance between themselves and the unwelcome caboose. Alma's baby-on-a-stick was a lovely bit of soft sculpture. The artist had used nylon stockings, I think, stuffed with quilt batting and sewn to craft a big, pudgy and smiling infant. Its diaper was made of stark white material with an oversized safety pin on each side. The bum of the thing was enormous, and the words "Wanted Baby" were painted on it in big, black, easy-to-read print. I saw Alma handing out pamphlets, too, with the free hand not carrying her puppet, and a woman from the pro-life side trying to stop her. There seemed to be an ongoing tug-of-war between them, which would have been comical if it hadn't been disturbingly vicious. The pro-life woman looked positively murderous. I tried to catch Alma's eye, but she was way too busy. I admired what she was doing, but it looked like a lost cause. She handed me a pamphlet as she went by, but the tug-of-war lady was pulling on the stick with the baby at the time, and I don't think she even saw me, just shoved the paper at me and turned to snarl at her opponent. It reminded me of elementary school basketball. The lady dogging Alma was just like the brutal girl from our rival, Sikwan Public School, who was always assigned to cover me in games because we were the same height. She used to come at me like a bulldozer in just the same way, slapping at the ball with big, meaty hands. I always figured she was the reason I got cut from the Grade Eight basketball team. This nostalgic image was reinforced by the fact that Alma looked so much like me and wore a look that was a mixture of fierce determination and a strong desire to be elsewhere. I knew how that felt—I'd loathed basketball.

People were emerging from shops and doorways to watch the marchers pass, most with vaguely interested or amused expressions on their faces, some looking outright disgusted.

"It ortn't to be allowed," one lady said, tossing the pamphlet she'd been handed into the gutter. "Spreadin' their filth."

A man with a megaphone in the centre of the marchers informed the onlookers that there were going to be speeches at the gateway to the Cathedral, and a special service inside, afterwards. It surprised me to hear that they'd be allowed to have a service. The staid Anglican tradition, you'd think, would be above that sort of thing, but maybe they had a special permit for that, too. I deked down a side street, having seen enough, and made my way through a maze of narrow, smaller lanes, hoping to get my Cathedral visit in before the mob took over the place.

*　　*　　*

Once I was inside, it quickly became apparent that no group on earth, short of a really large army, could possibly "take over" Christ Church Cathedral. I'd never been inside a really colossal place of worship before, and I have to admit it was quite overwhelming. You didn't need to imagine you were a twelfth century pilgrim to feel dwarfed by it all. It soared, it came at you from all sides in unspeakable splendour, it was mind-blowing. I wandered around (after having popped a couple of pound coins in the collection bin—you can't get to heaven for free, you know) with my head swivelling round and round like the quintessential bumpkin in the city, except that this city was indoors, and instead of skyscrapers, it was buttresses and stained glass, impossibly high ceilings, carvings, paintings and uplifting antiquity that had me rubbernecking, standing there with my mouth open.

Somewhere a mile or so away at the altar end of the building, a choir was singing. I could hear the voices of choirboys in a complicated, polyphonic tumbling of sound like a woven tapestry. I headed in that direction and found myself part of a small group being allowed into what I guess was an inner sanctum, a kind of church within a church, with its own small altar. A sign said Matins, 10:30 a.m., and seeing as it was that time on the dot, I realized I'd stumbled on a service.

This was obviously not the service the pro-lifers had advertised. As far as I knew, they were still marching and speechifying somewhere near the entrance gate. No, this was a solemn Anglican thing, and I was breaking all the rules, I figured, by pretending to be one and sneaking in. Nobody stopped me, though, and a stern-faced man in a black suit handed me a prayer book as I came in, directed me to sit in a row of ancient pews, like penalty boxes in an arena, two rows facing each other, and he didn't ask to see any kind of Anglican identity card, so I was okay. The choir filled most of the penalty boxes on the opposite side. They were all robed-up in white, with stiff collars and red frills, and there were little boys among them, singing like angels. I had walked like magic into the heart of something so utterly English, I was practically catatonic with delight. After glancing through the various leaflets included with the prayer book, I realized that the prayers were more or less the same ones I'd been brought up with, and this was just a service of psalms and scripture readings—no communion. I felt a lessening of interior tension.

I leaned back, closed my eyes and let the music wash over me, feeling the Sprog sort of stretch out in her cramped quarters, maybe putting her ear to the wall to hear better. At some point, I thought, I would have to think about the God thing in relation to the being-a-parent thing. That would be tricky, especially if I'd given her a taste for it early, by plopping her abruptly, in her seventh month of existence, slap bang next to a choir singing heavenly music in a church as old as time.

With my luck, she'd come out insisting on being baptized or something. Still, it was too late now. The choir finished their hymn, and the readings began. I suspended my carefully constructed disbelief and settled down to enjoy myself.

Sixteen

Any stress or trauma a mother experiences during her baby's gestation is automatically translated through her heart's code and body chemistry to her unborn child, and to her unborn child's heart codes and body chemistry. A shock response occurs when a life threatening danger is perceived by the reptilian brain, and the survival tools of fight and flight are insufficient to insure survival.
-From *Big Bertha's Total Baby Guide*

The Cathedral crypt at Canterbury is a marvel, and if you think a crypt is a stuffy basement, you'd be in for a surprise if you visited this one. It was vast and cool and deliciously echoey, mysterious and secret. The ceilings were surprisingly high and the lighting was discreet, so that there were shadows and dark corners, but you weren't in danger of whanging your nose up against a pillar. They keep a lot of the church treasure down there, too, in glass cases—ancient jewelled chalices and magnificent ciboria (it's a thing for the wafers) and candlesticks and complicated thingummies for incense. After the service, I had wandered down past the Thomas Becket shrine, which was surrounded by a Japanese tour group, three people deep. I planned to return when it was a little more accessible. The passageway led down into the crypt, and I went, expecting, as I said, a dank basement. Off to the left, there were a couple of tiny chapels hewn into the stone, and being in a sort of contemplative and possibly even religious frame of mind, I sat in one for a bit, probably looking quite prayerful to the one or two people who walked past. I gazed at the miniature altar, above which stood a statue of a saint in a little alcove, next to a glowing red candle. I was surprised at how Popish the Cathedral was—as far as I could make out, the Anglican tradition was as RC as anything I'd grown up with, and it made me feel strangely comfortable and at home, though I never would have admitted that to Aunt Susan. (At least, not sober.)

I could hear the advancing twitter and mutter of the tour group, so figured they had finished hogging the shrine and were now in the crypt. I didn't want to get stuck in the middle of them. I'd had enough of crowds, so I left my chapel pew and noticed a little wooden door at the far end of the narrow room, in the shadows. Being a nosy so-and-so, I tried the handle and found it unlocked. Ignoring the sign that suggested "Authorized Persons Only" were allowed to use the door, I opened it, stepped through and found myself in a narrow stone passageway, with stairs leading up and a light at the end. I was completely alone for the first time since early that morning and again felt that amazing sense of being cocooned in history. Above me, I knew, the cathedral tower soared to a height of 575-odd feet, where gargoyles glowered, carved by stonemasons hundred of years ago. The men who laid the walls beside me, stone-on-stone, lived and breathed and spat and hiccoughed like real people, bruised their fingers on the stone, left their sweat upon each one. I touched the walls as I climbed, wondering what it would be like to have extrasensory powers, to touch the stone and know, somehow, who else had touched them.

The stairway ended with a low, filigreed iron gate, heavy and thankfully unlocked. It squeaked as I opened it, and I found myself in a kind of courtyard, quite empty. It was like being in a monastery—I half-expected to see a hooded figure in a monk's habit, walking along its covered length, or sitting with a book of psalms in the square patch of brown grass in the centre. I suppose it was the cloisters, mentioned in the brochure, and I was amazed that there was nobody else there, that I was granted a private viewing. As I emerged and shut the squeaking wrought iron gate behind me, I heard a scurrying in a far corner, as if someone were just exiting, stage left. I caught the impression of a bald head and a dark garment—my imaginary monk, perhaps, tonsured and interrupted at his prayers. In the distance I could see some ruined stone work, the remains of an earlier version of the Cathedral, maybe. The age of everything felt suddenly heavy and dark, as if I shouldn't be there, that there was some danger that I hadn't anticipated. A moment later, I stumbled upon the baby.

It had been thrown into a corner, and for one very nasty moment, I thought it was real. It was Alma's agitprop baby-on-a-stick, and it had been sliced from nave to chops, its stuffing strewn here and there like dandelion fluff. I willed my heart to stop beating so fast and tried to calm down the Sprog, who all at once was drumming at my innards with her little feet. I crouched to get a better look, patting my tum and muttering sweet nothings at her, or at myself. Whoever had done the deed had almost beheaded the puppet, cutting it at the neck and obviously thrusting a hand inside to get at the stuffing. It was grotesque—the chubby baby face was all caved in, its smile a kind of rictus, its brains splattered. I remembered suddenly the tug-of-war between Alma and her Right-to-Life opponent, the "Let them live!" chant, and the film clip of the riot police in Karachi. I felt faint and had to put my head between my knees for a long moment.

If I had been a different kind of person, I might have screamed, I suppose, but I didn't. However, I didn't want anybody else to find the puppet as I had. Some elderly monk, perhaps, stumbling on it and having a coronary. I gathered up the pieces, trying to stuff the wayward batting back into the head (which was unpleasant) and picking the thing up in my arms like a corpse. My fingers were trembling like Rosie does when she's scolded. I figured someone had wrestled the baby away from Alma sometime during the demonstration—likely the woman she was doing the tug-of-war with. She would probably be looking for it. I gazed around me, searching for an exit sign, but there was none to be seen. I didn't know where the exit was, and I was afraid, the tingly feeling of touching the past having been replaced by a cold, clammy present.

I listened. Silence, like a tangible thing, except for the dripping of some water off the cathedral roof in an alcove, where there was a sign saying "Caution, falling masonry." I walked rapidly through the cloister, my footsteps echoing in a frantic little staccato, like a radio play soundtrack, and eventually I found a door, which I hoped would lead me back into the main body of the church. Another stone passageway, this time not filling me with the delight of history, but instead making me feel as if the veil of time between the now and that day back in 1170 when Becket was murdered was very thin indeed.

I emerged into chaos. There were dozens of people, giving off the kind of panic-energy that you can almost smell when there's been an accident. They were milling around and craning to get a look at something. I had emerged a few metres west of the door I'd taken to go outside, so the Becket shrine was to my left.

"Stand back, there, stand back," a strong, authoritative voice was saying. I didn't stand back—I pressed forward, the murdered baby puppet lolling in my arms. A woman beside me gasped at it and moved away from me. "Aaaaow, Arthur, lookit thaat," she said.

When I got to the front of the crowd, I could see the Becket shrine, dramatically lit by several well-placed spotlights. A still, huddled figure was crumpled at its base. I could see a head with brown hair, one arm flung out. I thought I saw blood. I knew at once it was Alma.

That was probably when I screamed her name. At least I think I did, because I got a lot of attention, very quickly. The man telling people to keep back was a priest, a proper one with a cassock, cinched at the waist by a thick leather belt, a priest's collar at his neck, a very handsome man whose distress had not made him lose one inch of his stature. He exuded control and competence.

"Do you know this woman?" he said to me, coming forward at once and taking my arm urgently.

"Oh, God, is she dead? Have you checked?" This was kind of dumb, but you never know. I rushed in close, stepping around the blood, which was pooling in an indentation in the stone floor where, presumably, King Henry and millions of others had knelt in prayer.

"Yes, I'm horribly afraid she is dead, my dear." He tried to pull me away. "She's hit her head on the stone, I think. We mustn't move her, you know."

"But she's pregnant," I said. "We have to do something to save the baby." Her body was curled in on itself, and she could easily have been mistaken for, well, just a rather large woman, rather than a pregnant one.

"The ambulance has just been called. Paramedics are on the way," he said.

"Did you tell them she was pregnant? Sometimes a baby can survive beyond the death of the mother," I said. I was crouching at her side, reaching for her distended belly, feeling for a kick, a sign that the other life inside her might have a chance. She was still warm. There was no movement under my hand, though. Her pregnant belly felt relaxed, soft, like a balloon that was losing air. I had to do something, but I didn't know what. Crying seemed to be a reasonable option, so I began that at once.

"Yes, we gathered that she was with child," he said, very gently. "The medical people will do all they can, you know." My own Sprog shifted in sympathy. A clerical person came forward just then with a dark cloth, which he draped over Alma's still figure as my priest friend helped me to my feet.

"Are you a relation of hers?" he said. I shook my head, unable to speak yet. "I wondered, you see, because you look remarkably alike."

"I only met her yesterday," I said.

"We just found her a few minutes ago," he said. Behind us, some junior priesty people were clearing the crowd back. "We'll have to ask you all to stay," one of them was saying. "Just until the police come."

The priest with me suddenly produced a cellphone from his belt. He punched a number and whispered to the person at the other end to seal all the exits.

Goodness, I thought, in a wry aside, swallowing my sobs. Bet they didn't teach him that stuff at theological school.

"Her name's Alma Barrow," I said to him when he'd finished. "She lives in Birmingham and was involved in the Right-to-Life march this morning. As a pro-choice person." It seemed important to let him know that—that she wasn't one of the fanatics. He made a kind of tssk sound with his mouth, as if he'd known these people would be trouble.

"And what's that you've got there?" he said, pointing to the puppet, which I had stuck under my left arm like a forgotten parcel. I explained what it was, and where I'd found it.

"It would have incensed some of the Right-to-Lifers, maybe," I said, clutching the ruined puppet close, "but not enough for them to do murder—to whack her on the head, eh? But they should question all those rally people first. Where the hell are the ambulance people?" He winced at the "hell" but let it pass.

"Now come and sit down, won't you—away from this. Look, they're just coming now, and the police are here, too." The paramedics assessed the situation as quickly as the priest had promised, realizing a baby's life might possibly be saved. There was a brief argument with the police, probably because Alma's body was very likely part of a crime scene, but the paramedics won. As they were putting her onto a stretcher, the dark cloth covering her slipped aside, and I had a brief look at her face. Her eyes were wide open, staring in shock, and the blood from a terrible gash on her temple made crimson tracks down her face. Had someone whacked her on the head before stealing her baby puppet? Where was the stick the baby had been carried on? Maybe it *had* just been a struggle, and she had fallen forward and cracked her head open on the step. Could that kill you? Perhaps it could, especially if you were pregnant and, well, delicate. Whatever had happened, intentional murder or an accident, Alma was dead, and it was too horrible to take in.

She had spilled her blood in exactly the same spot that Becket had, and I wondered if it had been at the behest of some Right-to-Life leader, suggesting that someone rid the demonstration of this turbulent woman. My priest friend muttered to a colleague just after they took her away that they would have to resanctify the place before the day was done. His words flipped me out more than seeing her gashed head. Where was God in all that? And would He come back again, after they'd scrubbed the place and maybe lit some candles?

I was lucky, as it turned out, to have found the baby puppet and to have stumbled in on the scene when I did. I was one of the first people questioned, which meant I was also one of the first people released. I had studied the crowd of people who were sitting obediently in the pews in the main body of the Cathedral, as instructed. It would take the police a long time, I figured, to sort out who was who and what was what. I watched them being separated into two groups—the Right-to-Lifers, who all wore fluorescent pink "Let them Live!" badges, and the tourists, who didn't. I didn't see the tug-of-war lady, but I confess I put the coppers onto her, thinking that she might be able to shed some light on what had happened.

I was interviewed by a British policeman [name tag: Detective Constable Potts], who walked me through my meeting with Alma the day before, my seeing her at the march, my discovery of the dismembered baby (to which he seemed gratifyingly to attach as much importance as I did, taking the thing into custody) and my subsequent emergence into the fray. He was impossibly young, I thought. With extremely fair hair and freckles across his nose.

"You say the shrine was full of tourists before you went into the cloisters?" he said.

"Yes, I didn't want to go there while there were lots of people," I said inanely.

"We're just trying to get the times down. There aren't many people here, except for that Japanese tour group, the demonstrators and the people who attended Matins," he said.

"I was at Matins," I said.

"So you've said. And the tour group was there when you went down into the crypt?"

"Yes. I spent about twenty minutes down there, and then the tour group came down to where I was in the chapel place, so I deked out to the cloisters through a little door."

"Deked?"

"It's a hockey term. Sorry. I meant, you know, snuck. Sneaked."

"A little door? Can you show me?"

I led Potts along the route I had taken, down through the passageway into the crypt, past the Church silver bits, into the little chapel, where I'd lit a candle (yes, I know, but heck) for my parents, and then back through the little door marked "Authorized Persons only."

"We mustn't go through there," Potts said, suddenly all young and awkward, as if he were still at the private school from which, judging by his accent, he had only just graduated. (That would be a public school, according to Brent Miller's British lexicon).

"Well, I know it says you can't go though there, but I did, and there weren't any alarms or anything," I said. He followed me through, albeit reluctantly. The iron gate squeaked again, ominously this time, I thought. Which reminded me of the scurrying figure in the corner of the courtyard who had left as I came out. I told Potts about that. I showed him where I'd found the baby puppet. It seemed much less scary and mysterious now that I had a solid policeman at my side. We found the place easily—there were still bits of fluff left, baby's brains, I called them, which really shocked Constable Potts, whose eyes widened for a fraction of a second. His next question was icy and professional.

"And you were here how long, madam?"

"I don't know. Not more than ten minutes, I guess." We traced my steps back inside, and on the way, I suddenly remembered that there had been no sign of Alma's pamphlets, unless they were underneath her body. Had the murderer taken them away and hidden them? Were they considered that controversial? Was reproductive politics that serious? Still, there were abortion providers who had been shot to death, even in placid and serene Canada, so I supposed the issue was—serious, that is.

"She was giving out pamphlets during the march," I told Potts. "If there weren't any at the scene, maybe the murderer took them with him—or her."

"We don't know that it's murder, you know, madam," he said, in a cautionary way. "Your friend may very well have fainted for some reason and hit her head on the stone. We'll have to wait and see what the medical people say."

"If it wasn't murder, who stole the baby and dismembered it, then? A Japanese tourist?" I said.

"I'm just cautioning you not to go about using the word murder," he said. "We don't need this matter all mucked up with the tabloids turning up, publishing screaming headlines. I must ask you to keep quiet about all this." He took down my personal information in his little notebook: where I was staying, how long I'd be in Canterbury and so on.

"I bet the case will be zipped up nice and neatly with 'death by misadventure' written on it," I said.

"You've been reading too many Miss Marple books," D.C. Potts said, favouring me with a little indulgent smile. "Look, I know you've had a dreadful shock, which is not good for a woman in your condition. Go back to your B&B and have a little lie-down, and if you think of any other details, give us a ring, all right?" I nodded, feeling patronized and trying not to let my temper get the better of me. I headed for the exit, but he stopped me with a final word.

"And we'd appreciate it if you would stay in the area for a few days. Keep us informed of your whereabouts and let us know when you're planning to return to Canada." Wonderful. Even when I was in a distant country, far from Kuskawa and my life there, I hadn't kicked the habit of stumbling upon dead bodies. It was never my choice, you understand, it just seemed to happen. And this time, I was on my own, a stranger in a strange land.

By then it was noon. Although I might have been forgiven if I had called the puppet conference people and told them what had happened and perhaps asked to have my seminar postponed to another day, the fact was that I hadn't known the victim at all, I'd just been a witness after the fact. We had no connection apart from a remarkable likeness to one another, and I still had my commitment to the CIPF, who were, after all, paying my way. Although I had witnessed a horrible thing, I still felt honour-bound to come through with my part of the bargain.

I wandered back outside like a zombie, still searching for the tug-of-war lady, who I had decided must have been packing a blackjack under her tweed skirt and had done the dirty deed while Alma was gazing at Becket's tomb. A wave of profound sadness washed over me as I walked slowly back to my B&B. I had a sudden yearning for a Canadian policeman and some stability, a yearning so strong it almost made me gag. And you know what? It wasn't Becker I was wanting, it was Morrison. Go figure.

Seventeen

Break car journeys every two hours and take a short walk. Make sure your seat belt fits properly; the top strap should go between your breasts and the lower strap under your bump.
   -From *Big Bertha's Total Baby Guide*

Someone came looking for you," Cedric Frayne said, as I stepped into the foyer of the Pilgrim's Rest.

"Really? Who?"

"Well, he said he was from the local comprehensive—coming about your puppet thing at the university. He seemed dead keen on attending it, although he didn't look much like a teacher, I must say. Still, it takes all sorts. I told him you were out and about, planning to watch that Right-to-Life March, as you said. I suggested he might be able to find you on the high street somewhere." I'd told Cedric about the march that morning, asking him if it were a common thing to have such demonstrations in Canterbury in the mid-winter. We'd laughed about it as he slid a beautiful spatula-load of sizzling blood pudding onto my plate.

"Oh, yes? Did he leave a name? What did he look like?"

"Blobby," Cedric said. "Big and blobby, but I suppose with youngsters these days, you'd want to be a bit meaty, to keep the blighters in line."

"He wasn't bald, by any chance, was he?"

"He was wearing a flat cap," Cedric said. "Couldn't tell. But I'll tell you one thing—he was driving one of those white vans, which I thought was most peculiar for someone who's a teacher at a comprehensive. Still, it might help to bung the little buggers in the back of a van with no air or light." He chuckled wickedly. It was clear that Cedric Frayne held the youth of Britain in no high esteem.

I had gone back to the B&B to pick up my puppet case containing my innocent policeman and pregnant lady puppets. I was a mess, having seen what I had seen at the Cathedral, and though I suspected that Cedric would want a full report of the goings-on later (I was the only resident at the B&B, apart from an elderly gentleman who was studying Roman antiquities at the museum), I wasn't about to fill him in right then. The most important thing for me in order to keep it together, I'd decided, was to go on with the program as planned. I would mourn for Alma later, after it was all over. I also planned to call up the police station and ask about Alma's baby, whether or not it had survived. But that would be later. Right then, I was determined to remain in a comfortable state of denial.

Cedric dialled the combination of the safe where he had stored my case, hauled open the thick, black iron door and handed it over.

"You've got your other things in there, too, don't forget," he said. I had forgotten and appreciated his reminder. I'd put my passport and return ticket in the case, as well as the velvet bag containing Edward Becker's ashes, none of which I'd be needing for my puppetry seminar.

"Thanks, Cedric," I said, opening up the case and handing him the extraneous items. "No sense in loading myself up with unnecessaries." My voice sounded ridiculously cheerful in my head, brassy and hyper, but Cedric didn't seem to notice. "I'm going to be late, you know. Do you think you could call me a cab?"

"Of course, I'll call one," he said. "Actually, even better—

I'll drive you myself. I'd like to attend your seminar, if that's all right by you, my dear. I'm an honorary member of one of the committees—I've forgotten which one. It won't matter my being out for a bit. Mr. Binterhof has his own key, and anyway he won't be back until this evening. He's studying some mosaics they've unearthed over at Greyfriars."

Mr. Frayne shrugged himself into an old grey cardigan and changed his leather slippers for a stout pair of boots, then he locked the front door and led me through a side door in the kitchen to a narrow garage beside the Pilgrim's Rest. The sun was still beating down in a most un-winterly fashion, and it had to be at least sixty degrees Fahrenheit. I thought for a moment that the weather might have at least had the courtesy of going all sombre and dark in honour of Alma. We came out into a small courtyard, which was surrounded by a tall wooden fence with a wide door in it.

"I'll need you to open the gate for me, if you don't mind," he said. I nodded and waited by the door that I assumed opened into the street. It had a spring lock that opened from the inside and would lock automatically when it was shut. Moments later, a strange, high-pitched coughing noise filled the courtyard, along with a belching of black smoke. It sounded like George's tractor on a bad day—George's tractor after inhaling a lungful of helium. What emerged from the garage was such a surprise, I found myself giggling again.

It was about the size of a bumper car at the Laingford Fall Fair. It was boxy at the back, sort of flat at the front, like the beak of a duck, and bright blue. It took me a moment to figure out why it looked so weird. Then I twigged. It only had three wheels. Two at the back, one at the front. He drove it, in fits and starts, past the big open door, which I closed carefully after he'd gone through.

Mr. Frayne leaned over and opened the passenger door for me, shouting above the descant chuggetty-chug of the engine.

"Hop in," he said. "I haven't taken her out in a while. She needs a tune-up, I think, but she'll get us there all right." I squeezed myself inside, feeling like a chick trying to crawl back into the egg.

"What on earth is this?" I said, as politely as I could.

"It's a 1973 Reliant Robin," he said, with pride. "I bought her for my sister—your benefactress, you know, and she gave it back to me in her will. I was the one to do the maintenance on her all these years—the car, I mean. She's frightfully good on petrol."

We were tootling along one of the back streets that ran past the Cathedral, and there were still police cars parked outside the gate.

"'Ullo, 'ullo—bit of bother at the church, it looks like."

"Yes," I said. "I was there, actually. But I'll tell you about it later, if you don't mind. I have to concentrate on the seminar now, or I'll make a mess of it," I said.

"Ah—an actor prepares. Yes, I know all about that. Right then—but I look forward to hearing about it. I do love a bit of excitement."

Cedric Frayne was one of those drivers who witters and looks at his passenger while driving. We narrowly missed a pedestrian, who shook a fist at us, but laughed as he did it. We weren't going very fast. In fact, in a race, the pedestrian would probably have won without breaking a sweat.

"Always get a lot of attention driving Maid Marian, you know," he said.

"Maid Marian?"

"That's what my sister called her. You know—Reliant Robin, Robin Hood, Maid Marian? Mary was always a bit fanciful, poor old dear."

"I guess."

"She was the one who started the puppetry conference, you know. Back in the eighties. She simply adored puppets. Which reminds me, I must show you her collection—well, some of it, anyway. Most of the pieces have gone to the Puppet Centre Trust in London, but I've kept her favourites. She had some very old ones, you know."

"I'd like to see them," I said, but I wasn't really listening. I was going over my notes in my head, trying to remember what the heck I was supposed to be talking about. Puppet construction—yes. Unusual accessories and marionette techniques. I wondered how I was going to keep a roomful of experts interested for a whole hour. What did I know? Why had they asked me to present something? I was in an agony of self-deprecation.

We stopped for a traffic light, and a weird thing happened. The driver of the car in front of us suddenly got out, slammed the door behind her, and walked away. I was about to comment on this to Cedric, who didn't seem to have noticed, and I was wondering whether we should be honking or something. I was getting into quite a froth about it, actually, until the light changed and the car in front proceeded, apparently all by itself. Then I remembered that the driver was the person on the right, not the left, and it had just been a passenger getting out. The driver, on the right side, was short, and I hadn't noticed him. This was to plague me all the time I spent in England.

We saw plenty of white vans on the road. I kept craning my neck to see if any of the drivers looked like my thug, but gave up after a while, because they all did. Every white van driver had a shaved head and a snarl on his face. It must have been one of the rules.

We made it to the university in one piece, but I had less than ten minutes to get to my seminar room and set up, so I excused myself to Cedric and left him with Phyllis (who had been getting into a froth herself by that time, thinking I wasn't going to show up).

The room was moderately full, about ten or fifteen people, and I hurried to the front, where my table had been set up, and dragged a chair over to stand on, so I could demonstrate my marionettes. The puppets had weathered the journey remarkably well, considering the hassle they'd had at Pearson airport, and thank goodness, the strings weren't tangled. I checked to make sure the little baby inside the tummy box of the pregnant lady puppet was okay (he was) and shuffled my notes a bit as a few more people came into the room. I noticed that two of the demonstrators from the *wayang kulit* group were there, which was very pleasing, and Blaise Killington came as well, which was an honour that left me feeling more than a little shaky about my material. Richard Seth arrived with a group of people, waved cheerily to me and took a seat near the front. It felt good to have him there—a bit of support from home. I hoped that his near and rather-too-attractive presence wouldn't be distracting, then wondered what on earth I was doing entertaining impure thoughts at a time like this. I winked at him, though. I couldn't help it.

Phyllis came up to the front to introduce me, and while she did so (saying all sorts of things that made me blush, making me out to be far more of an expert than I really was) another person slipped inside. It was the young policeman from the Cathedral, D.C. Potts. He was still in uniform, and some of the audience near the door eyed him curiously, but he didn't appear to be about to arrest me, just took a chair near the back and sat to watch with a lively and interested look on his face.

I presumed he'd come to talk to me and appreciated that he'd decided to wait until after my presentation was over. I wondered how he'd found me, but I suppose I had probably mentioned my reason for being in Canterbury, and he'd phoned to find out where I'd be. Then I was on, and I forgot all about Potts and concentrated on my job.

*   *   *

It was near the end of the hour when another person entered the room, and I barely noticed, being in the middle of a complicated manipulation, during which the policeman puppet had unzipped his trousers, removed his tiny little member, turned aside coyly and was pissing over the side of the table. The audience was laughing in a wonderfully gratifying way, and I risked a glance up to see if Potts found it funny, or was as shocked as he'd been when I'd talked about baby brains, back in the cloisters. He was roaring, which was a huge relief. That was when I noticed the other guy, hovering near the door. He was blobby, you might say. Big and blobby and wearing a flat cap, and he was looking at me with the kind of intensity you reserve for people you mean to harm. We stared at each other for what seemed like a very long moment, then I let my eyes slip sideways to look significantly at Potts. The flat-cap, whom I knew instantly as my breast-tweaker from Gatwick airport, took the hint, for hint it was, and left the room. Potts had caught the look and left a second or so later. I thought I heard running footsteps outside the door, but that might have been wishful thinking on my part. The whole thing had only taken a moment, and nobody in the audience appeared to have noticed much, except for the usual turning of heads that happens when someone enters or exits a hushed room. The policeman puppet completed his little whizz, tucked himself back into his trousers and turned back to the audience, bowing to the applause.

*   *   *

"Splendid demonstration, my dear," Cedric said afterwards. I had enjoyed some minutes talking to people after the seminar, and really, it seemed as if my not using PowerPoint hadn't mattered at all. I'd used the flip chart, drawing as I explained the basic construction of my puppets and the deceptive and complicated sort of physics of strings and manipulation bars and weight and angle-of-limb. People had a lot of questions, and it was great fun answering them. For that hour, at least, I had managed not to think of the horror at the Cathedral at all, except for a nasty moment when the pregnant lady puppet gave birth to her *papier mâché* cherub, and I thought of an emergency Caesarian in the ambulance, perhaps, a last ditch effort to save Alma's baby. It was only a flash, though. The manipulation of the puppet required my full concentration, the marshalling of more than a dozen strings, the tilt of the puppet's head, her hands hiking up her skirt, tenderly opening the tummy box, and the baby emerging and fluttering around her head like an angel. I had practiced the sequence for hours, getting it just right. I was not nervous. Funny that my eyes were full of tears, then. It was a moment of incredible hush. The audience members were perched on the edges of their seats, and I heard someone gasp as the baby came forth. I wished the real thing could be that easy.

Eighteen

It is often said that eating spicy food will help bring on labour—not true. There also is a myth that says having sex brings on labour. This also isn't based on fact, and there is no evidence to show that it is true.

-From *Big Bertha's Total Baby Guide*

I was still chatting with a few puppet-people when Constable Potts returned, looking like he'd run a marathon.

"Can I have a word, Ms. Deacon?" he said, and my companions melted discreetly away, although Cedric remained within earshot.

"Did you catch him?" I said. "I think that guy's been following me."

"I thought there might be something," he said. "No, I'm afraid I lost him in this blasted warren of a building. But I've radioed him in, and we'll be keeping a lookout for him, even though I only got a look at his back and the side of his head. He lost his hat, see? Recognize it?"

"He was bare-headed when I met him last," I said. "But Cedric Frayne, the man who runs the place where I'm staying, might help. I think the same guy came to the B&B looking for me earlier today. " Cedric appeared in a moment at my elbow.

"Some trouble here?" he said with relish.

"Is that the hat you saw my morning visitor wearing?" I asked. He took it from the policeman and peered at it, turning it over in his hands and looking for a label. It was a tweedy thing, a flat cap worn by all the characters in every rural

English drama you've ever seen.

"It might be," he said. "He was driving one of those white vans, you know. If that's any help. Although they all look the same, of course. Hundreds of them, all over the place." Potts nodded and noted the information down in his book.

"I caught a glimpse of the bloke's head when the hat came off," Potts said. "Shaved bald, with a football emblem tattooed on the scalp. Nice identifying mark, that. It shouldn't take us long to find him."

"A football emblem? Huh?"

"Yes—Manchester United. I recognized it at once—my brother's a big supporter."

"A devil with a pitchfork and the three blobs above it?" I said. He smiled.

"More or less. You've seen it then—had a good look at him?"

"Oh, yes. He groped me at Gatwick airport—tried to steal my luggage—and again at the train station in London. But how come you chased him? Is he wanted for something else?"

"I saw the way you looked when he came into the room during your puppet show," Potts said. "Your face drained white as a sheet. It was instinct, really. I just wanted a word with him, then he bolted, and when people run from a policeman, there's usually some cause to give chase."

"I see."

"And I wanted to ask you a few more questions, Ms. Deacon, regarding this morning's incident."

"What incident?" Cedric said.

"Someone died at the Cathedral," I said. "I'll tell you about it later, Cedric. It was pretty awful. Did they save the baby, Constable?"

"I'm terribly sorry," he said, after a tiny pause. "They did all they could, you know. But it was too late." I felt my eyes fill with tears. Two murders, then. At least, in my estimation they were murders, no matter what the police thought. All in the cause of pretending to protect the lives of the "unborn". How horribly ironic.

"Did you find the woman Alma was fighting with during the march?"

"We spoke to her, yes. She was as shocked as anybody, you know, and she was with her group the whole time. We don't believe she could have caused Ms. Barrow to fall and hit her head."

"You've decided it was an accident, then?"

"Well, we've ruled out a blunt instrument, you know. The head wound was consistent with the stone step where she fell. But she still might very well have been pushed, or grappled with. There were bruises on her arms."

"So someone beat her up. An assault that went too far?"

"That's why I came to find you," D.C. Potts said. "It occurred to me that it might have been a case of mistaken identity, you see. You looking so much like her. Perhaps someone frightened or molested her, thinking it was you. And if this bloke's been following you, that makes it all the more likely."

"But I didn't have anything to do with the Right-to-Life march," I said.

"I think you've got the wrong end of the stick about the protesters," Potts said, with a touch of exasperation. "It really doesn't follow that they had anything to do with Ms. Barrow's death. Now, you say that this bloke with the tattoo has been stalking you—trying to steal your luggage?"

"Yes, it seems that way."

"Why would he do that, do you think?"

"I haven't the faintest idea. I figured he'd decided that the puppet case, which is labelled 'fragile', contained something valuable."

"What does it contain?"

"Puppets. What do you think?"

"And some person or persons unknown attacked Ms. Barrow in the Cathedral, and the puppet she had with her was found torn apart in another part of the church. Doesn't that suggest a link to you?"

Now that he pointed it out, the link was obvious.

"The customs people at Pearson airport tore that case apart," I said, "just like Alma's baby puppet. Although they didn't dismember the puppets, they did x-ray them. There's nothing there. What the heck is this guy looking for?"

"Could be anything—drugs, gems, maybe. We'll have to have a word with him and find out. And I should very much like to examine that puppet case myself, if you don't mind."

"Be my guest—it's right there on the table. Though I'd appreciate it if you didn't dismember the puppets."

"I'll be very careful," he said, and we both went over to the case. I opened it for him, and he proceeded to do the same routine the Pearson airport people had done, albeit with a lot more care.

"You really don't think the Right-to-Lifers were involved?" I said, over his shoulder.

"It seems highly unlikely," he said.

"And did you find Alma's pamphlets? The ones she was handing out during the demonstration?"

"Not yet, no. They probably have no bearing on the case, anyway."

"I'll bet they grabbed her stuff, tore the puppet away from her and ripped it up out of pure spite. I saw how worked up they were about her being there. I still think you should concentrate on the lady in the tweed skirt."

"Well, they're a peculiar lot, I'll give you that, but no, we don't think it's likely they had anything to do with it, although we haven't ruled it out completely. The investigation is ongoing. But if the perpetrator was actually after you, Ms. Deacon, then we think you might be in need of some protection." He had finished his examination of the puppet case, carefully replaced everything and shut the lid gently. "We'll get hold of this tattooed bloke as soon as possible. He may very well be our man."

"If anything's a case of mistaken identity, the fact of this guy following me is," I said. "Maybe it's just that I look like his missing girlfriend or something. Oh—wait." I fished in my purse and brought out Old Reg's form from the train station. I explained the incident at the baggage lockers and the fact that the thug had apparently filled in Reg's "proper procedures" form.

"This'll be false information of course," Potts said, "but we might be able to get some prints off it, I suppose."

"It's covered in mine and the baggage guy's, mostly, I expect," I said. I wondered whether or not to tell him about the tiny glimpse I'd had of what might or might not have been my tattooed thug—what I'd seen from the window of a speeding bus on my way to the university the day before. It was hardly credible, just a fleeting glance, and the tattoo I'd imagined could very well have been just a shadow from the curtains. Potts was an observant fellow and noticed that my eyes had sort of glazed over as I weighed the pros and cons of telling him.

"There's something else, isn't there?" he said.

"Well, just this thing I thought I saw," I said, and then told him about it.

"Well, it's a strong possibility. Some criminals are remarkably stupid," he said. "He's clearly in the area, after all, and he's got to be staying somewhere. If you think you saw him in a flat on Castle Street, and that's the address he wrote down—well, it's too much to be a coincidence, isn't it?"

"I don't know," I said. "There have been an awful lot of coincidences lately."

"Well, we'll pay that address a visit right away," he said and relieved me of the BritRail form.

"I could have imagined it, you know. Jet lag and all that."

"We'll keep that in mind," he said dryly.

"Is there anything I can do to help?" I said.

"The best way you can help, Ms Deacon, is by having a bit of a think about your own situation. And be careful. You don't have a police record, by any chance, do you?"

I raised an eyebrow at him. "Whatever makes you think that I might?" I said, as stuffily as I could.

"Just asking. No reason to have people following you about to get information from you? To settle a debt? Nothing like that?"

"Constable, I am a lowly, insignificant and hopelessly innocent puppet maker from rural Ontario, Canada. I am not wealthy. I have never been arrested, and I am not known to Interpol. I don't consort with undesirables. Heck, I'm practically engaged to a policeman back home, as a matter of fact." I fished Becker's ring out from my cleavage and waved it about. He perked up.

"Ah. You're connected to the authorities in Canada, are you? That's interesting. Has your fiancé ever worked over here? Arrested anybody? Somebody who might bear a grudge?"

"His father was born here, but that was years ago. I don't think Mark has ever been to England. Certainly not in a professional capacity."

"Well, that makes no never mind, necessarily," Potts said,

cryptically. "The Internet dissolves borders, you know. What's his specialty?"

"He's a detective in the Ontario Provincial Police, doing some airport security stuff at the moment," I said. Potts wrote that down.

"Full name?"

"Detective Constable Mark Edward Becker—but jeez, don't be getting in touch with him, please. He'll flip out big time if he thinks I'm in trouble over here. He'll hop on the next plane and try to haul me home."

"That might not be a bad idea," he said. "When are you due, may I ask?"

I bristled. "That's rather a personal question, isn't it?"

"Well, yes."

"Not until the end of April. I don't plan on podding on British soil, if you're worried about immigration issues."

"That wasn't what I meant."

"Well, what did you mean?"

"Just that you ought to be careful, that's all. If I were pregnant, and there were some unpleasant bloke stalking me, who may or may not have caused the death of a woman who looks like me, for reasons so far unknown, I'd be watching my back. Or I'd be on the next plane home."

"Thanks for the advice—I'll be careful. But please don't get in touch with Becker. This has nothing to do with him. If anything, it has to do with the fact that some local English thug thought there was something valuable in the puppet case I was carrying around at the airport." We both stood looking at the case sitting innocently on the table. The "fragile" label was peeling off, and it looked a little battered.

"The puppets themselves sell for about five hundred dollars apiece, if that's any help," I said.

"Underselling yourself a bit, aren't you?" he said, which made me smile.

"Thanks. Starving artist, that's me."

"Well, that's all for now, I suppose. Our people will get this bloke soon enough, I hope, and your worries will be over," he said.

"Thanks. Do let me know, eh, when you do? I'd like to come by and maybe kick him in the crotch." Potts winced. "In exchange for the gratuitous grope at the airport, don't ya know," I said.

"We can't allow that."

"Yeah, well. Too bad."

"You're staying at..." he checked his notes, flipping back a couple of pages, "the Pilgrim's Rest? We can contact you there?"

"That's right," Cedric jumped in. I'd forgotten he was there. He had been hovering at my side the whole time, absorbing the conversation like an elderly sponge. "I'll look after her, sir. Not to worry."

"Right, then," Potts said, giving Cedric the once-over. I suppose he passed muster, although he didn't strike me as the protector type, but maybe the standards are different in England. I felt like I was being handed over. "We'll be in touch," he said and headed for the door.

*   *   *

Richard Seth had been waiting and moved in to take Potts' place. "I liked your presentation, Polly," he said. "Man, those marionettes make the usual Steamboat stuff look awfully clunky, eh?"

"Different techniques, I guess," I said and introduced him

to Cedric. We made puppet talk all the way out into the parking lot, where Cedric had parked his Reliant Robin in a space marked for motorcycles. It fit, quite comfortably. Richard invited us both to join him for dinner at a place in Canterbury called the Moghul, and we accepted. I love Indian food, and Brent had told me that the Indian food in England was to die for. He squeezed into the tiny space behind the front seats of Maid Marian, which looked painful, but he insisted he was okay. Better him than me, anyway.

At the restaurant, I allowed myself another Guinness. Okay—call me an abusive mom, but neither Cedric nor Richard commented, and the Sprog seemed to like it. Anyway, it was all rapidly soaked up by a thing called Peshawari naan, a kind of flatbread like a pita with a coconut mixture inside it, which I decided was the food of the gods. I gobbled two orders of it, in addition to a big steel bowl of chicken tikka and some gorgeous rice. One day, when I'm a rich and famous puppet maker, with untold millions and nothing to spend it on, I will beg and bribe some nice family from the city to come up to Kuskawa and open an Indian restaurant. I will foot the bill. I will subsidize it generously. There is nothing remotely like Indian food available in my neck of the woods. Oh, we have a couple of what they call Chinese/Canadian places, established during the lumbering days of the 1860s, and still serving fluorescent chicken balls and chow mein, but if you want anything more exotic than that, you have to go to Toronto. Oh, for an Indian restaurant in Laingford. Sigh.

I let the men talk while I stuffed my face. I learned that Cedric had studied theology at Oxford University and then thrown it away at the last minute, just before ordination, to become an actor in repertory theatre in the boonies of England. He'd enjoyed a modest career, touring India, actually, at one point. He seemed to know a lot about Indian food, and the Moghul staff treated him like a regular. He'd retired early, to come and help his mom and sister run the Pilgrim's Rest, which was one of the older B&Bs in Canterbury, and when his mom died, followed by his sister, Mary (who was widowed young), he went into the full-time hospitality business. He liked it, he said. It was quiet. He'd never married, and I had the impression, without him actually saying so, that he played for the other team, as it were. He and Richard got on like a house on fire, and they left me in peace to do my impression of a starving puppet maker.

I'd told them in the car about Alma's death at Canterbury Cathedral, as much as I could stomach repeating, and I made light of Potts' suggestion that it might have been a case of mistaken identity, that the assault had been meant for me. I was still kind of sandbagged by the whole thing, and while both men were obviously panting for more details, they respected my reluctance to dwell on it, which I appreciated. Over dinner, they gossiped about the theatre business instead.

Richard said he'd find his own way back up to the university, and we puttered back to the Pilgrim's Rest in the Robin, Cedric weaving rather erratically all over the road, probably on account of his having polished off most of a bottle of Chardonnay. He was only going about twenty kilometres an hour, though, and there was no traffic to speak of. If I'd got out and walked fast, I probably would've beaten him back home.

The first indication that there was something wrong was when I hopped out to open the gate into the courtyard. I knew I had carefully closed it behind me. I'd heard the lock click shut. Cedric had given me the key to it, but when I touched the latch, the door swung open by itself. Odd, and disturbing. However, I figured it was an old lock and unreliable. When we got to the kitchen door, though, and found that open, too, we got very worried, very fast.

"Did Mr. Binterhof maybe forget his key?" I said, referring to the other B&B resident, the one Cedric had said would be home in the evening. It was ten thirty by that point, and the house was totally dark, not a light to be seen. "Did he break in, do you think?" I hadn't met the man myself, but the name conjured a stern, Teutonic kind of fellow, possibly capable of a little B&E if he'd been left high and dry on a chilly February night.

"Mr. Binterhof is seventy-four and frail," Cedric said. "He would certainly not have forced his way in, my dear. I don't think we should go any further. I think we should call the police."

"Oh, please." I said. "We've had enough of them for one day, I think." It was probably the Guinness talking. I pushed open the door and groped around for a light switch. I found it at chest-height on my left and flicked it on. The kitchen was just as we'd left it, although I saw a mug on the counter, with a tea bag left in it. The tea was awfully strong, I noticed, black, really. A moment later, I noticed the pair of feet, sticking out at floor level behind the counter.

"Okay, Cedric," I said. "I lied. Call the damned police."

Nineteen

Special watch should be kept over our pregnant women during the year of their pregnancy to guard the expectant mother against the experiences of frequent and violent pleasures—or pains either—and ensure her cultivation of a gracious, bright and serene spirit.
  -Plato, as quoted in *Big Bertha's Total Baby Guide*

Excerpt from an email to Earl Morrison, OPP:

...and you'll be glad to know that Mr. Binterhof is perfectly fine, although he has a bit of a headache from being knocked out. I'm telling you all this, because I want to get my side of the story in before that eager beaver Potts gets in touch with you guys. Please let Becker know my version first. I'm certain that the break-in at the Pilgrim's Rest has no connection with me being involved with a policeman— so it's none of his business. This thug guy is obsessed with my puppet case, and that's that. Maybe I should mail the puppets back home in a box and leave the damned case out somewhere where he can steal it. Then he'll probably melt away and leave me alone.

And I'm also pretty sure that the nasty business at the Cathedral was connected to the Right-to-Lifers and had nothing to do with me. I'm quite happy to leave Potts to figure that one out, and I'm determined not to get involved in this one—in fact, I promise I won't, okay, Earlie? So don't go getting all worried about me. I'm fine, and I'm not playing Nancy Drew this time.

Perhaps, seeing as you're using Becker's

> computer these days, if an email comes in for him
> from Potts, you can pretend to be him and answer it.
> Or better yet, delete it.
>
> This morning, after a session on "Universal
> Language International Performance: Choosing
> Materials for International Performing in Puppetry"
> (which sounds like a real hoot, eh?), Richard Seth and
> I are going to go visit the Roman Museum, and then
> The Eastbridge Hospital, which is not a medical
> hospital, but rather a totally cool 800-year-old building
> used to house pilgrims. I'm looking forward to it.
>
> Love to everybody, and I hope you have a great
> cribbage game tonight. Watch out for George. He
> moves his pegs ahead when he thinks you're looking
> the other way. Polly

The night before, we had called the police as soon as we'd found poor Mr. Binterhof, who was out cold, but came to pretty quickly after Cedric had waved something in a small bottle under his nose. He had been whacked on the head from behind, but for all his age, he turned out to be pretty resilient. They took him away to the hospital, but he came back in the morning, perfectly fit except, as I said, for the headache. Cedric fed us both with a double order of fried breakfast stuff to celebrate his return, and Mr. B. said he would spend the rest of the day resting in bed, if Cedric promised to stick around in case the thug came back. Cedric armed himself with a cudgel thing from his wall display of medieval weaponry and said he would be delighted to provide protection. This was great for me, as it gave the host of the B&B someone else to play white knight for and left me to go about my business without a nanny. D.C. Potts (who, naturally, was the first on the scene after we'd called, with a really annoying "I told you so" expression on his face) had taken away Cedric's fourteenth century cosh, which had rather obviously been used to bean Mr. Binterhof, as it had been left on the floor by his head.

The burglar hadn't done much damage in the house, apart from trashing my room pretty thoroughly. I suppose it hadn't taken him long to find out which one it was, as Cedric had entered my room number next to my name in the guest book on the front counter. I hadn't locked my door, either, although that probably wouldn't have been much of a deterrent, as the burglar apparently managed to jimmy the locks on the courtyard gate and the kitchen door. Of course, the puppet case was locked in the trunk of the Reliant Robin at the time, but he couldn't have known that. He'd gone through all the stuff in my knapsack, including unrolling all my socks and pouring out the contents of my shampoo and talcum powder on the bed, which pissed me off, big time. He'd left a note on my bed, too, scrawled in pen on a scrap of notepaper: "YOU OWE US". I told Potts I didn't have a clue what that was supposed to mean.

"You owe us? Owe us what? And who is us? This is serious stuff, Ms. Deacon," he said. I was as baffled as he was and just shrugged.

"I'll have our handwriting people compare it to the BritRail form," he said. "We went to visit that address, but not surprisingly, the place was empty. It was a furnished bed-sit, and the lady who lets it said our Derek Smith had done a flit and owed her a week's rent."

"So he could be anywhere by now," I said. "He could be on the other side of the country."

"I don't believe he's going to give up that easily, actually. Has it occurred to you that this chap, who you think is a random thug, appears to know rather a lot about you?" I didn't answer, and we continued to sift through the mess in my room. There was nothing missing. Luckily, my passport and travellers' cheques were in the safe downstairs, and if the thug had attempted to get into it, he'd left no evidence of having been successful. It was still firmly locked, an ancient and black-faced iron thing, capable of withstanding a stick of dynamite, I'd bet. "This Smith knows your name, for example," Potts went on, "as he asked for you here this morning, and he knew where you were staying, correct?"

This worried me until we went back downstairs and asked Cedric what the flat-capped guy had actually said that morning.

"I think he asked to see my Canadian guest," Cedric said. Then he blushed. "I'm terribly sorry, but I think I must have blurted out 'oh, you mean Ms. Deacon?' or some such. You don't think, do you? I am sorry."

"How would he know you are Canadian?" Potts said, turning to me.

"He could have seen the Canadian flag on my backpack at the airport," I said. Although I remembered that he had confronted me when my back, and my backpack with the flag, were up against the wall. Still, he could have seen it earlier, if he was there looking for likely targets as I was coming through the arrivals gate.

"And he followed you all the way here from Gatwick? You don't think that's peculiar?"

"Of course, it's peculiar," I said. "Unless you take into account that he lives—or lived—right here in Canterbury, in which case, it was me following him home. But it still doesn't prove that he's out to harm me. In fact, if he were, he'd have had plenty of opportunity already."

"Like when you were alone at the Cathedral?" he said, meaningfully.

"I'm sure that what happened to Alma Barrow had nothing to do with me," I said. "That was the Right-to-Lifers, I swear, and I wish you'd concentrate on that and stop trying to link me to her. It doesn't make sense, and you'll never solve it by bugging me with questions I can't answer."

Potts left eventually, and Cedric (who had sobered up pretty sharply after we found Mr. Binterhof) made us a mug of Ovaltine. Then we turned in—me in a new room, not nearly as atmospheric as my attic room-in-a-trunk, but pleasant, nonetheless, and without a mattress soaked in Herbal Essence shampoo. Why on earth had the thug poured out my shampoo? Was he really looking for smuggled Canadian gemstones in the bottle? Maybe he thought it was maple syrup and had an over-inflated idea of how much the stuff was worth. I was perplexed as hell about it, but not enough to prevent me from falling asleep as soon as my head touched the pillow.

*   *   *

My email to Earlie was a ridiculously long one, and I hoped he would appreciate it, and hoped also that he would pass the information on to Becker, who still had not bothered to answer my original check-in thing. I was feeling a tad stubborn about it, actually. If Becker couldn't be bothered to answer my message, dammit, then I wasn't planning to send him any more of them. Let him get his news about Polly from his partner, who at least was willing to take the time to write. Yes, I know this was a radical change from the Me who said before I left that I wasn't planning to stay in touch at all, but people are allowed to change their minds occasionally, aren't they? Sheesh.

After sending the message, I finished my coffee, gave a cheery wave to the counter person at the Internet café (whose name tag identified her as Susannah, and who already regarded me as a regular), and headed out to the bus station to catch a ride to the university. On the way, I kept an eye out for Smith, in case he'd moved to another anonymous flat on the second floor, and was sitting there like last time, reading a paper. But he knew damn well he was being looked for and had probably absconded to northern Scotland to lie low. Which would be just fine with me.

The seminar that morning, "Choosing Materials for International Performing in Puppetry", was as wordy and academic as it sounded, but I felt obliged to attend, as I'd skipped off the morning previous. I took notes throughout, not because I was particularly interested in the subject, but to keep myself awake. Halfway through the lecture, Richard appeared out of the darkened aisle and sat down beside me, whispering a hoarse hello. I think he had only just woken up. He had a terrible case of bed head, and he sucked at his coffee like it was the only thing keeping him from passing out.

"Late night?" I whispered.

"There was a party in someone's room," he said. "It's too bad you aren't in residence. You would've enjoyed it. Bunch of people from Mermaid Theatre in Nova Scotia. Jeez. Party animals of the first order."

"I can't party these days, Richard," I said and patted my tummy significantly. Too bad, though. I missed that kind of stuff. The minute the Sprog made her appearance, I was intending to get well and truly loaded with a bunch of friends.

Someone next to me shushed, and we subsided into a kind of bleary silence as the presenter explained to us all that "the theatre of the inanimate transcends the need for language and what is required instead is a universal vocal tonality." The vocal tonality of the presenter, however, whose name I have since forgotten, was universally soporific, and I must have dozed off for a bit. Next thing I knew, Richard was poking me gently and telling me it was lunchtime, and did I want to grab a bite downtown before we hit the museum?

*   *   *

We grabbed lunch and a pint (yes, I had another Guinness—just a half) in a pub opposite the Roman museum. The little side street was cunningly called Butchery Lane, although there was not a butcher shop to be seen. Maybe a long time ago, the street had been filled with purveyors of animal flesh, with carcasses hanging from hooks in the doorways, like the illustrations in Dickens. Either that, or Butchery Lane was the hangout for Henry II's four murderous knights. Now it was full of twee little souvenir stores and places where you could buy bone china and Irish linen.

I was happy finally to be inside a real, honest-to-goodness British pub and gazed around with excitement, expecting a bunch of characters from *EastEnders* to emerge out from the woodwork. Actually, it wasn't that much different from the fake-o pubs they have in Canada, and I was a bit disappointed. There was the usual brocade red and gold carpet, moulded tin ceiling, and the horse brasses and miscellaneous antiques bolted to the walls.

There was a stunning selection of beers on tap at the bar, though, all with lovely names and decorative handles on the pull-things they use to draw your selection. I asked for a Guinness only because I had convinced myself that it was medicinal, and therefore good for the Sprog.

The tables were thick wooden ones, with matching armchairs, and each table held a nice, deep ashtray, which I suppose at least differentiated the place from your basic Toronto pub, where the smoking section could be found right over there in the dark corner next to the can, or more likely, out back in the alleyway. On the wall opposite the table we had chosen, a bunch of framed Victorian photographs overlooked the scene, probably picked up at a bargain price from an estate auction somewhere. I wondered what Great Aunt Effie would think if she knew her prim mug would end up front and centre in an establishment where liquor was consumed. I toasted her with my Guinness.

Richard had filled me in on pub-iquette the day before. You're never supposed to tip the barman or barmaid. You may, apparently, buy them a drink, but offering them your change is strictly not done and will brand you as a North American boob. I liked the fact that buying a barman a drink was quite okay— I had worked in enough bars during my theatre school days to know that in Toronto, at least, if you were caught drinking on the job, you were out on your ass. There is rarely table service in English pubs. If you want food, you order it at the bar. We had done so, selecting from a surprisingly extensive menu written on a portable chalk board flourished at our request by the barman [name tag: Harry]. Richard whispered in my ear that ordering fish and chips in a pub (unless it was right on the coast) is never a good idea, nor anything that involved cooked meat.

"Baguettes are safe," he said and ordered one with tuna salad inside.

I asked for the ploughman's lunch, a thing that in Toronto would have netted me a stale bun, a limp chunk of cheddar and a couple of pickled onions.

"You'd better help me with this," I said when it came. On a slab of wood were arranged four kinds of cheese—including a magnificent hunk of Stilton, a pickled egg, some relish and chutney, pickled onions, a wodge of lettuce, two fresh and crusty rolls, a pot of sweet butter and a handful of tiny tomatoes. We demolished the feast between us and deconstructed Professor whatever-his-name-was's lecture on the materials of international puppetry.

Richard was articulate and funny, and there was no point in pretending that I wasn't hugely attracted to him. This fact was pretty well established by the time we started arguing over the last pickled onion. (We cut it in half.) I figure I was suffering from the land-locked version of the shipboard flirtation—the kind of thing you indulge in because a person is handy and pleasant and away from home, just as you are. If we'd met in Kuskawa, at the Steamboat Theatre, for example, we'd have been professional and friendly and nothing more. It was just as well I was so hugely pregnant and not at all attractive, or I swear I would have interpreted his vibes as being of the "let's be pillow buddies" kind. Anyway, he was at least ten years younger than me, and probably thought of me as a nice aunt-substitute.

*　　*　　*

The Roman Museum in Canterbury is housed in a basement, which I thought was strange until we got down there and saw the excavated Roman house ruin that formed the centrepiece of the place. Once inside, you were invited to "follow the detective work of archaeologists"—through to the excavated Roman house site—and to the hands-on area with all sorts of real artifacts that you were allowed to handle. Way back, the town had been called Durovernum Cantiacorum, and it had been a going concern for about four hundred years. What I didn't get was where all the soil came from—if a Roman town had existed on that spot, how on earth had the earth piled up, all over the place, so that this stuff was only discovered after a bomb was dropped on the area during the second World War? I never did figure it out, but it didn't matter. It gave me the same kind of ancient shivers that the cloister had, and this time, I was in the company of someone who liked this stuff as much as I did.

The museum included a time-view of an early Roman town market, with trader's stalls and set out with real objects and authentic reconstructions. We spent a lot of time at that, because the drawings were so good. When we got to the "House Interior with room settings, including kitchen and dining room", we found a woman dressed up as a Roman matron and preparing Roman-type-food to amuse the museum-goers. She took one look at me and sort of shrieked, which made me shriek back, as I'd taken her for a wax statue. It was my old friend Maude, from the train.

"Oh, you didn't half give me a turn," she said. "I thought you were dead, dear."

"Did you? Why?"

"Well, the Cathedral. Everybody's talking about the pregnant lady who got murdered in the Cathedral just like Mr. Becket did ever so long ago, done to death right on top of his shrine, they say. Aaaaawful. Well, they said she was pregnant and had brown hair, and you remember I met you giving out pamphlets at the rally, and then they said you—well, naturally I thought it was you, didn't I?"

"Well, obviously it wasn't me, eh?" I said. "But, Maude, you didn't meet me at the rally. I wasn't giving out pamphlets—that was another woman who looked a bit like me—the one who died. Did you speak to her?"

"Only to pass the time of day, and I stood with her for the speeches, you know. Are you sure it wasn't you?"

"I'm sure, Maude." I introduced her to Richard, who was looking a bit bewildered, and Maude explained that she was a regular volunteer at the museum, "to help give it a bit of life, you know, dear." She peered through her coke-bottle glasses as if Richard were a particularly interesting Roman specimen. We made polite conversation for a bit, then made movements towards the next part of the museum exhibit.

Suddenly, Maude remembered something. "Look here," she said, "do you want your pamphlets back?"

"Huh? What pamphlets?"

"The ones you gave me to hold at the speeches, just before you went to the loo, dear. I held them for you, but you never came back for them, did you?" I realized she still hadn't quite grasped that I wasn't Alma, or that Alma wasn't me.

"The person you were standing with at the rally gave you her pamphlets, and you've still got them?" I said, very gently, so as not to rattle her.

"That's right. They're in my knitting bag in the cloakroom. They're a bit heavy, and I'd be glad to be rid of them," she said, looking aggrieved.

"Tell me, Maude, when the person handed over the pamphlets, was she carrying a big baby puppet on a stick at that point?" I asked.

"Oh, that thing—yes, you—well, she, I suppose—was. I remember saying it must be the thing you were carrying in that case you brought on the train. She didn't really understand what I was saying, but now I know why, because she wasn't you." She was looking more and more muddled, and I knew how she felt.

"That was the puppet that you found in the cloisters?" Richard said.

"Exactly—so she took it to the loo with her, did she?"

"I think so," Maude said. "It had come off its stick by then. I think one of the other marchers had a bit of a barney with her about it, and she was carrying it like it was a real one. It was ever so funny."

"And she didn't come back."

"No. I waited for quite a long time, even after all the people went into the Cathedral. I didn't go in, though—I'm chapel, you see. Don't hold with all that kneeling and standing and kneeling. I went home instead and had a cup of tea."

"You know, Maude, I think you might have been one of the last people to see Alma—that's the lady who was killed— alive. I think you ought to tell the police about it."

"Really? Me? Oooh, what fun. You really think so?"

"I know so. And you can give the pamphlets to them, as well. As evidence." Maude's bright little eyes behind their thick glasses shone like sea pebbles. Obviously, for some people, retirement in Canterbury didn't hold nearly enough excitement. She beetled off at once, presumably to collect her knitting bag and fish out her mobile phone. "When you call them," I called to her retreating back, "ask for Constable Potts. He's the investigating officer."

"Thanks ever so much," she twittered back, her footsteps pitter-pattering on the staircase up to the main entrance.

"That should keep Potts happy," I said with some satisfaction.

"You don't suppose that the person who assaulted Alma heard Maude ask if the puppet baby was the one in your case, do you?" Richard asked. He'd heard enough about the situation the night before to understand the mistaken-identity theory and its implications, if any. "Because if he did, then he could have followed her, assaulted her and grabbed the puppet, thinking it was you, carrying whatever he thought you'd brought into the country in that suitcase. That old lady has just made Potts's theory about you being in danger a whole bunch stronger, eh?"

Suddenly, everybody's a detective. And suddenly, my knees felt awfully weak.

Twenty

The Church's fear of sex was exaggerated and obsessive as well as fundamentally superstitious. It preserved the primitive magical belief in the power of sex to contaminate. It was for this reason that married couples must not only abstain from intercourse for three nights after their marriage, but having once performed the sexual act, must not enter a church for thirty days after, and then only on condition of doing forty days penance and bringing an offering.

-From the history section of *Big Bertha's Total Baby Guide*

The entrance to the Eastbridge Hospital is very low, and Richard had to stoop so he wouldn't whang his head. When it was built, the front door used to be at street height, but again, that weird building up of the ground had happened over the centuries, so now you had to step down into it. The front of the building was covered in a rough stone-like stuff, like stucco, but more ancient, which made the place stand out from its half-timbered neighbours. If anything, it looked older than you'd have thought was possible. A red sign over the door proclaimed it "The Canterbury Pilgrim's Hospital of Saint Thomas".

Our guide was the Master of Eastbridge, a gentle priest called Father David, who was also the rector of the churches in the city centre, St. Peter's and St. Mildred's. Father David explained that the place was established very soon after Thomas Becket was murdered, when his tomb and the scene of his death became a focus of pilgrimage, and the city suddenly had to provide accommodation for the hordes of visitors that flooded in.

"It's called hospital in the old sense of the word," the priest said, "a place of hospitality. It's given shelter and help to pilgrims, soldiers, local societies and schoolboys, and has been a permanent home to a number of elderly people for about four hundred years."

"Not the same ones, I take it," Richard said.

"Hmm? Oh, goodness me, no. Oh, not at all. But we do have a waiting list, you see. There are eight private rooms beyond that door, there." He pointed to a wing off to the right, marked private. I wondered what it would be like to live in an eight-hundred-year-old almshouse.

"Are there ghosts?" I said, realizing as I said it that probably every visitor who had ever dropped by had asked that. Father David smiled sweetly.

"Not so's you'd notice," he said. "You'll find the atmosphere is quite holy, really." He was right. We moved into the refectory, a high-ceilinged dining room that was originally used for the pilgrim's meals. It was now a meeting hall and library, with a thirteenth century mural on one wall. I had one of my time-travelley flashes that made my skin tingle. Seven hundred years ago, an artist had stood right here, a brush in his or her hand, a board with paint on it, probably hand-mixed, the brush made from squirrel hair, and had dabbed colour onto this very wall. The mural began at head-height and soared up to the ceiling. The artist would have had to stand on some scaffolding, and I wondered if he or she worked while the pilgrims were eating. I could just imagine the comments.

" 'Ere, that's a bit of orl right, that is. The eyes follow you round the room, don't they?"

Up a flight of steps, we were led into the chapel. The woodwork of the roof was amazing—like the ribs of a boat, upside down. There was a little altar and some wooden pews so old the wood was black, and the place smelled wonderful—that spicy scent of ancient wood and incense and prayer books. The chapel was still used for evening prayer and the occasional Eucharist on festival days. It had been used from 1569 to 1880 as a schoolroom, Father David said, but was now restored to its proper use.

A bell tinkled, and Father David excused himself. "We must have another visitor," he said and headed back to the entranceway.

"Have you seen inside the Cathedral yet?" I asked Richard.

"Yeah, I poked my head in on Tuesday," he said. "Although it's not really my thing—churches. I have what you'd call a secular background. It was pretty magnificent, though—architecturally, at least."

"But you know, I like this place better," I said. "This feels like there were really people here, crowded on the pews, bundled up in rags and glad of a warm place to sit down. People who had the kind of faith that makes you travel hundreds of miles on foot to touch a tomb."

"That kind of faith still exists," Richard said. "Ever seen pictures of the Kabaa at Mecca?"

"Yeah, or the Pope's shindigs at the Vatican, or World Youth Day—I suppose it's the same thing, isn't it?" We sat in silence for a moment, soaking up the atmosphere. Father David had called it holy, which doesn't mean a heck of a lot to me, but there was something, that tingling that I'd come to associate with very old things and places, the twinge of unformed excitement that I'd felt from the moment that taxi left Canterbury station and wound through the narrow, cobblestoned streets. I began to form an idea in my mind, a puppet show based on Becket's murder, a group of ragged pilgrim puppets at the tomb, seeing a vision played out before their eyes, the knights in dull, pewter-coloured armour, and the sagging figure of the priest as the swords did their horrible work. Then the vision was replaced by a modern one—Alma, being attacked by a masked figure. I shook my head to dispel the image and turned to Richard.

"Do you ever feel you're missing something, not being religious?"

"Sometimes," he said. "There's a lot to be said for having a path to follow. It's just that the paths I've come across so far seem to me to be full of human rules that don't make sense."

"Yeah—like those Right-to-Lifers."

"The ones who preach that abortion is murder but advocate the murder of abortion providers, you mean?"

"Yes, those ones. The ones who murder those who don't agree with them."

"An eye for an eye, eh? Not a very loving path."

"I'll say."

It was interesting having this conversation with Richard Seth, of all people, a man I'd only just met. It was the kind of discussion I'd often wanted to have with Becker, but we'd never seemed to get around to it. Becker was not a religious person, unless you count the religion of duty and loyalty to the law. I suddenly found myself doing the comparison-thing. Becker versus Richard. If it were Richard's baby, the Sprog nestling in my belly, we would probably have had a conversation about spiritual paths a long time ago. We probably would have discussed it in terms of the new person and how we were going to answer her big questions, like "why are we here?" and "is God real?" We'd discuss whether or not we would baptize her, whether or not the Big Guy really gave a damn about the business at all. I risked a quick look at Richard's profile. Gosh, but he was a good-looking man. But there was more to his attraction than his looks; he had a calm about him, a kind of settled peace that made the air around his body feel like a warm bath.

Becker's immediate presence was entirely different. It crackled with energy, a red-headed, do-stuff energy that could be irritating if you were in the wrong sort of mood. Becker's sexuality was like that, too—always present under the surface, and I'd learned that my reaction to it was oddly connected with confrontation. I was most frequently aroused by Becker when he was being forceful and confrontational. I'd thought that this was my problem—when I'd considered it in terms of a problem, that is, usually when I was alone and yearning for a bit of pillow-buddy activity. Richard Seth's immediate presence was, what? Comforting? Peaceful? Secure, even? It wasn't that I wanted to feel that way. I was perfectly aware of the inappropriateness of it, both in terms of time, place and circumstance. But it was out of my sphere of control. I was developing a roaring crush on this guy, and I couldn't do a thing about it. Awkward, very. He turned then and caught me full in the eyes with a smile that would melt rock. We didn't say anything. Just looked. It was a lovely moment and held a kind of promise that made my chest feel full. Poor Becker, I thought. I am such a flake.

* * *

Father David returned, looking bewildered. "Nobody there. It must have been one of our residents," he said. "Forgotten their side-door key, I expect. They do that from time to time." He continued our tour, speaking as he led us out of the chapel. "The Hospital was probably at its peak of use in the 1380s, when Chaucer was writing his *Canterbury Tales*. It would have been crowded, and probably smelly." He led us down a steep flight of steps, past another small chapel, into the undercroft, the first part of the Hospital to be built—the pilgrims' sleeping area. They may have called it the undercroft, but it felt like the crypt of the Cathedral, only mustier, full of the smell of cold stone. There was strong lighting down there, but it did nothing to dispel the sensation of entombment. To the right were a series of low-ceilinged cubicles, like cells, divided up by stone walls and archways. Stone platforms were built against the outside walls, long, narrow benches, which would in´the old days presumably have been covered in straw. Above each platform was a small, high window cut into the thick stone walls—a window that let in a chilly blue light from the outside, but in winter, in the 1300s, they would probably have been covered over with sacking and straw. The straw would have been alive with vermin, I imagined. It would have been like a barn. There would have been several people sleeping in each alcove, huddled together for warmth, snoring and farting in their sleep.

"Can you direct me to the facilities?" Richard said, suddenly and urgently, to our guide. "Sorry, Polly—the tuna baguette, I think. I won't be long." I patted his arm in sympathy. It's not only in Mexico that travellers get caught by Montezuma's Revenge.

"A touch of Becket Belly?" I said. He smiled wanly and followed Father David's instructions to find the door on the right at the top of the stairs.

Father David, in a fine, theatrical voice, quoted from an early archbishop's vision-statement as we made our way down to the end of the long room. "The Hospital is for the maintenance of poor pilgrims and other infirm persons resorting thither to remain until they are healed of their infirmities—for the poor, for persons going to Rome, for others coming to Canterbury and needing shelter, and for lying-in women."

"What on earth would it have been like to give birth down here?"

"Rather frightening, I expect. Though better than in a stable in the desert," the priest said.

At the end of the room, we turned back to head back upstairs, but I lingered and slipped into one of the alcoves for a moment, to sit on a platform and let my imagination have its way with me. Moments later, the lights went out, leaving the undercroft in eerie darkness.

"Oh, bother," Father David said. "The fuse has gone again, I expect. Don't move, my dear, or you'll come a cropper in the dark. I won't be a moment." He scurried out, and an utter and profound silence descended. Slowly, my eyes adjusted to the dim blue light coming from the narrow window above my head. I knelt on the platform and peered out of it—and saw a gravestone almost immediately before my eyes—a long-dead pilgrim, maybe. Maybe a lying-in woman who hadn't quite made it, her bones mere inches from me on the other side of the stone wall, buried deeply in the Canterbury earth.

I sensed the person behind me a split second before the hand came around to cover my mouth. I struggled, but only for a moment. He was very strong, and I could smell the distinct odour of fish.

"I'm right tired of following you about," the person hissed into my ear. "You was supposed to do the handover at the airport, and my people are sick of waiting." The handover? I tried to speak, but he wasn't going to let me. "No," he said. "You listen here. If you don't cough up sharpish, you'll be for it, see?"

I could hear a shuffling in the darkness by the stairway. Richard's voice pierced the dark. "Polly?" he said. "Are you okay down there?" The man tensed and tightened his hold on me, which hurt. The Sprog was squashed against the wall and kicked my kidneys in protest.

"So listen up. This 'ere's your last chance. Bring the stuff to Greyfriars at midnight tonight. Come alone, and you won't get hurt. Then you can go back to your bleedin' puppets, and nobody's the wiser. Got it?" He released me then, and I found I had been holding my breath and couldn't speak for a moment. I heard a back door slam and then the lights came on again. I put my hand to my belly. Sorry, love. It's all right, I thought at her.

"Polly?"

"I'm here. At the back." Footsteps, quick ones.

"What's going on? You look like you've seen a ghost," Richard said. I looked at him carefully. Had he faked his sudden indisposition in order to flick a switch and plunge the place into darkness? Was this all a set-up?

"I'm all right," I said, scrambling for something to say. "Just felt dizzy for a second. There. The lights are on again. It's spooky down here in the dark."

"Yeah, too much like a dungeon. Here's the priest." Father David had returned to us, shaking his head and making little placating movements with his hands.

"Oh, I do hope you weren't distressed being left in the dark like that," he said. "Quite extraordinary, really. The fuse wasn't blown, you know. Just came loose. I can't think why."

"Never mind," I said, my voice sounding a little shaky. "I got a taste of what it must have been like, you know, back in the days before electricity."

"Of course there would have been candles," Father David said. "Lamps and so on. It is eerie in the dark, though. Come on up out of this and into the chapel. You look a bit pale."

"She says she felt dizzy," Richard said. He was looking at

me intensely, and I could hear his subtext of "tell me what's wrong." The problem was, I wasn't sure whether or not I could trust him any more. I felt a sudden overwhelming need to lie down, preferably at the Pilgrim's Rest, with Cedric standing guard over me with his medieval cudgel.

We thanked Father David for his kind tour of Eastbridge, and Richard popped a ten-pound note into the collection box on our way out, which I thought was sweet of him. Father David's eyes bugged out a little when he saw it, and I remembered that the place existed purely on the basis of charity. We emerged into bright sunshine, and the horror of my encounter with the faceless thug receded a bit, though my knees still felt like water.

"Are you sure you're okay?" Richard said. "I was sitting there on the can, and then the lights went out and I got this really strong feeling that you were, you know, freaking out or something. Are you afraid of the dark? Claustrophobia?" He looked so earnest and genuine, I found it hard to imagine that he might have been in league with the thug, but before I could tell him about it, I needed a little time alone to work things out.

"Well, there was something, Richard, but I'm going to sit on it for a bit, if you don't mind. Are you going to the body-puppet show tonight?"

"The Czechoslovakian thing? You bet. They're supposed to be amazing."

"Why don't we sit together? And then I think I need to talk to you." His brow furrowed, which, on a face that beautiful, is kind of heartbreaking.

"Can't you talk to me now?" he said. "Is it something to do with the Cathedral thing?"

"Maybe," I said, "but I need some space, okay?" Oh—how many times had I said that to a guy? I need some space. Leave me alone while I wrestle with something on my own. Sometimes I was so predictable, I bored even myself.

"Dinner, maybe? Let me buy you dinner, at least. You'll be feeling better by six, eh?"

I agreed to meet him at the Moghul again for dinner before the show, and he escorted me back to the Pilgrim's Rest, where Cedric was at his post by the front reception desk, the cudgel near to hand.

"I'll meet you there," I said to Richard at the door. He left in a dejected kind of way, his shoulders down, and I felt bad for sending him off like that. We'd had a great day together, up until the moment the thug had put his smelly paw over my face. It wasn't Richard's fault. Or was it? I needed to think.

"I'm feeling a bit tuckered out, Cedric," I said, in response to my landlord's inquiring expression. "I'm going to go lie down for a bit, okay? How's Mr. Binterhof?"

"Sleeping like a baby," he said. "Do you need a wake-up call?"

"Please. Five-ish would be great."

"Five-ish it shall be," he said. "And in the meantime, I'll batten down the hatches and defend our ramparts from the advancing hordes." His eyes glittered, and I wondered as I mounted the stairs whether Cedric had been at the sherry. I felt a twinge of regret. A whacking great beaker of sherry would have gone down sweetly at that point. But still, I had the Sprog to think about, and what we both really needed was sleep.

Twenty-One

Dreams are like funhouse mirrors that reflect your emotional state. Since pregnancy can feel like an emotional roller coaster, don't be surprised if your dreams become more vivid and crazy than usual.

-From *Big Bertha's Total Baby Guide*

I am back in the undercroft at Eastbridge, which has somehow been relocated to the Cathedral and is now part of the church crypt. I know this, because Alma, who is painting a mural on the wall, has told me so.

"It's for all the lying-in women," she says, busy with paint and brush, speaking out of the corner of her mouth in a reverent whisper. "For us, you know." She is alive and well and as pregnant as I am. The picture she is painting is gruesome in the extreme—the Becket murder scene. I look down at her palette and the red paint is liquid—there appears to be an awful lot of it, and it's spilling over and dripping onto the stone floor.

"I don't want to have my baby down here," I say, panicked, because I know that the row of open coffins in the corner have been prepared for us, and I won't have any choice. We're locked in.

"There's a side door we can use," I tell her. "Stop painting, and let's get out of here."

"I can't stop, Polly. Look—the demonstration's coming, and we have to make sure the voice of reason is heard." Along the corridor, whose ceiling has become an upside-down boat, a parade advances. There are soldiers in armour with swords, and I can see a baby puppet being carried on a stick behind them. I know at once *that the demonstration will be horribly violent. I run for the side door, chased by the soldiers. One catches me from behind and puts his hand around my face, his gauntlet cutting into my neck. He hisses into my ear. "Silly bint. We've got a large coffin at Greyfriars for you, and we're expecting you to do the handover tonight. Nobody'll get hurt. Anyway, it's better than a manger in the desert!"*

When you're pregnant and bulgy, the option of sitting bolt upright in bed is not available to you. So I sat bolt sideways instead, sweating like a cheese.

"Miss Deacon? This is your wakeup call," Cedric said, discreetly tapping at my door. "I've got a cup of tea here, if you'd like it."

"Thanks, Cedric. Just a moment." I had curled up under the duvet fully dressed and only took a moment to rub my eyes, heave myself up and totter to the door.

"My heavens, dear, are you all right?"

"I'm fine, Cedric. Just sleepy, that's all."

"That's a nasty bruise on your neck." I reached up instinctively to touch the place where the thug's wrist had pressed into me, his hand on my mouth. In movies, people who have been manhandled by bad guys always get up right away, shake their heads, and carry on, perhaps with a cosmetic trickle of blood coming from the edge of their mouths, but only if they've been punched in the face. In movies, people who have had a hand placed over their mouths simply take it as a matter of course, and suffer no ill effects. In real life, such episodes leave traces behind. I was stiff, too. Achey.

"I must have slept funny," I said. "I bruise easily. Thanks for getting me up, and thanks so much for the tea, eh?" I smiled as best I could and closed the door gently, hoping I wasn't being rude. Cedric was a sweet person, and while I didn't mind his familiarity, I wasn't about to be inviting him in for a cozy bedside chat. I went to the mirror and looked. Yes, there was a mark there—though in the dim light of the hallway, I was surprised that Cedric had been able to discern a "nasty bruise".

I changed my shirt and added, for Richard's benefit, a pair of silver earrings that Aunt Susan had given me—little dangling puppet figures, which, if you pulled their tiny silver chains, would dance. I had an hour to kill before meeting him at the Moghul, which gave me time to pop into the Internet café, just to check for messages.

To: Polly1258@hotmail.com
From: oppmorr@kuskawa.com
Subject: RE: The Real Story
Date: Friday, February 15

Dear Polly,
We have heard from Constable Potts, and I think you should be careful. You may think this thug guy as you call him is after your puppet case, but maybe there's something more in it. Becker is in Calgary again, something to do with his sister, and I'm holding the fort. Potts wants to know if Becker ever worked with Drug Enforcement and thinks there's some outfit trying to pay him back for something through you. I may have to look at his files, because he's not checking messages like he should. Listen to Potts and don't do anything stupid.
    Regards,
    Earl

This message made me mad on several fronts. The first was that Becker had gone to Calgary, and I was the last person to know about it. Couldn't he have sent me an email? He still hadn't bothered to answer my Wednesday morning check-in thing, either. A second after I realized that I was pissed off about this, my conscience (that wretched little creature who sits on your right shoulder like the sparrow-sized angels in cartoons) suggested that I might be suffering from double standards. Hadn't I told him I would not be in touch, that I was only going away for a week, that communication was too much trouble and was silly? And here I was, having a nuclear meltdown because he wasn't sending me his schedule and letting me know every time he went for a pee?

The second thing that annoyed me was Morrison agreeing with Potts' theory about this stuff instead of mine. I had been on the verge of telling Earlie about the Eastbridge Hospital episode, but I thought better of it at once. It would only freak him out. I had figured how to fix the whole thing, anyway— nothing to do with Becker. My dream had told me the answer. All I had to do was get Richard to help me.

*   *   *

I sent Earlie a short "don't worry about me" kind of message and headed out into the Canterbury evening. Many of the streets of town had been what they call "pedestrianized"— which means that though local traffic is allowed, it's not encouraged. It lent a pleasant, historical aura to the cobblestoned and narrow laneways. Delivery trucks were allowed, though, and I counted no less than three anonymous white vans on my walk from the Pilgrim's Rest to the Moghul. One was parked next to a souvenir shop, another at "Ye Olde Fresh Meats & Fish" and a third outside a newsagents. After Cedric had mentioned that the thug who came looking for me was driving a white van, I'd been on the lookout for them. I was already aware that they were everywhere, the English equivalent of the yellow cabs in New York, and from what I'd seen of the local newspapers, the average Englishman detested them, and especially their drivers. I'd seen a letter in a tabloid I'd picked up in the Internet café, which read, in part:

One of those new Escort transit vans thought it could get in front of me on the M5 in heavy Friday evening traffic by undertaking me and trying to cut in after pushing someone else on to the hard shoulder.

Trouble is that not one of these girly shirtlifting tosspieces will never read this newspaper, because they can't. Being illiterate is a requirement for the job.

I liked "shirtlifting tosspiece", although I marvelled at its actually being printed in a newspaper, because I suspected that it was a tad rude. There were no signs of any van drivers near the white vans spotted in my walk, though. Perhaps they were inside the shops they were delivering to, trying to read their purchase orders.

*　　*　　*

The Moghul looked quite full from the outside. Obviously Friday night was curry night for many Canterburyites.

"It's okay, I made reservations," Richard said, arriving on foot a moment after I did. "Been waiting long? Did your landlord drive you?"

"No, I walked," I said. "The pregnant lady requires regular exercise, all the books say."

"You shouldn't be walking around by yourself, you know. Not after dark. Not after what happened."

"Not after what happened?" I said. Aha. Maybe he'd just

given away that he knew about the Eastbridge thing. It could have been a set-up. He might be in league with them, whoever they were.

"After the cathedral thing," Richard said, surprised. "And the guy the cop chased at your demo. Come on, you don't think there's something to be worried about?"

"Tell me about the lights-out at Eastbridge again," I said. "How come you left suddenly and then the lights went out? Tell me you had nothing to do with that."

"You think I turned the lights out? What? Why would I do that?" I was testing him, in the most blatant way I could imagine, because I wanted to make damn sure about him. This was partly because I was more than a little attracted to him, and I didn't want to do anything stupid, as Earlie would have said.

"Maybe you popped the fuse to give the guy the opportunity to jump me," I said.

"What guy? Hey, something did happen back there, didn't it? Why didn't you tell me? We could have called the cops. Somebody jumped you? Are you okay? What's that on your neck?"

Now, on a scale of one to ten, I would have given that performance a clear 9.5, and Richard was a puppet maker, not an actor. Okay, maybe the whole thing was subjective as hell, but I believed him at once. He had passed the Polly-test.

"Let's go eat," I said. "And I'll tell you about it."

* * *

In North America, restaurants with buffets will put up a sign that says "All You Can Eat." In England, they're way more refined. It was buffet night at the Moghul, and the sign said, "Help Yourself To As Much As You Like." I thought that was a much classier way of putting it, even if it meant the same thing, that you could gorf out like a pig if you wanted to, and nobody would mind.

Over something called Butter Chicken (even the name makes your mouth water, doesn't it?) and a double order of Peshawari naan, I spilt the beans about the Eastbridge episode.

"So obviously the guy came in while Father David was showing us around upstairs," Richard said. "But how did he know how to turn the lights out? How did he know where the fuse box was? He must have some connection with the place, eh?"

"It's open to the public, you know. Maybe he cased the place first."

"Then how did he know you were going to be there?"

"I don't know, Richard. He was following us, maybe. Maybe he heard us talking about it."

"And he said he—or 'his people'— expected a handover of some kind? Your puppet case, right?"

"That's what I think, yes. I think they thought I was bringing something in—drugs or guns or something—well, we kind of wondered about that yesterday, which is why Potts searched the puppet case again. I think the thug has got me mixed up with some smuggler-type. That's why they were so pissed off when I didn't 'hand it over'. He was expecting me to be in on it, don't you see? That's why he's been following me, but not actually attacking me. He's expecting me to live up to my side of the arrangement."

"So you've got a gang of some kind who think you've got guns or drugs in your puppet case, and they're expecting you to give it to them at some deserted place at midnight, and you don't want to tell the police about it? Are you crazy?"

"I don't have much luck with the police, Richard. They tend to mess stuff up."

"I thought you were marrying one."

"I haven't made up my mind about that. I told you. Police officers are difficult people."

"They're not the only ones," he muttered. "Look, you need to tell the police about this as soon as possible, Polly. Then they can set a trap for the guy at Greyfriars."

"He said 'come alone'. If he sees the cops, he'll just hide."

"So? They always say that. But the cops are usually pretty good about being discreet."

"How do you know? In my experience, most bad guys can smell a cop a mile away."

"Have you ever been to Greyfriars? Do you even know where it is? Or what it is?"

"I was hoping you could tell me, actually. And maybe come with me, as well."

"He said 'come alone'," Richard said, trying to sound like me, a small smile on his face.

"Puppeteers are usually pretty good about being discreet," I shot back.

"What are you proposing to do? Tackle the guy bare-handed?"

"I'm going to hand over the puppet case and let him see for himself," I said. "That's what he wants, right? I'll tell him I don't know what the hell is going on, and let him tear the thing apart if he wants. I'll be honest. I'm going to use the voice of reason. Then I'll ask him what he's looking for. When he realizes I'm the wrong person, he'll stop bugging me. He'll see that he's barking up the wrong tree."

"Are you on crack?" he said. "You think being 'the voice of reason' to a psycho is going to make him shake your hand and say no hard feelings and then go away? Have you forgotten about Alma?"

"Alma was killed accidentally by the Right-to-Lifers, I'm sure of it, Richard. It has nothing to do with me."

"Yeah, right. And they tore apart that puppet baby she had for no reason. Jesus, Polly, I can't let you do this," he said. "You're nuts."

"If we let the cops know about this midnight meeting, they'll show up with floodlights and police cars, and this white van man will not show up, he'll just keep following me until I'm on the plane home," I said. "I want it to be over now, right now, and this is the way I want to do it."

"And what do I do, lurk in the shadows and jump the thug when he tries to clobber you?"

"He won't try to clobber me. Trust me on this one, Richard. And tell me about Greyfriars."

We ordered tea, and Richard got out his handy dandy guide book—one he'd bought at the Roman Museum. Under Greyfriars it said:

This building, located behind the private Franciscan Gardens in Stour Street, near the Post Office, is not commonly open to the public without special permission. Greyfriars is somewhat decayed, but still quite an architectural wonder, the last monument of the Greyfriars or Franciscans, once the most popular of the monastic orders. This little house occupies no land, for it is built on arches over a branch of the Stour, and its slender supporting pillars rise from the middle of the river bed.

"There's a little laneway you have to take to get to it," Richard said. "I checked it out when I was exploring, yesterday. It's sort of in the middle of a field. There's an archaeological excavation site next to it. It's lonely and deserted, Polly. You don't want to be going there alone at midnight."

"I won't be alone," I said, looking at the lovely watercolour illustration that accompanied the text. "You'll be with me, right?"

Richard looked extremely unhappy, but he nodded his head. "I'll be with you, yeah," he said.

"And if you tell Potts about this, I'll never speak to you again. Now we'd better get the bill and boot it. The Czech show starts in half an hour. You want to split a cab?" On the way out the door, it occurred to me that saying "I'll never speak to you again" to a guy I'd only known for two days was a bit foolish. There's no point in threatening to cut off communication with someone unless you thought that communicating with them was important. He put his hand on the small of my back as we hurried out onto the street. It felt warm and intimate and far more significant than was proper for a woman in my circumstances. I experienced a sudden roaring blast of lust that made my face burn, a follow-up to that moment at Eastbridge that had more urgency than anything I'd felt since before Christmas, when Becker had stopped touching me and started treating me like I was a fat and fragile porcelain vase.

It didn't help when Richard kissed me in the back of the taxi. It didn't help at all.

Twenty-Two

Some women will find that their sex drive significantly increases during their pregnancy, while others will experience a decreased interest in sex. The same holds true for fathers. The most important thing here is to be open. Talk freely with your partner and continue to build upon your warm, healthy relationship.

-From *Big Bertha's Total Baby Guide*

The Czechoslovakian puppetry company, Sidewalk Weeds, claimed inspiration from the tradition of subversive performance known as "daisy shows", which proliferated in Prague during the Second World War. While the Nazis were in occupation, puppet theatre was apparently a way to keep the spirit of resistance alive. Probably far more sensible than taking out ads in the local newspaper. It took a long time for the Gestapo to figure out that puppets weren't just a kind of kiddie entertainment, since the guys in jackboots didn't spend too much time attending theatre for young audiences. Nazis weren't big on metaphor. However, when the Nazis finally clued in that the puppet shows were attracting large audiences over the age of six, they cracked down, and the stuff went underground. Instead of theatres and beach-side black-boxes, the shows, enormously political, were performed in private homes, alleyways and basements.

The program notes explained the name:

The performances were known as "daisies", named for those tiny, determined flowers that have the strength to force their way up through concrete in order to find light. By the time the war ended, the "daisies" had almost entirely disappeared, and so had their creators. More than 100 Czech puppeteers died under torture or in the camps during the Nazi occupation.

Sidewalk Weeds' production of "The Development" is a tribute to those dangerous performances.

The Development was not a kiddie show. The villains of the piece, corporate businessmen-characters in pinstriped suits, carrying huge briefcases, were represented by puppeteers working with larger-than-life body-puppets, a version of the North American sports team mascot. They moved slowly, ponderously, with enormous power—dangerous giants. The regular folks, whose property and community were being confiscated to make way for a new factory, were represented by marionettes, fragile figures with fragile strings, who skittered away from the giants like mice dashing for cover at the lion's approach. It reminded me of those old Japanese Godzilla movies, but it was way more frightening. The dialogue was simple, fairy-tale stuff, which added to the feeling of oppression and hopelessness. Richard and I held hands throughout the show, like small children. The applause at the end was thunderous. It was not an uplifting piece, and it didn't have a happy ending, but it was damned good.

"That sort of puts the *Hunting and Fishing Is Our Heritage* show into perspective," Richard said, blinking in the glare as the houselights came up.

"Steamboat Theatre used to do great stuff, you know," I said. "At least, before the Tory government stopped funding theatre companies."

"Yeah. But the province is funding this one. With support from the Federation of Anglers and Hunters."

"What exactly happens in it?"

"A little guy is taught to fish and hunt by the ghost of his great-grandfather. There are singing and dancing fish and deer, and there's a scene where an Indian comes along and explains the concept of honouring the earth for her bounty and the Creator for making food available to the people. So the little guy carries on killing things, but he does it mindfully. Big finish at the end when the kid bags his first deer, and there's a chorus of ancestors like the heavens just opened. It's going to tour the school system in September."

"Charming."

"Yup. Gotta love it." You might conclude that the bad guys had finally realized that the best way to fight subversive performances was to co-opt the enemies' techniques and make them your own. Propaganda, the next generation.

* * *

We went to the student pub afterwards with a number of other conference people, the cast of the show we'd just seen, and some of the CIPF organizers. The gang from Mermaid Theatre of Nova Scotia were there, too, and Richard had been right—they were party animals. Very funny, very friendly, and I was soon feeling homesick for the east coast, where I'd spent some wonderful years before moving back to Ontario. Although the convivial atmosphere made it really difficult to say no, I stuck to Perrier with lime, mainly because if I'd had one Guinness, I'd have had four.

After about an hour, even then, I was ready for a nap.

"I should go back to the B&B for a while, or I'm going to be toast by midnight," I said in Richard's ear. One of the Mermaid people was doing a mini-performance, animating a couple of beer bottles as if they were puppets, which had the table in stitches.

"Why don't you come over to my room in residence?" Richard said. "You can rest there, and then I won't be worrying about you, and it'll be easier for us to go to Greyfriars together, rather than meeting later."

"You got any etchings over there?"

"Huh? Well, I do have a sketchbook you might want to look at."

"What are we waiting for? Lead on, MacDuff—if you're sure you don't mind."

"Why would I mind? I'm about ready to leave, myself. After all, I'm playing bodyguard later, right? And I don't need any more Old Speckled Hen." That was the beer he'd been drinking. I'd taken a sip, just to taste. It was wonderful, rich and smooth and slightly sweet. How tragic that I was in England, the Land o' Great Beer, and unable to do more than take a couple of taste tests. Sigh.

It was dark and cold, and I was glad of my trusty curling sweater. Even so, Richard put his arm around me—you know, to keep me warm and all that. Because we were in a university setting, there was a peculiarly undergraduate feeling to our journey, as if we were doing something illegal and slightly naughty. As if we were nineteen again, and sneaking around. Or maybe it was just me. I'd never lived in a university residence myself, and though I knew there was a rule-bound, cloistered quality to such communities, (an impression acquired from movies and TV), I'd never actually experienced it myself. Maybe I felt like I was sneaking around because I was having impure thoughts about Richard, because Becker would not have approved, and because I was pregnant with Becker's child and frankly considering fooling around with someone who wasn't him. Which was goofy, really, because we were going to Richard's room to rest, right? To have a catnap before meeting a thug at midnight.

We walked along Parkwood Road, which ran across the top of the campus. The night was clear, and there was a fat, full moon hanging in the sky like a silver apple. There was nobody about but us, and we could see our breath.

"It's blizzarding in Kuskawa, I bet," Richard said.

"Mmmm. And my aunt and George will be curled up on the sofa in front of the woodstove, with Lug-nut and Rosie squashed in there, too. And Poe on his shelf, his head under a wing, snoring like a freight train."

"Ravens snore?" I'd told him about my family, the beasts as well as the people.

"Poe does. But then he thinks he's human."

"Do you miss your dogs?"

"Yes, a little bit, although it's nice once in a while not to have the responsibility—you know, walks, feeding them, paying attention to them—all that. I know I'm really lucky to have Susan and George take them while I'm away. I'd be wallowing in guilt if I'd had to leave them at a kennel."

"Separation anxiety, eh?"

"Yeah. And you know, once this is out," I said, patting my belly, "I suspect that the babysitting service is going to be a little less abundant. This feels like my last crack at freedom for a while."

"You're happy about the baby, though, aren't you?"

"Most of the time I am, I guess. More like overwhelmed though. Scared as hell. Wondering what on earth I think I'm doing, and what kind of mother I'll be."

"I think you'll be a great mother. Not that I know you, but what little I do know, you'll be great. Feisty, inventive. Incredibly loving."

"Wow," I said. "Thanks. I don't believe you, but thanks."

We headed down another road, which led towards a group of attractive, low-slung buildings, flanked by trees and shrubs. A sign said "The Courts", and gave a list of dozens of names of "courts", which I presumed were residences.

"I'm in Farthings Court," he said, and we veered off to the left. "Have you chosen a name for him or her yet?"

"I think it's a her," I said. "Well, I know it is, actually. Not that I had a thingy done—I've been a pain in the neck to my doctor, who wanted to do all sorts of tests because she says I'm a 'mature primagravida'—and doesn't that sound like a skin condition? I hate that medical science treats pregnancy like a disease."

"You strike me as the midwife type," he said. "You planning to have it at home?"

"I'd like to," I said. "At least, home meaning the farmhouse—not my place. It would probably be good to have, you know, hydro and running water."

"Yeah, that might be a good idea. So—names?"

"There's a fashion right now for calling kids by the place name of where they were conceived," I said. "You know, like Dakota or Africa."

"Uh-huh. So you're going to call her Kuskawa? Think there are any kids called Wawa? Moosonee?"

I snorted. "Becker's condo is on Dill Street," I said.

"Dilly? Hey—Pickle! Pickle's cute."

"I bought one of those baby name books, but it didn't help. They're all made-up things with weird spellings. I thought about naming her after my mom, Cecily, but there was way too much baggage."

"Hmm." Nice of him not to press for details.

"In my mind, she's the Sprog."

"That's a new one on me. What's it mean?"

"It's a family word for child, British slang, I guess. My aunt used it on me when I was small. It's sort of affectionate and goofy at the same time."

"You can't call your baby Sprog, Polly."

"No, it wouldn't look good on the school registration form, would it? Sprog Deacon."

"You'll never get her into private school that way."

"Seriously, though, I think Elizabeth is the best name for a girl, because she has all those options as an adult if she wants to change her name. Liz, Eliza, Betty, Beth, Lizbeth. And I like Bess. Bess is strong, I think."

"Bess Deacon. Has a nice ring to it. What does her father think?"

"Do you know, we've never discussed it."

"Really?"

"Really. We've been in a kind of stalemate for a while. We don't agree about the most basic stuff, like where she's going to live—where I'm going to live. Stuff like that."

"I see."

"Anyway, no—we haven't discussed the name. And Becker has a son already, whom he apparently is seeing right now, because I found out this morning that Becker is in Calgary, where his ex and his son are, although he didn't bother telling me, and I'm sorry, I shouldn't be blithering on about people you don't know."

"I don't mind. We're here. After you." Richard used a key to open a glass-fronted door which led into a pleasant lobby area. There were mailboxes, a reception desk (unattended), and carpeted floors—the usual middle-class apartment kind of space—cozy and reasonably clean. A short trip down a hallway, and Richard ushered me into his room, which

208

probably had its equivalent in every university in the world. On the left was a desk, a window, a closet with a mirror and a narrow single bed. On the right was the mirror image of the same thing.

"There's no roommate," he said. "Welcome to my private suite." The desk was covered with brochures and buffle from the conference, sketching materials and a small sketchbook, open at a lovely drawing of the Cathedral.

"When did you have time to do that?" I said.

"After you went back to your B&B," he said. "I carry that stuff with me all the time. It's better than a camera. I take rotten photos, and I think if you spend your time taking snapshots, you don't really see things. When you sketch them, you take the time to absorb all the details."

"May I?"

"Go ahead." His drawings were wonderful, clear, clean lines, just the right amount of shading. He stood behind me, quite close, while I looked though the book. At the beginning were some sketches of Kuskawa, including the Sikwan Falls as seen from Steamboat Theatre, a view I'd seen myself many times.

"These are amazing, Richard. Hey—you do have etchings. Hah! Of a sort."

"Explain that, would you?" he said. He was massaging my shoulders from behind, and my train of thought got thoroughly derailed in a matter of moments.

"It's one of those catchphrases. You know—'Do you want to come up and see my etchings?' The suave sophisticate seduces the innocent maiden?"

"I'm not all that suave."

"And I'm obviously not all that innocent." I turned around to face him. His eyes were very large and sort of luminous. He'd turned on the desk lamp, whose shade cast a golden glow over us. We kissed, long and slowly and deeply. He was quite a bit taller than I was, and his height seemed to make up for the sort of sideways cant we had to make to avoid squashing the Sprog. Or Bess, I suppose I should start calling her. "Is this a good idea?" I said.

"Well, we do have a couple of hours to kill."

"I'm way older than you, you know."

"Like that really bothers me."

"And you're not grossed out by my, you know, my being pregnant? It's hardly sexy."

"Are you kidding? You're so sexy it hurts." Five little words was all. Five little words I realized I'd been aching for—from Becker—heck, from anybody who was willing to tell me that I wasn't just a vessel all misshapen and grotesque, stretched out of all imagining by the load I was carrying. That I was Polly Deacon, a person in my own right, with or without the Sprog. And here was this incredibly handsome and interesting and intelligent (and young) man, touching me, caressing the back of my neck, telling me I was, well, attractive. And nothing short of a fire alarm was going to turn off the response it called up in me. Put the brakes on? Call a halt? I'd rather have eaten my own foot.

We moved to the narrow bed and stretched out on it. It was crowded, but it didn't seem to matter. Gently, we removed each other's clothing. The steam radiator by the window hissed companionably. Richard's body was thin, lithe and wiry. He had no body hair to speak of, except a soft nest of dark curls between his legs. He played his sensitive, artist's hands over my belly, smoothing and stroking.

"This is going to require some positioning," he said. "Excuse me, ma'am." He wasn't talking to me, either. The Sprog didn't appear to mind the company at all, as it turned out.

Later, we snoozed a bit. Richard had set his alarm for 11:15, to give us enough time to pick up the puppets at the Pilgrim's Rest and take a cab down to St. Peter's Street, where he said there was a path leading to the deserted Greyfriars. "One good thing about this," I murmured, before slipping away into sleep. "There's absolutely no chance of me getting pregnant."

Twenty-Three

Some change in eyesight is the case for some women—maybe a 10-20% deterioration or so. Within a few months of getting pregnant, they pull out the glasses that they wear ONLY when they're pregnant, and once their baby is delivered, the glasses go back into storage. But this change doesn't happen to all women.
-From *Big Bertha's Total Baby Guide*

"Won't the guy want to see the puppets, too, before he'll believe you?" We had made our way back into Canterbury and stopped off at the Pilgrim's Rest to pick up the puppet case. It was late, and there was no sign of Cedric or Mr. Binterhof. We tiptoed in, not wanting to make Cedric think there was another burglary in progress. I'd asked my host to take the case out of the safe for me earlier in the day, and I'd stashed it under the bed.

"I suppose he will, won't he?" I said. The police-puppet and the pregnant lady lay in their little coffin, face-up, looking a little apprehensive, I thought. "And he'll want to tear them apart, too, if he's looking for stashed drugs or secret microfiche or something."

"I really don't think this is a good idea," Richard said.

"It's the only way, you know. To make this crazy stuff stop. Trust me."

"I'm trying to. So, are you going to let him have the puppets, too?"

"I wasn't planning to let him have anything," I said. "I was just going to show him that the case was just a puppet case and nothing more. My theory is that if I brazen it out and really explain that I don't have what he's looking for, he'll get the picture."

"What about 'his people'? The ones he's working for? They may not take his word for it, you know."

"I guess you're right. Okay, he can have the case. But he's not getting the puppets. I'll take them home in a cardboard box." I lifted them out and placed them on the bed, side-by-side, their heads on the pillow, then closed the case and picked it up.

"And what if he does attack you, Polly? What if—just humour me for a second—what if you've read this thing all wrong, and he really is the guy who attacked Alma, and he really is a dangerous and ruthless criminal? There won't be much I can do about it if he pulls a knife on you or something. Or a gun. Have you really, really thought about what you're doing?"

I sighed and sat down on the bed. "I've been thinking about nothing else, Richard. This whole situation has totally wrecked my trip so far—I know that's selfish, seeing as at least I'm still alive and Alma isn't. But point one, I don't believe what happened to Alma had anything to do with the thug and the puppet case. And point two, if I don't confront this guy, he's going to wreck the rest of my trip, too."

"What about point three, that if you'd called the police, they'd be there to back you up and arrest the guy?"

"If the police were involved, they wouldn't let me near the place. You know that, and they'd just scare him away. Then he'd wait to get me alone again, and he'd be pretty mad when he did, and then he might really hurt me."

"You really don't have much confidence in the police, do you?"

"Frankly, no. I have too much experience with the real thing. They don't always get their man, you know."

"Well, at least take something with you for defence, just in case this guy turns out worse than you think."

"You have a gun handy?" I said.

"I have this," he said and handed me a small can of pepper spray.

"Where the heck did you get that?"

"I've had it ever since I started hiking in bear country," he said. "I keep it with me when I travel, too, in case of muggers."

"And how did you manage to get this past customs?"

"I keep it in with my deodorant and stuff. Nobody's noticed it yet."

"You know, this could get you a week or two in Guantanamo Bay, if you tried to smuggle it onto a U.S. flight," I said.

"That hardly applies here, Polly. Will you take it?"

"I'll keep it in my pocket, yes, if it'll make you feel better."

"It will. Thank you," he said. Actually, it made me feel better about this escapade as well, but I didn't say so.

I sighed once more, for effect, and got to my feet. "Okay, let's go."

*　　*　　*

The full moon painted the scene silver. It was eerily bright until we got to the alleyway that would lead us to the ruined monastery house. Then the shadows kicked in. Richard had a keychain flashlight, but I wouldn't let him use it. "We have to split up now," I said. I was feeling nervous, but tried not to let it show. "Is there another way in to this place?" We were whispering.

"There's another path along the river that leads to a private house on St. Peter's Street," Richard said. "It ends in someone's garden, and it's blocked off from the main road the same way

Cedric's courtyard is, with a high wooden fence you can't climb over. The guy will probably come this way himself, but Polly—he's probably already here, waiting for you."

We stepped as quietly as we could along the path and came to the river—a trickle, really, with walls on either side—a deep channel cut into the earth. The moonlight glinted off the sluggish water below. There was a little bridge over the river, and in the near distance, Greyfriars, a black outline against the sky. The weird thing about moonlight, especially when it's really strong, is that it leaches out colour so that everything looks like a black and white photograph.

"I'll go on ahead, Richard. You follow me, but do the cloak-and-dagger thing, okay? Be stealthy. Don't be seen. He'll be looking for me, but I don't think he'll expect me to have a companion."

"You don't, eh?" he whispered. "How naïve can you get?" I chose to pretend not to hear him. Okay, I was being naïve. And probably really stupid, too, but I had got it into my head that the only way to shake off my pursuer was to meet with him and tell the truth. Too many situations get weird because people make mistakes about each other, good guys and bad guys alike. If the thug was under the impression that I had been supposed to hand over some pre-arranged something-or-other, and I hadn't, well, he was perfectly justified in feeling frustrated about it. Okay, maybe his tactics lacked refinement, but we can't all be James Bond. I suspected that he was just some dumb mook who had been hired to take delivery of a package and wanted to do a good job. You may think that this line of reasoning was insane, but I believed (and I still do) that even the villains of the piece thought that their actions were reasonable.

As I approached the Greyfriars building, I got one of those living-history neck prickles—a nice feeling, in spite of the gothic context. It was a beautiful structure, a tall and thin house of ancient brick, built, as the guide book had said, directly over the river, which ran underneath the double arches at its base, both pointed at the top like church doorways. There were no lights showing, which was no surprise—I didn't expect that the thug had a key to the place. The guidebook had suggested that it was a ruin, but it looked pretty solid to me. I wondered what it would be like to live there—it had been built hundreds and hundreds of years ago. Would it creak with memories? Would you be able to hear the trickle of the water beneath the floor? And what was buried in the silt in the river? Coins and bottles and broken pottery, I'd bet. Stuff that people, maybe the monks, had tossed out the window and into the river, or dropped by mistake. Museum stuff now, but then, it had just been something to throw away. And hundreds of years from now, people will be regarding the stuff we throw away in a similar light—excavating our landfill sites, all excited to find a preserved newspaper or an ancient, twentieth century shoe. The garbage of history is thrilling because it confirms that our ancestors were just like us, litterbugs and hopelessly human.

I wasn't trying to be stealthy. In fact, I was making sure I could be heard and seen, swinging the puppet case at my side, like I was going on a midsummer picnic, not a care in the world. I didn't want the thug to miss me. On the opposite side of the river, across from the building, there was a small field, a meadow, really, then a fence backing onto the gardens of private houses on the street beyond. The field looked empty, just an expanse of dry grass, with a mist rising from it. It was not cold, but I was shivering anyway. On my side of the river, there were trees, the walls of a garden much closer to the river, above which I could see the tops of some old greenhouses. And beyond that, a number of trenches dug into the ground.

That must be where the archaeological excavation was going on, the one that Mr. Binterhof was working on. There were trees and deep shadows, and I suddenly rather wished I had asked Richard for his flashlight. But of course, he was right behind me—just out of sight. I didn't dare turn around to see. It would have given him away. But I was glad he was at my back, because I felt exposed and a tad vulnerable.

That was when I tripped. Polly goes down with a thump, not hurting the Sprog, thank goodness, but grazing her knees. I scrabbled to grab the puppet case, which teetered on the edge of the riverbank. There was a jingle of change as the contents of my pocket spilled out on the ground. I scooped up earth and coins and shoved it all back in again. It would have been rotten to lose Earlie's lucky ha'penny at that point—I needed all the luck I could get. And of course it was right then that I had a flash of Alma's body, crumpled at the foot of Becket's tomb, oozing blood, and I started to waffle about my certainty that she had been attacked by the Right-to-Lifers.

I walked as boldly as I could up to the entranceway of the Greyfriars building. Still seeing no sign of movement in the shadows, I found a low stone wall and sat upon it. Then I waited. I suspected that the thug was probably waiting, too. Maybe hiding out there somewhere and watching me, although I didn't feel watched. The place was profoundly empty. I listened with all my concentration, could hear a car pass by on the street beyond the line of houses on the other side of the field, listened for footsteps on the dry grass, or a rustling in the hedge on the other side of the trenches, but there was nothing. The moonlight was quite strong enough for me to see the face of my watch, a clunky thing that I'd had for years, and both hands pointed straight up. Exactly midnight.

According to the guidebook, the Greyfriars monastery had

stood long ago on the grounds in front of me. Four or five feet below the surface, they had found a floor of black and white clay tiles, beautifully preserved, and the traces of a colonnade, what must have been a cloister-walk. Seven hundred years ago, little monks in dark habits had paced about among the arches, praying perhaps, or scurrying off on some important errand, humans going about their business. Again, as when I'd been underground in the subterranean Roman museum, I was struck by the peculiarity of the earth, the way it built up, seemingly all by itself, and buried what had originally been at the surface. Further below, there was the Roman stuff, then the medieval layer on top of that, then the Renaissance layer, each subsequent era sandwiched together like a cake, with chocolate loam and chalky clay in between. In another few hundred years, the twentieth century layer would be covered over, too. And our precious linoleum floors and discarded washing machines would be discovered with whoops of delight by future diggers, lifted out carefully ("it fell apart in our hands, but I think it was an early device for sending messages, what they called a typewriter") and displayed in museums. Costumed interpreters, dressed in ancient bell-bottoms and quaint tank-tops, would explain to schoolchildren how the people in the olden days used to sit in front of this box, made of a material they called plastic, and watch the pictures that flickered across its screen.

There was a disturbance in the quiet. I felt it more than heard it. Beyond the hedge, the setting-down of feet, heavy steps, steps that weren't trying to be silent. He was coming. I gripped the handle of the puppet case tighter and stood up so he would see me. A chilly sweat broke out on my forehead and I found I was panting. The Sprog, Bess, did a little loop-de-loop and drummed at my bladder.

"There's no sign of him," D.C. Potts said and switched on

a powerful flashlight, pointing it straight into my face and blinding me. "We've had the area secure for more than two hours. You've been stood up, Ms. Deacon."

Richard appeared then, along with another two police officers, and then a few more. One popped out from behind a bush, another from an alcove in the stone wall, and two from the trenches. The place was alive with cops. The only thing that prevented me from having a huge hissy fit was the fact that I hadn't sensed them at all. I'd been convinced the place was empty, deserted. Unless the thug had been psychic, he wouldn't have known either, I was sure of it. Unless he'd seen them getting into position two hours beforehand.

"I'm really sorry, Polly," Richard said. "I couldn't let you risk it, eh? And I'm no good in a fight."

"When did you call them?" I said through clenched teeth. He was about to find out how well he could manage a fight, because he was about to have one.

"At the pub, when I went for a whizz. I had to—you do get that, don't you?"

"What I get is that you're someone I shouldn't have trusted," I said and turned my back on him. He'd been wonderful in bed—tender and considerate and remarkably sensitive. Too bad it didn't extend to the upright position.

"We'll leave the case here, Ms. Deacon," Potts said, taking it from me and placing it carefully on the stone wall. "You never know, he may still attempt to pick it up, and we'll leave a couple of men to watch it. And if you'll come with me, we'll get a statement from you about this little incident this afternoon at Eastbridge. We've already talked to the priest."

"I should think he's probably miles away at this point—not the priest—the thug," I said. "He'll wait until this dies down, and then come looking for me again. Thanks a lot."

"You didn't really think you could just give him your suitcase and he'd toddle off all happy, did you?"

"Well, actually, yes, I did. Now he knows that the police are involved, which will probably piss him off and make him think that whatever-it-was is still in my possession," I said.

"And what do you think that whatever-it-was might be?" Potts said.

"I don't know. The whole thing is a mistake—a misunderstanding."

"Well, come along. Let's get a hot cup of tea into you. You're shivering."

Richard came too, but I was not speaking to him.

*   *   *

I was in bed by two. I'd answered Potts's questions, signed a statement and given yet another description of the thug. They had a police artist work up a sketch of him, which was reasonably accurate, I thought, until the artist herself muttered that it looked like every single white van man she'd ever seen wreaking havoc on England's motorways.

"I'd arrest the lot," she said to Potts. "It would make everybody very happy." Maybe she was annoyed because she had been dragged out of bed, I don't know.

I eventually accepted Richard's apology. Maybe the midnight tryst had been a stupid idea, but I was still privately very pissed off.

"Will you let me take you to lunch tomorrow?" he said. "There's a seminar on glove puppetry at two we could check out."

"I'm going to be busy with something," I said. "But we can go to the banquet together, if you want." The wrap-up of the conference was planned for Saturday night, with a gala show presented by the Muppetworks contingent (I adore Muppets) and no doubt a bunch of interminable speeches from the organizers. By Saturday night, I figured I'd be over my snit. But I didn't want to see Richard until then. Besides, I was planning a little side trip, and I didn't want him along.

I was feeling guilty (predictably) about getting romantically (or at least carnally) involved with a non-Becker person, and I'd promised my wayward Canadian policeman a favour. I had some ashes to scatter, and I decided I'd take the train over to Eastbourne to do the thing on Saturday. I also wanted to look up Becker's great aunt, whose address was stashed away in my bag. If she wasn't too frail, perhaps she would like to come with me. That task completed, I'd be able to attend the final puppetry banquet with a clear conscience. Sort of clear, anyway, because I admit I did think that Richard might possibly be interested in another, you know, catnap, after the public festivities were over. I was mad at him, but not that mad. That probably means I'm a bad person, or at least an immoral one.

In spite of what the child-Catholic in me would have called a state of sin, I had it in mind to attend the service at the Cathedral in the morning on Sunday. Then I had a flight back to Canada that night. That's provided the thug, the one who stood me up, didn't interfere with my plans. I was thoroughly disgusted with the whole business, to tell you the truth, and grumpy as hell. At the same time, I was still buzzing from having enjoyed some extremely satisfying sex with Richard. This was a weird combination of emotions, which may very well be the reason for my clouded judgement, at least in retrospect.

Richard seemed pathetically pleased that I was willing to join him at the banquet. "We'll sit with the Mermaid people," he said. "It'll be the Canadian table, eh?" It suddenly struck me how young he was, and I squirmed a little. He was like a Labrador retriever puppy, all bouncy and eager. There were times when Becker's remoteness and involvement in his own affairs were exactly what I wanted. Conflicted? You bet. I bade Richard goodnight at the door of the B&B and did not invite him in. Then I tiptoed upstairs and crawled into bed, so wiped I didn't even bother to move the puppets, just shoved them to one side. Then I fell asleep with my hand on the policeman puppet, cuddling him to me like a teddy bear.

Twenty-Four

In Elizabethan times, records of the area around the Borough of London estimated that approximately 38% of women accused of felony during the early modern era claimed to be pregnant in order to escape the gallows.

-From the history section of *Big Bertha's Total Baby Guide*

Edward Millbank Becker weighed about four pounds, in his cremated and pulverized state. The blue velvet drawstring bag he came in would have served as a very nice purse or shoe bag for somebody, once he no longer needed it. I had gone out to the shops early on Saturday morning and purchased a small day pack, put Mr. Becker Senior at the bottom of it, and a few sundries on top, including my toothbrush, wallet (the new one that was wide enough to carry those enormous English banknotes), the Pez-phone (because I was taking the trine) and an extra pair of socks, in case my feet got wet. My aunt Susan had taught me that. While the writer Douglas Adams maintained that the most essential item in the traveller's arsenal was a towel, Aunt Susan knew better. You'll always be glad of a dry pair of socks, and you can't wear a towel on your feet.

The railway person behind the ticket counter was extremely helpful when I asked about the most direct route to Eastbourne. Although the trip as the crow flies was only about eighty kilometers (about the distance from Laingford to Barrie, in Ontario terms, an afternoon's shopping trip), I was told I would have to change trains twice, and it would take two hours. Still, I didn't have a car, and while Cedric had offered to drive me there in his Reliant Robin, I declined, shuddering at the notion of sitting in the three-wheeler on a major motorway, just asking to be squashed by a white van man. I bought a ticket at the Canterbury West station, hopped aboard the 9:44 (which was so empty, I didn't have to use my Pez-phone at all) and settled back into my seat with a sigh. In a way, it felt good to get away from things for a bit, to escape the sensation of oppression I'd had since the visit to the Eastbridge Hospital. My delight in things ancient had been replaced in the ensuing hours with a closing-in feeling, exacerbated by the dark, narrow streets of Canterbury. I wanted some open spaces, and according to Richard's guidebook, which I'd borrowed the night before, Eastbourne was just the place.

Eastbourne is situated at the foot of the South Downs in East Sussex. The South Downs run from Winchester in Hampshire to Eastbourne and are designated an Area of Outstanding Natural Beauty.

Beachy Head is the most famous part of the Eastbourne Downland. Beachy Head rises 162 metres (530 feet) above the sea below and is the highest chalk sea cliff in Britain. The main reason for Beachy Head's popularity is the wonderful panoramic view that can be seen from the cliff top. If you look east you see the beaches and town of Eastbourne, the Pier and the Harbour, and then on to Pevensey Bay and Hastings and, on an exceptionally clear day, Dungeness in Kent, nearly 40 miles away.

What the guidebook didn't mention, but Cedric did, was that Beachy Head was England's most notorious suicide spot. Apparently, throwing yourself from the top of a 530 foot cliff was a pretty foolproof method of dispatching yourself, and people did it all the time. Luckily, Mr. Becker Senior would suffer no ill effects from his own encounter with the cliff, although it occurred to me that I'd better be damned careful where I put my feet while I was in mid-scatter.

Cedric had packed me some sandwiches, which I munched reflectively as the train rattled through the Kent countryside. The region was, even in February, a place that lived up to its guidebook billing as an area of "outstanding natural beauty". Kent was known as the garden of England. There were lots and lots of farms, hop-kilns like pointy hats rising out of the landscape, vineyards and orchards. As the train moved towards the downs, beautiful soft hills rose and fell, pastel-coloured in the cool winter sunshine, gentle browns and weary greens and the occasional golden patch. The trees in England are so very different from Canadian ones. They were tamed, somehow, as if they'd had to put up with the proximity to humans for so long that they'd knuckled under and agreed to behave themselves. They were bare of leaves, of course, but uniform and rounded, creating vistas and views that were straight out of pictures by Constable. I set the picture I saw out of the train window against my mind's eye view of Northern Ontario, as seen from a VIA rail car on the way to Thunder Bay, a trip I'd once taken to work at Magnus Theatre. Then, I'd been staggered by the sheer expanse of uninhabited forest, hectares and hectares of tall pines and dense, muskeggy thickets. I suppose that England, once, had been like that. Back in pre-Roman times. Back when the English forest was alive with boars and stags and, if legend was correct, lions. (Probably not true about the lions. Dragons, maybe, though.)

It would be another seven hundred years or more before my Canadian landscape looked so thoroughly managed. By which time, the layers of history, as they were in Canterbury, would be striated and layered, each layer telling something about the people who had cut down the trees, tamed the wilderness and struggled to survive. A railway person came down the aisle at that point, offering drinks and snacks from a cart. I had a hankering for a bag of chips [packet of crisps— ref. Brent] and reached into my trousers pocket to find a handful of change, mixed with the earth I'd inadvertently scooped up the night before, on the grounds of Greyfriars.

I fished out a pound coin for my crisps, and before putting the whole mess back in my pocket, made sure Earlie's lucky ha'penny was still there. It was, and in addition, there was something else. Another coin—an unfamiliar one.

It was small and dirty. I spat on it and scrubbed it clean with my sleeve, revealing a picture of a person in profile, wearing a crown and a ruffle around her neck. The lettering said Regina Elizabeth and some other Latin that I couldn't make out. On the other side was a shield and some more Latin stuff. My hand shook a little. This was not something from a Cracker Jack box. It was an Elizabethan coin. Elizabeth reigned in the 1500s, I knew, more or less. Which meant that the scrap of metal in my hand had been pocket change to somebody, five hundred years ago. And how had it come to be sitting on the path at Greyfriars? And what remarkable circumstance had made me, in the dark, pick it up? Had it lain there in the grass beside the River Stour for hundreds of years, missed and ignored by centuries of visitors, centuries of passersby? Had some poor Elizabethan soul dropped it out of his or her pocket? Had it made a difference to lose it? Maybe it had been coughed up from below—heaved up from its Elizabethan layer of earth by the frost. I would never know. Before I'd cleaned it, it had just looked like a lump of earth, a thin pebble, or a bottle cap. It staggered me. It also made me feel incredibly lucky. I had found a treasure, although it was probably only worth a few dollars on the numismatic market—if that. But I had found it, or it had found me, in the dark. Now I would have a lucky coin to give the Sprog. Bess, I mean—named after Good Queen Bess herself—a splendid omen.

I changed trains at Ashford, and again at Hastings, by which point I could watch the sea from my window, the great, pewter-grey expanse that was whipped up into stiff waves by the February winds. It was clouding over a bit, and it looked like there might be rain or even snow on its way. It was going to be nippy atop the cliff, and I had a sudden image of trying to scatter Becker Senior and having all his ashy bits blown back in my face. Comical, but not very pleasant.

It was freezing cold outside the train station, and for the first time since coming to England, I absorbed the fact that it was winter, and while the country didn't have the kind of snow I was used to, it was still pretty bitter. I remembered my conversation with Dimmy at the pub back home, when I'd insisted that I wanted to do some walking on the trails in England. I had nurtured this mental picture of myself, with a hickory stick in hand, a kerchief over my head like the Queen wears when she's out with the corgis, striding along the top of some heath covered hill. Har de har. At least it would be unlikely that I'd have company up there on the famous cliff. And I didn't think I'd be hiking to get up there—I'd be taking a cab.

But before I scattered Becker Senior, I had to go and visit Becker's great aunt Edith. I had her full name and address in the zippered pocket of my purse, where I'd put Earlie's and Mr. Fogbow's business cards. I took it out now and peered at it.

Edith Taylor, it said, the sister of the deceased man's mom. She must be at least a hundred, I thought, but Becker had said she might still be alive, although she hadn't responded to his message about his father's death. She and Becker's dad had exchanged Christmas cards, that was all. Becker had said she was pen pals with his mom, but not with Becker Senior, and obviously, she and her great-nephew had not done any major bonding in the short time they'd had together in Canada, when she'd come to attend Becker's Mom's funeral in '97. Becker had told me that she stayed overnight in a hotel in Calgary and had flown home the next day. They'd shared a word or two at the reception, and then Becker's dad had helped her into a taxi, and off she'd gone. Still, he figured he would have heard if she had died.

I tried to do some math in my head, but that never works for me, or at least, I make horrible mistakes, so I fished out a pencil and did some subtraction. Edward Senior had been seventy at his death and had been evacuated to Canada during the Second World War, when his father was a Royal Air Force pilot. If he was the child of very young parents, let's say in their twenties, they might both be in their nineties if they were still alive. If Becker's deceased grandmother had a younger sister, Edith, she could be anywhere from seventy to ninety—I knew some families had aunts and uncles that were younger than their nieces and nephews, or the same age. It all depended on the longevity and fertility of their parents. This family tree stuff was alien to me. I had never researched my own roots, choosing instead the path of least resistance, denial and selective memory loss. I didn't have any living relatives in Ireland or in Canada except Aunt Susan. She had told me so, and my curiosity went no further.

So, I was looking for a seriously senior citizen, Edith Taylor, who lived at 52 Mossy Lane, in Eastbourne. There was no telephone number. I went to a public telephone kiosk (not one of the famous red ones, I'm afraid. I still hadn't seen one and feared they must really be extinct) and looked her up in the phone book. She wasn't there, at least there were three Taylors, a C., a Fred and a Dr. K. I didn't bother trying them, as none of their addresses was Mossy Lane. But an elderly lady might choose not to be in the book, or she might even choose not to have a phone. I decided to risk an unannounced visit, anyway. If I couldn't find her, I would still scatter her nephew's remains. I just thought she might like the chance to join in. It would feel strange to do it by myself, considering that I'd never even met the man. I hailed a cab and gave the address to the cab driver [the license on the back of the seat said: Hassan], who nodded silently and did not speak a word for the entire journey. It began to rain. The cab was stuffy and the windows steamed up at once, as Hassan had the heating set on tropical. I was obviously destined to arrive at every place I visited in England in the midst of a downpour, so I couldn't see where I was going, nor where I'd been.

The cab stopped, and Hassan turned around and glowered at me.

"Is this Mossy Lane?" I said, inanely. He nodded and growled "two pound." I handed over a two-pound coin and a fifty p. tip—not that he'd been a delightful travelling companion, but driving a cab in Eastbourne, or anywhere, has got to be a drag, and tips make it easier.

"I'll wite if y'wonk," he said. This surprised me, until I wiped a clear space in the passenger window and looked out. The street was taken up by a long row of council houses (I knew the term from watching *EastEnders*), what we'd call projects or municipally subsidized housing. Each front door was about nine feet from its neighbour, which I figured would have made the interiors indescribably narrow and probably very dark. The front doorsteps attached directly onto the public sidewalk. There were no front gardens, and no privacy either, although most of the front windows were covered in lace curtains, football flags or blinds. The sidewalk was littered with broken children's toys and dustbins. What had prompted Hassan's offer to stick around was the obvious fact that nobody was living at number 57. The windows were boarded up, for one thing, and the sooty marks above the windows indicated that there had been a fire. The houses on each side of 57, oddly, didn't seem to have been damaged by the blaze, though, and I saw a flicker of movement at number 59, next door.

"Oh, I see. Thanks. Yes, would you mind waiting? I'll need a ride back to, well, I don't know, but I'll need a ride somewhere, and it's not a day for walking."

"Beastly out, innit?" Hassan said. "Corsall wite, luv." His Cockney accent was so thick, it took me a moment to understand him. I gave him a cheery grin and squelched out onto the street. I knocked at the door of 57, more for form's sake than anything else, and listened for any movement inside, but there was nothing, and anyway, the hiss of the rain on the street and the sound of children's wails coming from next door were too loud to have been able to hear anything else. A small pane of glass had once graced the door, but it was boarded over, too. I peered through a crack where the wood didn't quite meet the frame and saw nothing but blackness beyond. As I moved my head away, I caught the distinct whiff of burned things, a wet and horribly lonely smell that caught at the back of my throat.

My knock at the door of 59 was answered immediately by a young, thin-lipped woman with unlikely red hair scraped back from her face into a ponytail. She looked tired and defeated, and the two small children hanging from her like limpets suggested the reason.

"Looking for Miss Taylor, are you?" she said. "I figured you was. Nobody takes taxi rides round here."

"There was a fire, I take it," I said.

"Last month," the woman said. "Luckily, she had one of them smoke alarms, and they got it in time, so the whole row wasn't burned up in our beds."

"And Miss Taylor?"

"Oh, she's all right, though by rights she shouldn't be. Daft as a brush, that one, and better off where she is now. She left a pot on the cooker, didn't she? Could have killed us all."

"I'm glad you're all okay," I said. "Where is she now?"

"You American?" I experienced that familiar bristle that Canadians feel when accused of being a U.S. citizen, but I suppressed it and spoke gently.

"No, Canadian."

"Relative, are you? She was always going on about her nephew in Canada. You ought to have visited before she went barmy, though. Not much use now. She won't know you."

"She wouldn't know me anyway," I said. "A friend of mine's her great-nephew, that's all."

"Well, she's in Fairview Hospital," the woman said. "And she's not long for this world, so you'd better hurry. And if you came expecting anyfink out of her, you're wasting your time. She lost the lot."

"I was just hoping to talk to her," I said.

"Well, best of luck," she said. "I'd ask you in to tea, but our Doug has got the flu, and I've got my hands full."

"No, I see that," I said. "I, er, thanks for telling me about Miss Taylor. And I'm glad the fire wasn't worse."

"You're not the only one," she said. "The National Health ought to have taken her away long ago—she was a danger to herself and the rest of us. Still, she was right enough before she went dotty. Refined, like. Used to have us to tea." A masculine roar came from the back of the house, along with a waft of cat's pee and the smell of cooked cabbage. "That's Doug," the woman said, rolling her eyes. "Be seeing yer." She closed the door and I stepped back, placing myself directly underneath a cold cascade of water from the little roof over the front step.

"Where to, then?" Hassan said, when I climbed back into the welcome warmth of the taxi, where I immediately began to steam, like a pudding.

"Fairview Hospital," I said. Not that I expected much of the visit. In the course of a five minute conversation, my red-headed informant had referred to Miss Taylor as daft, dotty and barmy. I didn't need Brent's lexicon to figure that one out.

Twenty-Five

There will be trouble for the pregnant woman who attends a funeral.

-From the "Superstitions" section of *Big Bertha's Total Baby Guide*

I don't like to mention it," Hassan said, "but I thort you'd like to know that there's some bloke bin following us since I picked you up at the station."

I twisted around to see, but the rear window of the cab was all fogged up.

"White van," Hassan said. "Tosser's bin on my tail, waited round the corner when you was at the door of that house, and he's still there."

"Oh, Lord," I said. "Can you lose him?" Hassan gave me a most beautiful smile, as if he had been waiting all his career for a line like that. " 'Ang on," he said. The next fifteen minutes were some of the most frightening of my life. Hassan obviously had experience as a stunt driver in the movies. He floored it, spinning his tires, deked into a back alley, deked again into what seemed to be somebody's private courtyard, knocking over a potted plant, and then back out on the street again. He hopped curbs. He did loop de loops in side streets, and I lost all track of where we were (not that I know downtown Eastbourne at all, but you know what I mean). Eventually he ended up down by the beachfront, in front of an imposing, Victorian brick building. I uncurled my hand from the handle-thing thoughtfully provided above the rear window and flexed my fingers.

"Orl right?"

I nodded, unable to speak.

"Lost 'im back there somewhere," Hassan said. "And this is Fairview. 'Op out quick, and I'll see if I can find him again and give him another bit of a chase."

"You are a prince among men," I said and pushed a lot of money into his hand.

"If you need a cab again, call this number and ask for me special," he said, handing me a card.

"I will. Thanks." I hopped out quick, as instructed, and he screamed away in a shower of pebbles and water. I scanned the horizon for white vans and didn't see any. Instead, I saw a genteel neighbourhood, full of elegant houses set back upon landscaped lawns. This was a posh district, and I wondered if I'd been directed to the right place. A sign certainly informed me that this was The Fairview Hospital, but if this was a "National Health" institution, a government funded place, it certainly didn't look it from the outside. It was a sprawling building, set in the middle of an extensive property. There was a brick wall, shielding it from the street, and beyond it, trees and shrubs, not overly manicured, but kept presentable, probably to keep the upper-class neighbours happy.

The entrance was forbidding, with a massive front door, but as soon as I was inside, I recognized that this, for all its external dignity, was a warehouse. No amount of disinfectant and cleaning fluid can mask the smell of the ill and elderly, no high ceilings or marble floors can hide the depressing atmosphere that gathers around a bunch of people waiting to die. I was directed by a uniformed receptionist down a long, echoing corridor and into a public ward. There were beds lined up in rows on each side of the ward. Curtains provided for privacy of a sort, but most of them were open, and the people lying in the beds were all very old, most of them motionless. There was the occasional mumble or cry, which was amplified, echoing like the sound track for some film about Bedlam. In the distance, I could hear the clatter of dishes. It must have been nearly lunch time, and there was the smell of soup in the air—institutional soup, mixing with the smell of age and illness. Between each bed, tall, narrow windows reached from waist height to ceiling, letting in the grudging grey light from the February rainstorm outside. I felt like I'd been transported back a century or more. The nurses all wore the kinds of uniforms with those apron things across the bosom and stiff white caps.

"Can I help you?" a nurse asked, touching my shoulder from behind me.

"Yes—um. Yes. I'm looking for Edith Taylor, please."

The nurse nodded, once, and led me down the rows, coming to rest at a bed like all the others, the curtains open, and a very small, white-haired figure lying perfectly still upon it, her hands folded on the sheet which covered her. Her eyes were closed, and she was snoring.

"Edith's not had any visitors since she arrived," the nurse said. [Name tag: Nurse Hopkins.] "She's lucid today, so you're in luck. We'll just wake her up, then. Are you a relative?"

"Her great-nephew's a friend of mine. I came to ask her something. Is she able to go out, at all?"

"Oh, no, miss. She fell, you·know, in the fire. Her hip's gone, and she can't get about."

"Too bad. She's lucid, you say. What's she…er, got?"

"Well, she's not all there, you know. Senile dementia, really."

"Alzheimer's?"

"Similar, though that's not quite it. Edith? Edith, there's someone here to see you, dear," Nurse Hopkins said, gently touching the sleeping woman's shoulder. At least she wasn't shouting, so maybe Edith Taylor's hearing was okay. That was good, I reflected, a trifle selfishly. I didn't want to have to bellow at her.

The woman's eyes flew open at once. They were a pale, milky green, with a sparkle in them that made me think of Becker in a frisky mood. "Someone to see me? Nonsense. Who on earth would want to see me?" she said. Her voice was strong and imperious, with a refined accent, as the red-haired neighbour had suggested. She sounded like the Queen Mum.

"Henrietta? What have you got yourself up in that outfit for, you silly girl? And where's my tea?"

"She sometimes thinks I'm her maid," Nurse Hopkins whispered to me. "I just go along with it. It makes her happy." Aloud, she said, "Your tea is just coming, Madam. You have a visitor." Then she nudged me.

"Miss Taylor, my name is Polly Deacon," I said. Miss Taylor sat up slowly, helped by Nurse Hopkins, who plumped up her pillows and settled her comfortably, making pleasant little nursy-noises the while. For all its dreariness, the Hospital at least had caring staff. I wondered how long Edith would have lasted on a stone platform in the undercroft of the Eastbridge hospital, back in the days of Thomas Becket.

"Polly Deacon," Miss Taylor said. "I don't know you, do I? Where's your calling card?" She squinted at me and cocked her head to the side, like a white-haired terrier.

"No, we've never met. I—just a sec." I rummaged in my purse for one of my cards, and then handed it over. She took it impatiently and glared at it.

"This should have been presented on a tray, you know. You can't get good help any more." She tossed the card down on the bed. "So—speak up, girl. What do you want?"

"I'm a friend of your great-nephew, Mark Becker, in Canada." Something slid away from her eyes, as if they had been a set of windows, and someone had drawn the curtain back. Her face changed, softened.

"My sister's grandson? The policeman? Fancy that. I've not seen him since his mother's funeral. Lovely woman, his mum. Is he here, too?"

"No, but he asked me to get in touch with you. There's some sad news that you might not have received."

"I'm eighty-eight years old," Miss Taylor said with some spirit. Whatever past moment she had been reliving was gone, I thought. She was here, now. "There's no sense putting on that special voice for my benefit. Someone's died, I expect."

"Well, yes."

"Hmmph." She made a little snorty noise through her nose, the kind Mr. Fogbow on the plane had made. And Cedric, too. It must be an English thing, like that conversational tic "sort of" (pronounced as one word—soot-uv, with the double 'o' as in book), that everybody seemed to use, adding it as a filler for a pause, like our interrogative "eh?". "There's hardly anyone left that's not dead," Miss Taylor said. "Who is it this time?"

"Your nephew, I guess. Edward Becker. He died in October."

"Oh, yes. I expect I was told about that," she said. "I went over there, you know, when his wife, Emily, died. Lovely woman. She wrote such delightful letters, and I wanted to see Canada before I popped off. It's a very flat country, isn't it?"

"Parts of it," I said. Miss Taylor was hardly what I'd call dotty, I thought. A bit repetitive, perhaps, but sharp as a tack, otherwise. At least, some of the time.

"My sister, Gertie, always wanted to go to Canada after her boy emigrated, but she never quite managed it," Miss Taylor said. "I went for her sake, really, though at eighty-five, it was a bit of a palaver. Nephew Edward was done up with grief over his wife, poor dear, but wouldn't let it show, of course, being a Becker."

"Becker men are like that," I said.

"And he did so hate everything English, you know. Including me, I'm afraid to say. It was rather awkward."

"He hated England? Didn't he always want to come back and visit?"

She snorted again, which set off a fit of coughing that made me glance around for Nurse Hopkins, who had glided away on crepe-soled feet. Miss Taylor waved a very thin, claw-like hand in the air to tell me she was okay. "No, no," she gasped. "I'm all right. Just pour me a glass of water, there's a dear. You made me laugh, and that always brings on the old dreaded lurgy." I did so, and she took a swig. After a moment, she took a deep breath and settled down into her pillows again. "Edward Becker most certainly did not want to come and visit," she said. "Why, he wouldn't even come back for his mother's funeral, although I offered to pay his way. I was," she added, fixing me with a beady eye, "quite well off in those days, you know. Before I lost it all on the stock market."

"That's odd," I said. "Mark—your great-nephew—said his dad wanted his ashes scattered at Beachy Head. That's why I'm here, and why I came to see you, actually, to see if you wanted to come with me. I never met him, eh, and I feel kind of funny doing it by myself."

"Nonsense," Miss Taylor said. "That little lad was terrified of heights. He hated the cliffs around here. I remember we took him up to the head for a picnic the day before he was evacuated, and he had the screaming ab-dabs and had to be taken home. He was about eight, then. A very peculiar little boy. He never really forgave Gertie and Horace for sending him away, I think. Went back to Canada after the war just as soon as he could."

"Becker said he used to play up on Beachy Head."

"Hmmph. Not on your life. He liked fields, did little Edward, fields and cows. He was always very fond of cows. Which I suppose is why he liked your big, flat Canada so much."

"That's very weird," I said. "He could have, you know, changed his mind about it. Maybe a bit of nostalgia?"

"I don't think that boy would be capable of changing his mind about anything," Miss Taylor said. "He wouldn't know a bit of nostalgia if it bit him on the bottom. Else he'd have come over when Gertie died. And when Horace did. And he would have answered my letters, which he never did. His wife did, instead. Dear Emily. No, you mark my words, he wouldn't come back while he was alive, and he certainly wouldn't have wanted to come back when he was dead."

"You wouldn't like to come up to do this scattering-thing with me anyway, would you? We could take a taxi." I really liked her, this Miss Taylor. And I couldn't imagine why anybody might think she was dotty, or barmy or whatever. I wanted to take her home with me.

"Sweet of you to ask me, dear, but I can't even manage a trip to the WC these days," she said. "I fell, you know, and there was something about a fire, and now look at me. Sitting in storage courtesy of the National Elf." She gave me a wicked, gap-toothed grin. "Have you got him with you? Old Nephew Edward?"

"Right here," I said, hefting my day pack. "You want to see him?"

Snortle again. "No, no. I've seen enough ashes to last me out, I think. But do come back after you've done the deed, and have another little visit, won't you? It's nice to have a visitor. I'll have Henrietta turn out the blue drawing room, and we can have a proper tea."

"I will. Do you need anything? I could bring it when I come."

"Just a new body, dear. That would be nice. This one's getting a bit shopworn." She snorted again, then fell suddenly fast asleep, as if someone had turned a light off. I panicked for a moment, thinking our conversation had killed her, but Nurse Hopkins was there, right behind me.

"It's all right," she said, softly. "She does that. And when she wakes, you know, she'll not remember a scrap of what you both said. I'm glad you caught her on a good day."

"So am I," I said, heaving myself to my feet and picking up the remains of Edward Becker Senior. "So am I."

Twenty-Six

Remember that it is very important to discuss your plans for exercise with your health care provider. If you are experiencing any problems with your pregnancy, exercise is not advised.
-From *Big Bertha's Total Baby Guide*

I wandered back down the echoing hallway of the hospital, wondering what on earth to do next. Should I go up to Beachy Head and scatter the remains of Mark Becker's father or not? According to Edith, that would have been the last thing he would have wanted. According to the dead man's son, it was his final and dearest wish. Now, I'm not one to set much significance on a pile of ashes. I figure that once a person has died, what's left is just an empty shell of organic material, and it doesn't much matter what's done with it. Funerals, in my opinion, are for those of us who are left behind, in order to assimilate the fact that the dead person is, well, dead. However, it had seemed very important to Becker that I do this thing, and I'd given my word that I would. I may not be particularly superstitious about human remains, but I am about promises. I was feeling guilty about my indiscretion with Richard, and although I admit I was open to the possibility of repeating it later that evening, I also had a sense that it wouldn't be so bad, wouldn't seem like such a betrayal, if I completed my task first. Okay, I know this was unsound thinking. In retrospect, it reminds me of that long-ago relationship I'd had with the concept of the confessional, the notion that you could do a bad thing, confess it and get absolution for it, and then go out and do the bad thing all over again, because you had a clean slate, and what was the point of wasting it? I wasn't planning to go to confession, but scattering Edward Becker's ashes from the top of a cliff seemed like the next best thing.

I called Hassan's taxicab number from the payphone in the hospital lobby. When I requested Hassan specifically, the dispatcher told me that they weren't permitted to send one driver over another. It depended on which cab was closest. "Anyway," she said, "he's not called in for ages, and he's probably on a break. Do you still want a taxi?"

I told her I did and gave her the name of the hospital. I guessed that my friend was probably leading the white van driver in a merry chase all over Eastbourne, and I smiled to think of it. I'd go up to Beachy Head by cab, tell him to wait, admire the view, dump Becker Senior and then come back to the hospital to say goodbye to Edith. Maybe I'd give her the nice blue velvet bag as a memento. Then I could go back to Canterbury, and the CIPF banquet with Richard (and whatever transpired afterwards), with a clear conscience. Sort of.

The cab driver was heavily bearded, with thick glasses like Maude's and the inevitable flat cap. The driver ID hanging over the back seat identified him as Hassan—another one. I guessed that there were probably several Hassans in every cab company in England, and the dispatcher had done her best for me, and just picked the wrong one. It was too bad. I would have liked to have seen my friendly cab driver again. I told him I wanted to visit Beachy Head, and he nodded and pulled out of the hospital driveway very carefully, looking both ways, first. I don't think I'd seen a cab driver do that since I'd landed in England, but then with glasses that thick, prudence was probably called for.

"Odd sort of day for sightseeing," he said, in a strained and gravelly voice, as if he had a cold. He spoke without turning his head, keeping his eyes on the road. It had stopped raining, but there was a bitter wind coming in from the sea, and grey clouds were moving in like tanks.

"Well, at least it won't be crowded," I said. I saw his eyes in the rear view mirror dart a quick glance at me, as if I'd said something really strange.

"Probably not," he said. "Wind's strong up there, you know. You mustn't go too near the edge, mind. The wind can snatch you off the cliff like the hand of God."

"I'll be careful," I said. The passenger window was open a crack, letting in a strong scent of the sea, a fishy smell that made my nose tingle. I figured that there must be a fishing operation somewhere nearby and decided to try and find a restaurant down on the seafront before heading back—a place where I might be able to get real fish and chips, not the pub-version Richard had warned me about. Maybe I'd get an order to go and take it to Edith. Better than institutional soup, anyway.

The road up to the lookout point on Beachy Head was single-laned, paved but bumpy. At the top, there was a car-park, and signs for a walking path that led towards the cliff top. The carpark was empty, and the wind was setting up little clouds of gravel, tossing them about like miniature tornadoes. I could hear the scream of seagulls. It was a lonely, bleak but beautiful spot, and I was glad I'd come on a day when nobody else would be there. Especially since I wasn't certain that scattering ashes was strictly legal.

"They don't let cars beyond this point," the cab driver said. "You'll have to walk to the view. Do you want me to wait?"

"If you don't mind. I won't be long, I don't expect."

I got out, and immediately my breath was torn away by the

wind. That morning, when buying the daypack, I'd also bought a Queen Elizabeth dog-walking scarf. I put it on and tied it under my chin, zipped up my curling sweater, hoisted the pack onto my shoulder and headed along the path, which was flanked on both sides by gorse bushes that broke the wind a bit. This was it, my "hiking in England" fantasy. I didn't have the stout stick the traditional picture required, so I hunted about along the underbrush and found something that would do—more of a twig, really, but it helped the illusion, and carrying it added to my sense of balance. I figured that once I got beyond the bushes, the wind would be fierce, and the stick would be some added stability. If I was going to scatter the ashes properly, I'd have to get pretty near the edge, I thought. Either that, or most of Mr. Becker Senior would end up on me, flying up my nose and into my eyes.

Behind me in the distance, I heard a car door slam. Damn—more visitors, which would mean I had to do what I had to do quickly, if I wanted privacy. I picked up the pace a bit, beginning to feel breathless, although I was walking downhill, not up. I was out of the bushes, suddenly, and oddly, the wind subsided a bit, probably because the lookout point was a little bit lower down than the car park was, so I was no longer quite at the summit.

I stopped for a moment to catch my breath. The view was spectacular.

I could certainly see the beaches and town of Eastbourne, far below, but beyond that was obscured by the cloud bank, which must be fog, I realized, moving in fast. The wind, luckily, was even quieter now, replaced by an eerie silence, disturbed only by the sound of seagulls a long way off. I made my way carefully to the edge, as close as I dared, and sat down out of sight of the path, with my back to a shrub, in case the new arrivals happened to catch up and wonder what on earth I was doing. It amazed me that there was no railing or anything, just a couple of signs warning sightseers that the cliff edge was unstable, and to take care. Everything's always so understated in England, I thought. In Canada, they would have put up a great big chain-link fence. I liked that they hadn't done that. It was a kind of trusting, as if the authorities were prepared to treat the public like adults, and if they fell off, it was their own fault. That, I suppose, was one of the reasons Beachy Head was a prime suicide spot.

I reached into the bottom of my pack and pulled out Edward Becker Senior in his blue velvet bag. I put my hand into the bag and touched plastic—a package, wrapped up in tape. I pulled it out and hefted it in my hand for a moment. Just the shell of a mortal.

Be he alive or be he dead, I'll grind his bones to make my bread. The lines from the old nursery story popped into my mind—ground bones. Yum. I sat there, trying to decide the best method for a reverent and mindful disposal of Becker's dad. Should I toss the package over all in one piece? Nope— that would seem too much like littering—as there was the plastic involved. Anyway, I'd been asked to scatter, and scatter I would. Should I open the bag, grab handfuls and throw them over, one by one? That would mean getting my hands all covered in human-bits, but it wouldn't really matter. I decided to toss out one handful, with a little word spoken into the wind—something about ashes to ashes and dust to dust—and then I'd crouch down and empty the rest over the edge—or as near the edge as I could stomach, being a little leery of heights, myself. I undid the tape, unrolled the bag and peered in. The crematorium guys had obviously done a great job of pulverizing the remains. I'd expected a gravely sort of stuff, like kitty litter. This was a fine white powder. At the very back of my mind (finally! you're saying to yourself, aren't you?), a little alarm went off. I licked a finger, reached in and brought it out with a bit of powder on it and tasted it.

I heard footsteps on the path behind me, then, and without turning around, I knew it was the cab driver. The fishy smell—that hadn't been the sea coming in the cab window, it had been coming from him—the same fishy smell that the tattooed thug from Eastbridge had carried about with him. The guy in the train, too, according to Maude. A white van man, delivering fish to that Meat and Fish Shop in Canterbury. The thug who for some reason knew that I was carrying around about four pounds of pure cocaine. His beard and glasses—I couldn't believe I'd fallen for it. What a maroon, as Bugs Bunny would say. The hand-off? Yep, I could suddenly see why "his people" had been so upset when I missed (apparently) the rendezvous at the airport and toddled away with the booty. And four pounds of cocaine would be worth killing Alma for, if they thought she was me, right? And that much coke would fit very nicely in a puppet baby, wouldn't it? They must have been really teed off to find it empty. My mind refused to go any further. The question of how the cocaine had come into my possession—there was really only one answer to that, and it was so outrageous, I couldn't stand to think of it.

And now I was on a deserted clifftop (530 feet, the guidebook had said) with a guy who had maybe killed once already to get the stuff I now held in my hands. The fog was rolling in for certain, now, and my best bet, I decided, was to stay huddled up right where I was. Maybe the cab driver would fall off the edge by accident, another one to chalk up to the chalk cliffs of the Sussex coast. Beachy dead head. I was panicking. My hands were shaking, the Sprog was squirming like a worm in my belly, and I tasted copper in my mouth. There was no cavalry on its way to save me, nobody to protect me. I was on my own, again. Just like always. I remembered the first time I'd felt like this. I went back there, then. Just for fun. Because I didn't have any choice.

*   *   *

It is a bright, golden day, a high-summer day from early childhood, with a deep blue sky, the world in crayon colours, clean and uncomplicated. The Kuskawa craft fair spreads its glory out upon what in England would be called the village green. In downtown Laingford, it is called Memorial Park.

My mother is very busy. I am six, and the morning is mine.

Over by the band shell is the weaver lady's stand. The year before, she let kids sit at a loom as big as a tree fort and weave a bookmark by themselves. She sent mine in the mail to me in the fall, my first ever letter with my own name on it. My mother told me that the weaver lady would probably be happy to see me again.

Before I make another bookmark, though, there is the rest of the fair to see. The fair is a paradise for kids.

I sit on the steps of the war memorial to have my can of pop and revel in the luxury of a plastic straw, which I will keep to make a little doll with later. The man who comes to sit beside me is old, with white hair but wearing a smart suit.

He thinks I am pretty and tells me so. I smile at him because I know I am. What is odd is that I feel a sudden tightness at the back of my throat.

The white-haired man looks like an important person you mustn't be rude to, and so this wary moment is already complex.

"I'd like to take a picture of you," the white-haired man says. "Is

that all right?" He has not offered me any candy—I know I'm not allowed to accept sweets from strangers. Although my throat feels funny still, I nod and smile and stand and pose for him. Afterwards, he asks me my name and my age, and he writes it down in a little notebook. He pats my knee, lightly, as if it's a small animal that might startle and make a run for it. Then his grip tightens. I can feel his sweat making my knee wet. "Yes, you're a very pretty girl. Would you like to come for a ride with me in my car?"

"No, thank you," I say. I cannot move. "I have to see the weaver lady."

"Well, some other time, maybe," the white-haired man says, and his hand releases my knee. He has left a mark there.

It has all taken a minute or so. My can of soda pop is still quite cold and heavy in my hand. I stand and head for the bandshell and the loom, walking a little bit outside myself. I turn around and see that he is following me, smiling. Then I run. I run very fast, the word Mother thumping through my blood like a prayer. And when I find her, sitting placidly behind a display of muffins, I tell her everything, including how afraid I was.

"Don't be silly," Mother says. "You're always imagining things. Don't be so vain, Polly."

*   *   *

I learned that day that when I am frightened, I am alone. And on a clifftop in Eastbourne, I remembered. I was on my own. I stood up slowly, the fog swirling around my feet like dry ice in a Broadway show. There was no point in scattering the ashes of Becker's dad. That's not what was in the blue velvet bag. The problem was, I had completely lost my sense of direction. The fog silenced everything like a big quilt thrown over the world, and I couldn't even hear the sea, couldn't tell which way the precipice was, and which was the path. I sensed, rather than saw or heard, a presence to my right. My breath came in short spurts, as if I'd been running, and I tried to control it in case he heard. Why hadn't he held me up in the cab? Why had he waited to drive me up here? And I knew the reason for that, of course. So he could grab the drugs and toss me off the edge. CANADIAN WOMAN FALLS TO DEATH. MATERNAL DEPRESSION CITED. My knees were like rubber. Where was the damned path?

I dropped down again and started to crawl as quietly as I could along the line of shrubs which I hoped delineated the path I'd been on. I had the stick in my hand, still, and I'd stuffed the plastic bag back into my pack. I'd left Richard's tin of pepper spray back in the B&B. If I'd had a mobile phone, I could have called 911 (Did they have 911 in England?) But all I had was my stupid Pez-phone, which could make a nice phone-like noise, but wouldn't help me now. I also had my spare socks, but they wouldn't be much use against a murderous cabbie. Had the fish thug caught up with the real Hassan and stolen his cab? It seemed likely, though how he knew I was here in the first place completely baffled me. Anyway, it was irrelevant.

I pushed through a thicket, realizing as I did that it could very well have been on the cliff-side, in which case I'd come out right at the edge, the earth would crumble away, and I'd have a quick trip down to the everlasting bonfire. On the other hand, it might be on the path-side, in which case, I'd have somewhere to go. Maybe the thug had left the keys in his cab. Maybe I could get there before he did and escape. I found myself reciting a prayer—the simplest one in the world—"please, please, please"—over and over again. My hands touched gravel. Miracle. I scrambled to my feet and started running. There was a shout behind me—a grunt, really, awfully close, as if he'd been waiting only a few feet away, and then we were racing for the car park. I tossed the stick behind me, hoping he would trip on it. The fog had cleared a bit, and as we neared the top, the wind came back. That's when I saw the other figures coming down the path. I cannoned straight into the arms of the biggest one, grabbed him, squeaked out a "help" and fainted.

Twenty-Seven

The more mature your baby is at birth, the more likely it is that she will not have any problems, so that babies born at 26-29 weeks have a much better chance of surviving and growing up either normal or with mild or moderate problems.
  -From *Big Bertha's Total Baby Guide*

"Here she comes," somebody said. "Welcome back, Polly." I figured I must still be off in la-la land, because it was Morrison's big, friendly face that swam into view. I blinked a couple of times, and my vision cleared a bit, and it was still Morrison.

The next thing I was aware of was an absence. Somebody who was supposed to be there, wasn't. I craned my neck to see, and there was nobody else in the room, which wasn't a room, actually, but rather an enclosure of curtains. A small room. A tent, sort of. Then I made out a face—a dark one, floating disembodied at the foot of the bed. No, it was attached to a body, of course it was, a body dressed in white to match the curtains. Very clever.

"Henrietta, what are you wearing that silly outfit for?" I mumbled, but I don't think it came out that way, because what I heard was a sort of spluttery groan, and Morrison hadn't said anything, so it must have been me. I tried again.

"Water, please." The dark Henrietta person came forward and produced a cup with a bendy straw in it, and I drank. Then in a horrible wave of knowing, I guessed who was missing. My Sprog. Bess. My hand, after touching my belly, which felt like jello, or a burst balloon, started searching

251

frantically amongst the bedclothes. She'd fallen out. I had to put her back in. Oh, God—maybe she'd gone over the cliff. I tried to sit up, but nothing below my chest seemed to be working properly. "Bess. I—where's Bess?"

"It's okay, Polly. Don't worry, it's okay," Morrison said. His voice sounded funny, like he was talking around a mouthful of crackers. I turned to look at him. Someone had thrown some water at him. He was all wet. He was covered in fog, like the last time I had seen him, coming out of the fog like a monolith, a stonehenge person, the one I'd slammed into. Right behind him, then and now, was the face of Richard Seth. Impossibly young and full of some emotion I couldn't begin to understand. He reached a hand towards me, then let it fall.

"Your baby is all right, Ms. Deacon," the dark, disembodied face said and touched my shoulder, pressing me down into my pillow again. "Premature, but perfectly fine." She/he was doing something to a tube in my arm. "Sleep now, everything's all right."

"Earlie?" He was disappearing into the fog again.

"Polly, don't worry. She's beautiful," he said, and then I fell over the cliff and into a warm sea.

*   *   *

Coming out of sedation feels like you've lost years, even if it's only a few hours. I woke, and it was night. My first thought was panic again, as I felt the physical void in my middle—the part-of-me lump that I'd lived with for twenty-eight weeks. Earlie Morrison was still there, sitting in a chair drawn up to my bedside, his eyes luminous in the light from the monitor thing attached, I presumed, to me.

"Hi," I said.

"Hey," he said. "It's me."

"I know it's you. How did you get here?"

"On a plane, then I drove," he said. "It took a while to track you down."

"How come you came?" I said.

"Instinct, maybe. I found some stuff that worried me. And I thought, you know, that you could use some help."

"Nice timing, Earlie."

He grinned then, a sheepish grin.

"A little tight, I thought."

"Tell me about Bess."

"Is that what you're calling her? She's in the neo-natal unit, in intensive care. It's okay—they're really good, here. You can go see her in the morning."

I felt a tight ache in my breasts, and suddenly had a really strong stab of sympathy for Julian of Norwich, George's prime dairy goat, whose udder, when full, ballooned out like one of those exercise balls. At the thought of her, something gushed, and I felt my chest grow damp. "She's really okay? Tell me the truth, Earlie, please."

"The doctor said they'll have to monitor her for a few weeks. There's stuff about preemies that you need to know. He thought I was, um, her father, so he probably told me a lot that he shouldn't. But she's big, for a little guy, if you know what I mean. And strong, he said."

"How big?"

"Three pounds, two ounces," he said.

"Oh, my God."

"No—no. That's good. He said he thought she should be smaller, considering. But she's got some growing to do—I won't try to explain it. Let him do it. But you're not supposed to worry, Polly."

"Really?"

"Really. Now you gotta rest."

"Nope. I'm wide awake, now. And my, excuse me, my breasts are killing me. Can you buzz somebody?"

*   *   *

Earlie stepped outside the curtains while a nice nurse [name tag: Nurse French] introduced me to the joys of the breast pump. She said that Bess would enjoy what we produced (and I felt like Julian again, let me tell you) at breakfast time in a couple of hours. "When can I breast feed her myself?" I asked. Nurse French shot me a look.

"Has the doctor talked to you yet?"

"No."

"Well, it'll be a while before you can do that, luv. But don't worry. Your milk will go to her in the meantime, and there's nothing better." She carried the pumped milk away with her, and I had a sudden flash of Eddie and me in the barn, weighing the goat's milk and noting down in George's book which song we had sung and how much each goat had produced. I resolved to sing to myself next time, to see if it made any difference.

Earlie came back in, after the nurse had helped me change into a fresh gown-thingy—the kind that did up the back with string. Apparently, my premature Sprog had appeared in the conventional way, as I couldn't find any sutures on my belly, and there were parts of me that felt like I'd been run over by a truck. Still, I was in one piece.

"You've seen her? Bess? You've seen her?" I asked him.

"Yep. I've been going to check on her every so often," he said. "I haven't told them that I'm not, you know—that we're not, you know."

"Good," I said. "Don't tell them. I need you here." He smiled and blushed a little. He was wearing a big green sweater and baggy jeans. His hair was rumpled, and he had a growth of stubble on his chin. How long had we been here? I didn't like to ask. I could do that later.

"So, what does she look like?"

"She's about this big," he said, holding his hands an impossibly short distance apart—nine or ten inches, "and she has black hair, although they say that'll probably fall out and get replaced. Her eyes are closed, so I can't tell what colour they are."

"Aren't all babies' eyes blue?"

"I haven't got a clue," he said. "By the way, Susan and George are all set to come over if you want."

"No, they don't need to do that. The goats, and everything. We'll be home soon enough, right?"

"It'll be some weeks, Polly. You can't fly with an incubator. She needs to get stronger, first."

"She will, though, right?"

"With a mom like hers? She'd better." We smiled at each other. A nice moment.

"Did I see Richard here, earlier? Richard Seth?"

"Yeah," Earlie said. "He insisted on coming down with me. I found him when I was trying to find you, eh? At the Bed and Breakfast place. He helped fill in the details, and then when I said I was driving down here, he got into my car and wouldn't get out again, just sat there with his arms crossed, so I let him come. He really cares about you, eh? He told me some personal stuff."

"He did, did he?"

"Yep. And he feels really guilty about letting you go on this trip by yourself. He said he wouldn't have let you go if he'd known."

"It's not like he could have stopped me," I said.

"Nobody can ever stop you from doing what you want, Polly. But maybe if you'd let him come, it would have turned out different."

"Maybe. Where is he now?"

"He went back to Canterbury—to the conference, and he didn't want to miss his flight home. He said he'd get in touch with you back in Kuskawa."

"That may not be a good idea," I said.

"Huh. Well, whatever. You should know that he stayed here watching over you like I did all the time you were unconscious, though, eh?"

"Nice of him," I said. Then there was a pause. I asked the question that hung between us like a dark shadow, like the disembodied face of the doctor or whoever it was I'd seen in my first wake-up moment.

"Where's Becker?" I said.

"He's, uh. He's detained right now. He would have come if he could."

"Detained?"

"Well, yeah. Sort of an investigation thing he's involved in."

"Typical," I said. I wasn't sure how I felt about that.

"I guess I should fill you in, eh?"

"Please."

*   *   *

On secondment to the Pearson International Airport people, Becker had been helping redesign the security system—I knew that. What I didn't know was how far he was prepared to go, in order to test it out.

"You know he didn't want you to make this trip, right?"

Morrison said. I nodded.

"So, he decided to use you as a guinea pig."

"Go on," I said. I knew what was coming. All that stuff about his dad wanting his ashes scattered off Beachy Head—all that had been made up. It was a story to get me to try to take the contents of the blue bag through customs. And the contents? Four pounds of premium grade cocaine. The kind that, if you're caught with it, sends you to prison for a long, long time.

"He said he'd worked it all out with the airport authorities beforehand. It was supposed to test their search procedures and so on," Morrison said. "When they found it, they'd arrest you, but your file would be computer flagged, and he'd be right there to cover the thing—you know—spring you and identify you as someone working with the OPP."

"I see. Except that I didn't know I was working with them."

"That was the idea. They wanted you to be a typical drug mule—someone who doesn't know she's carrying."

"Charming. A mule. Hee haw. So, what happened?"

"Well, you got through, didn't you? They didn't find it."

"And was he there, in the airport?"

"Apparently. And he was plenty pissed off that you got through, I should add."

"Jeez, Morrison. It was right there in my knapsack with my toiletry bag. Right out in the open." I told him about the security people ripping my puppet case apart and x-raying my puppets.

"Yeah, well, I guess the system still has a few bugs, eh?"

"So how come the thug-people were involved? Was that Becker testing his drug connection policies?"

"He made the mistake of sending a lot of the information via email," Morrison said. "That's how I clued in to it. I was using his computer, you know, while mine was busted, and I got into the file by mistake."

"And I guess somebody else got into the file too, eh?"

"Yep. The guy at Pearson—we figure he was the first—a runner for a Canadian biker gang that does a lot of hacking into police computers. It's hard to track. But he was just small-time. The guys at this end—well, we're working on that. But they tracked you from the moment you got off the plane, I guess. And they hacked into your Hotmail account to find out where you were going and what you were doing. You know—that stuff you sent me about your itinerary. While you were keeping us in the loop, you were keeping them in the loop, too."

"So when I got through security, why the hell didn't Becker get in touch right away?"

"He said he was dealing with damage control at his end. Seems he didn't exactly have authorization for the thing to begin with. At least, not the cocaine part."

"Where did he get it, then?"

"We're working on that. Becker's not talking."

"Ah. So he's, um, detained right now?"

"Big time."

"I hope he gets life," I said. There was a nasty little pause. Morrison didn't disagree with me, either.

"What was all the stuff about the hand-over, then?" I said. "You've talked to Potts, right?"

"Yeah, he's here now, dealing with the guy we nabbed up on the cliff. The English guys think the gang over here intercepted the information from the Canadian gang—or maybe they're linked—we don't know yet. We figure they thought it was a legitimate drug-mule delivery—well, legitimate to their way of thinking, and they were told to connect up with this Canadian puppet maker."

"So the thug was told to expect cooperation from me?"

"We think so. That's not clear, yet. Probably won't be, either."

"So, who attacked Alma?"

"The woman who looked like you? Same people, probably the same guy, Polly."

"And you've got him, right? And 'his people'?"

"Not really. It's only in movies where all the bad guys get caught at the end. But they're working on it, Polly."

"I can't believe that Becker set me up like that."

"Me either. But remember, as far as he was concerned, it would all have been fixed at Pearson International, and you'd have come home, perfectly safe, the way he planned it. But it's a lot to get over, eh?"

"What makes you think I'm planning to get over it?"

"He made a mistake, that's all."

"A mistake? You call that a mistake? Jesus, Mary and Joseph, Earlie, that was more than a mistake. He used me as a goddamn pawn in some weird little police game, and even if it had gone the way he planned, I would have missed my flight and probably missed the conference, and I would have killed him with my bare hands right there in the airport terminal."

"No, you wouldn't. You would have forgiven him eventually, Polly."

"Hah. No way. Not in a million years. I'm glad he gave me Bess, and I'll always be glad about that, but she's the last thing he'll ever give me, and if he thinks he's going to have anything at all to do with her, he's nuts. I'll tell her that her father is dead. Or beamed up by aliens. Forgiveness? I do not think so."

Earlie just looked at me, an expression of inestimable sadness on his face.

*　　*　　*

A week later, after our usual morning visit with Bess, who was fighting apnea, jaundice and a host of other maladies that preemies are heir to, we took a trip, Earlie and I, back up to Beachy Head.

It was a sunny day, and the sky was a heartbreaking blue, the sun a lemon yellow, and I was wearing my Queen Elizabeth head scarf. Hassan waited in his cab for us, wearing a white bandage on his head, where he'd been coshed by the thug that stole his taxi, after a chase scene that didn't, apparently, turn out like they do in the movies.

We hiked along the gorse-lined path and out to the edge— not too close, but close enough. It was a clear view, and, like the guidebook said, you could see the beaches and town of Eastbourne, the Pier and the Harbour, and then on to Pevensey Bay and Hastings. We could even see Dungeness in Kent, nearly forty miles away.

"You sure you want to do this?" Earlie said.

"I'm sure." I reached up and unclasped the chain that I wore around my neck. I took one last look at Becker's ring— quite a pretty one, really, if you liked diamonds. Then, with all my strength, and emitting a grunt like a shot-put athlete, I threw it over the edge and out to sea.

Epilogue

I did meet Mr. Fogbow, the anthropologist, again, just as he had predicted. He was in Eastbourne researching the phenomenon of Spanish girls coming to England to learn the language, working for slave wages in the restaurant trade and trying to meet an English husband. We met by accident on the street and ended up having lunch together (real fish and chips) in a seaside resort place. I filled him in on my own personal mating habits, which had come to a dead end in a most spectacular way, and we parted cordially, promising to stay in touch.

I stayed in England for another five weeks, until Bess was big enough and well enough to travel. She is very, very small, and I have been warned to expect any number of health problems arising from her premature birth, but nothing nasty has transpired so far. I'm living at the farmhouse, for the time being, and George and Susan are head-over-heels in love with my daughter, as I am.

Before I left, I visited Edith again. As soon as I walked in, she hailed me as Lady Deacon, and shouted for Henrietta to bring on the tea. I had brought some nice pastries from an Eastbourne bakery, and we had a great time in fantasy-land. Nurse Hopkins was a sweetheart, playing along like an extra in *Pride and Prejudice*. I went back a couple of times and promised to write when I got home, although Nurse Hopkins told me that I shouldn't be too upset if I didn't get an answer. I think people underestimate Edith, though. I think she's only as loony as people want her to be, and I bet she lasts a good few years yet, provided the institutional soup doesn't get her.

There was an internal investigation about Becker's Great Drug Exploit, but nothing much came of it in terms of his job. There was a hearing. He was reprimanded, and Morrison told me that, in spite of it all, Becker apparently got a commendation as well, after the Canadian biker gang connection was followed up and resulted in an arrest or two. Morrison had had more to do with that than Becker did, but then life is never fair. Though I was told I had every right to press charges against Becker for more or less framing me and endangering my life, I didn't bother.

We met on neutral turf, the Tim Hortons, of course, next to the cop shop. I'd had a difficult time deciding whether or not to bring our daughter with me, and I'd asked Susan for her advice.

"Some people," Susan had said, "naturally hanker after things they can't have. If you keep Bess hidden away from Mark, he will quite understandably want to see her. Given the circumstances, you have every right to keep her away from him, but let him see her at least. You owe him that."

"I don't owe him a goddamn thing," I said, but I brought her with me anyway.

"After this," I said, stirring a large coffee to go, "I don't want to see you ever again."

"I understand that," he said. He had hardly looked at the tiny angel in the baby carrier beside me. Maybe it hurt him too much to look, I don't know. But it hurt me that he didn't, too. He didn't even want to hold her.

"She was always your baby—never mine, anyway," he said.

"You do realize, don't you, that because you set me up, and because the bad guys in the U.K. got hold of it, a woman called Alma Barrow and her baby died? You realize you're responsible for that?"

"You may think so, Polly. But that's ridiculous." I knew he wouldn't be willing to take responsibility for that, but I had to say it. It would help lessen the burden I felt myself. In a way, I—and Becker by what he had done—had killed Alma. That was a thing that could never, ever be forgiven.

"What I'll never get is why on earth you did it in the first place," I said.

"I didn't think it was safe for you to go," he said. "I told you that, and you wouldn't listen. And I needed to test out the new system. You were a perfect agent, that's all. You would have been doing something good for your country."

"And you thought I'd forgive you after I found out what was going on?"

"Yeah—I thought you would. I guess I was wrong."

"I guess you were." He got up and left not long after that. My coffee to go was cold by that point, and I tossed it into the bin. The trash. Whatever.

He transferred to Calgary in the late spring. Maybe he's getting back together with his ex-wife—who knows? And, as Cedric would say, I don't give a toss.

Lug-nut and Rosencrantz don't seem to be terribly jealous of Bess, although sometimes her wails make Luggy roll his eyes to the ceiling and sigh like an old man. He used to do that with Rosie when she was very small, too. I've explained to him that Bess will eventually learn to bark properly, and he just has to wait awhile.

Eddie's court case about the marijuana was dismissed, on

account of the fact that by then, Becker had transferred to Calgary, and Morrison claimed he didn't have sufficient evidence to proceed. This was probably an unethical fiddle on Morrison's part, but we were willing to forgive him. I think the episode scared the daylights out of Eddie, and he told me he'd never touch the stuff again. I'm not sure I believe him, though.

Alma's death remains unsolved, at least officially. The tattooed guy, whose fake beard had fallen off when he was arrested at Beachy Head, was charged with all kinds of things, including clobbering Hassan and stalking me. He was a legitimate white van man, apparently. His fishy smell came from his part-time job delivering plaice to restaurants and grocery stores in the Canterbury area. His connection with any kind of gang was hard to prove, according to Potts, who was keeping in touch with Earlie. The guy insisted he was working on his own, though that made no sense. I guess he'll go down loyal to "his people" and come out of jail a hero at some point. They're still collecting evidence to connect him with the thing that happened at the Cathedral. However, Morrison got an email from Constable Potts the other day, with the news that Maude had identified the guy from a mug-book as the person who had tried to steal my puppet case from the train, and also as someone she thought she had seen in the Right-to-Life crowd, just before Alma went to the loo. Not enough to go on, considering that Maude's eyesight was so bad, but a beginning, anyway.

The English tabloids had a field day with the whole thing, dubbing it, predictably, "Murder in the Cathedral." Cedric wrote to say that his B&B was full up with thrill seekers, and the Becket tomb had never been busier.

Richard is still working with Steamboat Theatre, and we've seen each other a couple of times. I thanked him for having been part of the rescue squad, and for hanging out in the hospital while I was capering about in coma-land. We've agreed to write off our Canterbury dalliance as one of those strangers-in-a-strange-land things, and I think we're both fine with that. He's pretty good with Bess, though he handles her as if she's a fragile piece of priceless stuff, which of course she is. We're just friends, though. He's way too young for me, for one thing, and for another, my heart has lodged elsewhere—a development that I couldn't have predicted at all.

Earlie Morrison has been around here a lot. Bess fits into his lap like a small cat, and he's trying to teach her cribbage, which is ambitious, as she's only two months old. Still, she adores him, and you know what? So do I.

H. Mel Malton was born in England and emigrated with her family to Canada. She grew up in Bracebridge, Ontario, and has resettled in the same area. She spent ten years touring North America in the theatre business as both actor and stage manager, but has also worked as a government forms designer, a newspaper reporter, a waitress, a receptionist, a clerk in a candy store, a singing teacher and a church secretary. None of these jobs has harmed her. She lives in a log cabin in Huntsville, Ontario, on ten acres of swampland with her two dogs, Karma and Ego.

Mel has published short stories, poems and articles in numerous periodicals and literary journals, including the *Toronto Star*, *Chatelaine*, *The Malahat Review* and *Grain*. Her crime stories have appeared in *Menopause is Murder* and *Fit to Die*. Her first Polly Deacon novel, *Down in the Dumps*, was shortlisted for an Arthur Ellis Award for Best First Crime Novel. Her second Polly Deacon novel, *Cue the Dead Guy*, was published in 1999 and the third, *Dead Cow in Aisle Three*, in 2001.